S.J. DAVISON

Angel of Money

1

It wasn't the thick black coat disguising what he wore underneath that made Hazim sweat as he tried to steady himself against the swaying of the carriage. Neither was it the proximity of the other tightly packed passengers rushing from work to enjoy what was left of the evening. He also knew the oversized coat he was wearing didn't single him out. It may have been warm in the airless, London Underground carriage, but everyone was dressed for the sharp cold awaiting above ground.

The sweat rolled from his armpits because of fear. When he let go of the metal bar, he felt his hands tremble. If someone glanced at him, Hazim was sure they would see the guilt in his eyes. He might not be the one who was going to use the device, but he knew only too well the damage it would cause. People were going to die for a cause he didn't believe in, but if it kept his precious family alive, then so be it.

The train drew to a halt at the next stop, and he squeezed up, allowing a mass of people to exit onto the platform. With fewer people entering the carriage, he slumped into one of the free seats before his shaking legs gave way. An old woman opposite with a bright orange shopping bag on her knee smiled at him. He didn't smile back. Instead, he looked down at his black shoes.

Hazim tried to calm himself with some deep breaths, but they were ragged and short. He felt worse.

"Are you okay, dear?" the woman asked him. "You look as though you're going to be sick."

"Long day," Hazim mumbled not looking up. Did she know? Could she see in his eyes the horror he was burdened with? He tried to check that his coat hadn't opened to reveal the vest underneath. He didn't want to touch the jacket. Despite what he'd been told, he didn't trust that it wouldn't go off by accident.

The next station beckoned with the loud announcement that it was Bank Underground Station. Not usually his stop, but the instructions had been clear. Was someone watching his every move? Were they reporting back to those holding his family?

Avoiding eye contact with the woman, Hazim hauled himself towards the train doors as they slid open. Moments later, he was hurrying up the escalator towards the exit. It was a part of London he used to know very well. He'd been to the bar, which was the rendezvous point with his contact. It was a world of money and respect that was in a distant past, when Hazim worked for Global Money. A huge financial house, he now realised, was the worst company in the world. One lousy quarter of financial results because he'd been ill. That's all it had taken for them to fire him after ten years of service. The fact he had been in the top percentile for half of those years meant nothing.

One weak quarter, and you were out.

A message arrived on his phone as soon as he hit the frigid November night. He thought he was going to vomit as the woman had suspected. Swallowing back the bile, he saw a picture of his daughter sleeping in her cot. The text under it told him to stay focused, and his family would remain safe.

The sick bastards. The sick, sick bastards. Hazim wanted to hurl his phone at the wall. He wanted to run to the nearest policeman and confess everything. But he knew that would mean the end for those he loved the most. The bastards were so far gone with their stupid beliefs that killing babies meant nothing to them.

If there was a chance they would let his family live, Hazim had to take it.

The man who had contacted him had said all Hazim needed to do was deliver the vest. There was also the promise of financial reward. Enough to pay off the loan sharks that dogged him, with some left over so his wife and daughters could start a new life out of London.

"Sorry, mate." A large, coloured man in a sports jacket bumped him. Hazim stumbled and dropped his phone as the man moved on with an apologetic face. For a moment, Hazim froze, expecting the world to blow apart.

Nothing happened.

Stooping to pick up his phone, he found the screen cracked. Pissed, he thought about going after the man. Glancing at the time, Hazim realised he needed to get going if he was to get to the handover point in time.

Slipping the broken phone into his pocket, he hurried through the thinning crowds, down Cornhill Street, towards his destination. He was sure the vest felt heavier, as if it was Frodo's burden in *The Lord of the Rings*, weighing him down with each step. There were two police officers on the corner of Whittington Avenue. Hazim nearly panicked; he wanted to turn back. Maybe he could dump the vest in a bin and go. But there would be grave consequences if he did.

Sucking in some of the chilled air, he hung off the back of a group of smartly dressed men making their way down the street until they passed the police. Once under the roof of Leadenhall Market, the crowds increased in size, and he moved away from the group, heading towards his target, The Lamb Tavern.

His contact had spoken about the infidel bankers being led like lambs to the slaughter. Hazim wasn't sure if that had been some sort of joke or just stupid ISIS propaganda.

It might have been early in the evening, but there were still plenty of people making for the various watering holes to enjoy a well-earned drink. It had been a long time since Hazim had been able to afford to drink in these swanky bars and restaurants.

A further thirty metres along the street, he saw the tavern. Suited men and women huddled around heaters while a combination of smoke and vape fumes curled towards the high roof of the covered market. They ignored Hazim as he passed through the doors and into the main part of the bar. It was early enough for there not to be a bouncer to question him.

Inside, it was more of the same—city traders in their thousand-dollar suits and power-dressing women holding their own in a world of male testosterone. It confused him as to why this would be a handover point as he manoeuvred himself towards the bar as instructed. He received disgusted looks as he barged through the crowd.

Reaching the front, Hazim tried to catch the attention of the bartenders. It seemed an age before one of the girls, sporting a tight top and a tired smile, came over.

"I need to speak to Saeed."

"Who?" she shouted, looking puzzled.

"Saeed," he repeated. "I have a delivery for him. I was told he works out back."

"No, mate, no Saeed here. Are you sure you have got the right place?"

He knew it was this pub. It wasn't something he was going to forget. "This is the place. I must speak to Saeed."

"Look, mate," the girl started to get irritated, "I've worked here a year, and there has never been a Saeed."

Hazim felt a vibration in the vest, and the world vanished before his eyes.

2

The man in the black hooded jacket sitting outside a small snack bar was disappointed with the blast. He'd been promised something more spectacular by the bomb maker and felt he'd paid a premium for a more visceral explosion. His vision had been for the whole of the bar to burst outwards, hurling glass and debris onto the street, injuring as many as possible. The man hoped there might have been some severed limbs caught on camera, which always made for good online streaming. The enclosed element of Leadenhall Market had helped funnel the blast down the narrow passages, but it was still not what he'd hoped for.

As the sound of the explosion died away, the night became filled with intense screaming. Moments before, there had been the sound of laughter from the chattering crowds, who thought no harm could ever come to them.

The man had chosen his seat outside a café with care. It was east of the Lamb Tavern and not under the fancy roof of the market square. The Regis snack bar was only open so late because they were struggling for cash—hardly surprising by the state of the sandwich that lay untouched on his plate.

A few yards away, victims, showered with glass, were fleeing, while in the opposite direction, smartphone-armed gawkers were rushing to document the human misery. Facebook feeds, YouTube, and Twitter would soon contain macabre sights that earned money for those who were quick enough to upload their content. Perhaps the social media giants would take some of the more graphic streams down, claiming they genuinely had a moral compass. But why take them all down when they would be generating so much traffic?

The man felt utter contempt for people who profited off such content.

Two of the snack bar staff appeared between the tables, not to clear them—that would be too much effort—but to join the onlookers. One of them already had her phone out. The man turned his head away despite the inner lining of the hood obscuring most of his face. Perhaps the staff would remember the strange man in the black jacket sitting outside their café on a cold November night who'd refused the offer of heaters. But they wouldn't be able to describe his face.

He rose from the table and slipped into the throng of people surging away from the bar and down the street. He kept his head down and hands buried in the ample pockets of his thick jacket. Knowing where the CCTV cameras were positioned meant disappearing among the crowd was simple. When he approached London Bridge, he pulled a phone from his pocket and dropped it over the metal barrier into the inky blackness of the water below. His stash of old-style phones, ideal for this sort of work, was nearly gone. There were only two more left, and they would be used over the coming days.

Then a different, more modern device appeared in his hand, from which he selected a number.

"Are you ready for me?"

"Ooh, I'm always ready for you, lover boy." He winced at the

American woman's attempt at an alluring voice, but he kept the irritation from his tone. Lilly had been fun for a while, but he was rapidly tiring of her, and while her usefulness was coming to an end, there was one last important role for her to play.

"I'll be there in twenty minutes. Are your bags packed?"

"Always so practical." The woman's voice turned back to normal. "Packed and in the hall. Do you want me to call a cab?"

"There should be one on the way already."

"Have you seen the news?" she asked.

"Can't miss it, so we need to get going before they lock everything down."

"Okay, see you soon."

He hung up before lengthening his stride as the crowds thinned. Crossing the Thames, he headed down to Blackfriars, where owning even a small place cost the better part of a million pounds, a sum that meant nothing to Lilly's family.

The man concentrated on the plans he'd made for the rest of the night. He had a small bag at Lilly's that would, no doubt, be dwarfed by her belongings, even though she also had an apartment in New York. They would throw their luggage in the taxi and soon be sitting in the airport business lounge sipping cocktails while the rest of the world was trying to piece together the events of the evening.

3

"I think there's something wrong with these numbers, Henry. You need to look." Terry held the phone under his chin while his free hand continued to scroll through the figures on the spreadsheet. He had spent the last two hours checking and re-checking but was sure he was right.

"Jesus, Terry, can't it wait till tomorrow? Get your arse down here and get drinking. We'll even go to a strip club. It's about time you lost your cherry."

Terry ignored his comments. They were always having a dig at his lack of sexual prowess. It was one of the many reasons he didn't reveal his sexual preferences to his work colleagues. Terry swivelled around in his leather office chair, trying to get more intensity into his voice. "You should look at them now. There could be some massive fraud going on in the company. It could be ENRON all over again."

"Look, mate, I applaud your dedication, and I know you've been working hard on this, but whatever you've found can wait until the morning." There was a loud cheer, and Terry could hear his boss was having more drinks shoved in front of him. "I gotta go, get yourself down…"

The line cut out. Terry didn't bother trying to call back, turning instead to examine the calculations to see if he could figure out the root cause of the fraud. It should have been impossible for anyone to trade in the way the numbers were showing. What's more, they bypassed all the risk parameters the models were supposed to be regulating.

In the background, he heard a door open, and the sound of a vacuum grew louder as the cleaners entered to do their nightly rounds. Perhaps Henry was right. It looked as though this had been going on months, years even. What difference would a few extra hours make?

It was already late, and he'd spent countless nights alone in the office fine-tuning his algorithms trying to zero in on the anomalies. There had been plenty of nights when he'd first started at Global Money that Terry had gone out with the others for beers, trying to be one of the lads. But that wasn't his kind of life. Terry was happier with a spreadsheet full of numerical problems and some hard rock on his headphones. He always wanted to get some drumsticks, like the guy who bet against the housing market before the 2008 crash. Only, he wasn't sure that would go down well in the office. He was hardly in the same league.

Terry had felt the numbers were wrong a week ago. Something didn't add up, even when on the face of it, everything did. Then, he'd found discrepancies in the data he'd previously dismissed as a statistical anomaly.

The gut feeling hadn't gone away.

More results threw off his revised calculations, even if it was only a fraction of one percent. It gnawed at him because what Terry loved about mathematics was its symmetry. He needed to know what was skewing the numbers. For three straight nights, he'd worked on the problem, and while he still couldn't nail the exact source, all the pointers were telling him one thing. Secret trades right under the company's nose; money being made off the books.

Almost impossible to detect. Almost but not quite.

Only that could never happen. Could it?

"Screw you, Henry." Terry had little love for his immediate superior. Henry had used him as the butt of most of his jokes—an act he suspected hid his boss's inadequacies. A public-school nephew of someone in the firm, Henry certainly hadn't gained his place at Global Money on merit. And that pissed Terry off. That and the fact Henry took credit for the team's work. Terry liked his job as a data scientist, and Henry didn't have a clue what that meant. So, fuck him.

Picking up his desk phone, he punched in the number of the next person in the chain of command.

"Christ, Terry, you still in the office?" the gruff voice of thirty-year company veteran Brandon Walsh came from the other end. "I thought there was some do tonight?"

"Not my scene."

"No, I suppose not." Terry could tell Brandon was driving. Despite working in London, his boss suffered the traffic every day so that he could drive his beloved Porsche. "What's so important you need to call me at this hour?"

"There's something wrong with our models. Trades are occurring outside the rules set in the system. But done in a way they're almost undetectable."

"Go on. A little more for those who aren't data gurus."

"It's as though the trading algorithm has been tampered with." There was a pause, and Terry could almost hear his boss thinking.

"That's impossible," Brandon said at last.

"No, only improbable, sir. When you run the numbers

against what we should have been doing, they don't add up. It's close, but it's not what it should be."

"Bottom line?" Brandon said.

Terry took a deep breath. "I think someone is stealing money from the company."

"Fuck me. How certain are you?"

"Pretty convinced." Terry tried to sound more confident than he was. "It's the only inference I can make from the data I have so far."

There was a hesitation on the line. Terry could hear the radio in the background; the announcer sounded urgent, but he couldn't make out what she was saying.

"Where did they go tonight?"

"What, the others? The Lamb Tavern again. I just spoke to Henry a few minutes ago."

"I'm coming to the office. Ring him back and see..." Brandon sounded panicked. "Just try and get hold of him." The line went dead.

Terry was puzzled. Dialling Henry, the call went straight to voicemail. A shiver went down his spine. The gut feeling that something was wrong was back again, but this time, not about the numbers. Despite being a highly rational man, Terry still considered himself attuned to his intuition.

The cleaners had stopped vacuuming. They were staring at one of the screens on the wall that streamed twenty-four-hour news. Terry tried calling again.

Voicemail.

He tried Alan, who sat at the desk opposite during the day. Same thing.

Grabbing his mouse, Terry flicked one of his screens onto the news channel, and he knew his life was never going to be the same again.

4

Zack slid the package across the table to the overweight American opposite. The man had swaggered into the office dressed in his Saville Row suit and sporting a litany of chunky gold rings. Arrogance radiated from everything he wore and every movement he made. Zack had taken a dislike to the American the first time they'd met. But, turning down money because you disliked someone didn't pay overdue bills.

It was the second time Zack's client, Hank Williams, had walked into his office and surveyed it with utter disdain. He knew the businessman looked down on him and the small detective agency, but he didn't look down on the cheap rates. One crucial thing Zack had learnt over the last week of surveillance was that despite the pretence of bling, Hank Williams was a cheap bastard.

"So, what's the verdict? She a cheating bitch?" the American demanded.

"Take a look for yourself." Zack nodded towards the package.

Hank Williams flipped back the flap and pulled out the photographs.

"What the hell is this?" he exclaimed sifting through the large images.

"They're pictures of your wife going about her daily routine." Zack tried not to sound smug.

Hank frowned as he continued looking through the photos; his multiple chins rubbed against the collar of his expensive white shirt. "There's nothing here."

"Exactly." Zack tapped the table. "So, you'll be pleased to know your wife is as honest a woman as you'll ever meet." He sat back and smiled.

"What the fuck? This is not what I wanted."

"Really?" Zack feigned surprise.

"You know that, you little fuck." Beads of sweat started to pop out on Hank's forehead. "I wanted the dirt on what she's been up to. She's having a fucking affair, and it was your job to prove it."

"But there is no evidence that she is," Zack knew that wasn't the whole truth, but it was hardly an affair.

Hank's face started turning red. "Only because you've not done your fucking job. These are fucking useless." He hurled the pictures across the room.

"I thought you'd be pleased." Zack smiled again.

"I want my money back, you fuck. I want all of it back."

"We've investigated your wife as you asked. We've done our job." Zack examined an invoice on the desk in front of him. "Now, about the rest of the payment."

"The rest of the fucking money." Hank stood and leaned forward, pressing both knuckles on the desk. While he remained in his chair on the other side, Zack tensed in anticipation of his client getting violent. "I want every fucking penny back."

"That's not going to happen, Mr Williams, and I think you should leave the office and consider paying the rest of what you owe. My agency has carried out the job as requested. We cannot be held responsible for photographing what doesn't exist."

Zack knew he was probably antagonising the man, but the fat bastard deserved it. All Hank Williams wanted to do was ditch his current young bride, an up-and-coming British actress, so he could hook up with a new one until he was bored of her. And Hank wanted to do so with the least possible expense. The truth was his wife was going to a friend for comfort. Driven there by the shit Hank had become once they were married. Zack wasn't sure he believed she wasn't having an affair with this friend as she'd told him. But he had also watched the American and discovered he was having numerous flings while treating his young wife like she was nothing.

Apparently, Hank Williams could be sweet and kind when it suited him, but Zack only saw an egotistical bastard who spent his life taking what he wanted.

"Why you..." Hank launched himself across the desk and was left floundering as Zack propelled his chair out of reach. After a moment, the American stood, adjusted his tie, and stormed back across the office. At the door, he turned his angry, red face back towards Zack. "You've not heard the end of this!" he screamed as he slammed the door.

"Guess we're not getting paid then," Zack said to himself before retrieving his phone from the drawer. He messaged the soon-to-be ex-Mrs Hank Williams.

It's done.
How did he take it?
Not well.
Thank you.

16

4

You're welcome. If you get a reasonable settlement, then remember me.

I will. Thank you so much.

He might go to another detective.

But I have the photos you took of him. My lawyer says we'll get a deal. I'll pay you then.

Zack knew it would be probably too late for the agency by the time any settlement money came through. Two more red letters were crumpled in the bin. The money from the job he'd just messed up would have kept the wolves away for a while. He wasn't sure how he was going to tell Chloe that his desire for fairness had crippled the business. But the guy was a prick, and he'd seen for himself Hank slapping the poor girl, even got it on camera, so Zack hoped she took him for everything she could.

Putting his hand on the table, Zack could feel the tremble without having to see it. He glanced at the clock. It was two hours before his next dose of prescribed pills that were nestled in his drawers. But he could feel the pressure building inside him. Sense the walls closing in.

"Fuck it." Opening the drawer, he fished out the small bottle and flipped off the white plastic lid, dropping two yellow pills onto the wooden desk. He stared at them for a while. The bottle was nearly empty, it was almost a week from his repeat prescription, and going early would tell the doctor that he wasn't coping like he said he was.

"Fuck it," he repeated before tossing the two pills into his mouth and dry swallowing them.

Almost immediately, there was a wave a relief that Zack knew was more about his mental state than physical dependency. There was the number of the therapist in the drawer

17

he'd promised the doctor he'd get in touch with, and Zack knew there wouldn't be a chance to get his prescription renewed early unless he'd at least booked an appointment.

But then again, there were other means of getting the pills he needed.

Swinging around in his chair, Zack looked down onto the street where people hurried about their business under the threat of the dark grey clouds. The agency's office was on the second floor of a building between Covent Garden and Leicester Square in London. Although it sounded a glamorous location, the offices were on one of the forgotten streets of London where progress seemed non-existent. On the plus side, it had been as cheap as you could get in the centre of the UK's capital and had given them enough space to start the detective agency.

The agency had been Chloe's idea.

Zack had been asked to resign quietly from the police force after the newspapers had finally exhausted reports about the events at Oakwell. The explosion and fires that had rocked the previously unheard-of English town had caught the world's imagination for a brief time, as had the antics of Detective Inspector Zack Carter in rescuing his daughter and another woman from a criminal's lair. Zack had tried to keep himself out of the news, frustrating the media who wanted to portray him as a hero.

But it had taken a lot of work to keep quiet the fact he had been running around an English town with a gun he had no right to have. The police's top brass didn't want to see him investigated, and Zack had already concluded his time in the police was at an end.

Besides, he'd already been spending his time trying to track down the man who'd abducted his daughter, Miley. How could he feel she was safe with the mad bastard who had caused so much destruction in Oakwell loose in the world? So when Chloe Evans, the other woman abducted, suggested they start a detective agency, whereby they could keep trying to find the man behind it all, Zack decided it was a good idea.

The killer they knew as Alex Ryan had eluded every law enforcement agency in the world. But Chloe and Alex had been determined to keep up the hunt. They knew they could also use Zack's detective experience to work on other cases to pay the bills.

London was the place to be. It helped that Chloe worked in the city with her father who had the Oakwell by-election to become a Member of Parliament at the second attempt, the first vote having been disrupted by Alex Ryan destroying the Town Hall.

London was also where the clients with money were.

Zack had initially moved from a London police station to Oakwell with his daughter to escape the violence that had nearly taken his life one night when responding to an incident. Now, he was back in the Capital as a private detective, and he'd found himself looking for marital infidelity or people who had disappeared owing substantial amounts of money. Not exactly the sort of investigating challenges he'd hoped for, and even that side of the business had slowed down to a mere trickle.

Plus, every lead on Alex Ryan had gone cold.

A light drizzle fell onto the window pane as Zack tried to rehearse the words he was going to use when Chloe came over to talk business. There seemed to be no straightforward way to say they were going bust, and she'd lose all the money she had invested.

Zack closed his eyes and tried to fend off the wave of despair that threatened to engulf him. He had let Chloe down. He had let everyone down.

On the desk, his phone rang. It was Adam, the intern who'd helped the police in Oakwell with data analysis. He'd worked for them in London until they couldn't afford to pay him anymore.

"Hi, Adam." Zack tried to sound upbeat as he answered.

"I'm on my way to see you." The excitement was evident in Adam's voice. "On the train. Can you be in the office at six thirty, maybe seven?"

"I've got a call with Miley before then, but I can wait in the office, no problem."

"Good, I'll be with some potential clients from the city. Could be a big one this, Zack."

5

With the sun climbing into a cloudless sky, the myriad of fall colours from New York's Central Park dazzled James with a beautiful array of yellow and oranges.

He'd always liked the penthouse office that soared into the blue sky next to Central Park. Being able to walk through a small patch of nature from his homes to get to his office was one of the little luxuries being rich afforded him.

Most of the morning had been taken up dealing with the London office. With nearly an entire floor wiped out by the terrorist bomb, they had to work out how to keep the money rolling in while seeming to be a benevolent, caring company to the press.

James had considered it a random act, and the fact their employees were caught up in it an unfortunate coincidence until the latest anonymous message had arrived on his phone.

"Isn't it what I pay you for? To stop this sort of thing." He turned to face the two people in his office. The dark-haired man wore a suit perfectly tailored to his muscular body. Next to him, a petite woman with sharp features looked pensive. James knew she had only started to work for the company a few months ago.

"You do, sir, but in this case, there's no trace of the calls or emails." It was the man who spoke. Brad Reynolds, the head of the security team who'd worked at Global Money for ten years.

"How can there be no trace?" James moved away from the window and walked towards them. "Everything is traceable these days; even the NS fucking A is listening in to all our calls if Fox News is to be believed."

Brad shifted his feet. "In this case, every measure was taken to hide the sender's identity. The messages were from cheap pay-as-you-go phones bought with cash. The emails were from one-time, generic accounts created through proxies, so no one can trace their origins. Even our best guys can't crack these."

"Then get better guys," James growled pacing across the room between two large leather sofas. He didn't understand most of what Brad was saying, but it didn't matter. It was obvious they had nothing.

"We've got the best money can buy," the woman protested. James glared at her, and she looked down at the carpet. Marian Simmons had been hired for her cyber security skills, and right now, James thought it was a mistake.

"It's probably just some nerd jockey hacked off at losing some cash on the markets and looking to troll," Brad added.

James now turned back to his head of security.

"Some fucking nerd. A nerd who knows things about my family no one else does. A nerd who hides his tracks so well your best," James threw out some air quotes, "guys can't track them down. This is serious; now go and take it seriously or go and find other jobs. Do I make myself clear?"

"Yes, Mr Goldstein," Brad said. "And we are."

James raised his hand. "I don't want to hear it. Hire more

people if you need to, but find out who's behind this and nail them."

The two employees looked to be almost bowing as they backed out of the room and away from the CEO of Global Money. It would do them good to be fearful of their jobs if they didn't deliver. He hadn't fired anybody for a while, and James thought he should start re-exerting his authority. The staff were beginning to get complacent.

Fixing himself a drink from the extensive bar, he moved back to the window and gazed out.

"You're out there somewhere, you fucker." James sipped on the single malt. The sharp taste flooded his mouth, giving him some momentary pleasure.

None of the messages made any sense. They indicated corruption within the company and that Global Money cared little for its own staff, never mind the rest of the world. Each message seemed to be part of a more significant statement, cryptic pieces to confuse him before revealing the whole. James wasn't a stranger to threatening messages. You didn't get to the position he occupied at one of the biggest financial houses in the world without upsetting a few people on the way.

Because of this, the first two emails had gone unnoticed, filtered out by his secretary. The third communication was a message to his personal cell and the fourth to a private email which only a few people should have known about. That's when he took notice and reviewed the other messages. There were six now, and while there'd been no direct threat to his life, they'd talked of bringing the company down together with all guilty parties—though the messages hadn't specified who the other guilty parties were.

The last message, the one open on his laptop, hinted at something more specific. Suggesting James was to blame for what happened when he ran the London office during the financial collapse.

They were brutal days, James recalled—hundreds laid off and thousands losing every penny they had. The company had only just survived, and he knew it was down to the ruthless culling of staff. Since then, James had introduced the most advanced automated trading platform he could find, and now, Global Money was on its way to being one of the biggest finance houses in the world.

If it was a disgruntled ex-employee behind the messages, there were plenty of them. But why now?

The fact his team couldn't find anything deeply troubled him. He knew they were good; the company took its cyber security very seriously, investing more in it than most of the other financial institutions. After all, they were using one of the most sophisticated computer systems money could buy. So, how had this person been able to get around all the safeguards and remain untraceable?

Glancing at his watch, James saw it was getting late, and he'd lined himself up a rather special anniversary dinner with his wife. A table had been booked together with an exceptional suite in a very exclusive hotel.

Gulping down the rest of his drink, he headed to the bathroom. For tonight at least, James would forget about his cyber stalker.

6

Miley entered the communication room and waved to the teacher with a short blonde bob sitting behind a desk at the head of the long, narrow room.

"Hi, Mrs Robinson," Miley said.

"I hope you are well, Miss Carter." Mrs Robinson adjusted her glasses, nodded to the console she wanted Miley to use, and then looked back down at the smart pad on the desk in front of her.

Miley skipped across the room and slid into the chair by the workstation.

She'd struggled to concentrate all morning knowing she was going to be able to call her dad. It had been tough not being able to speak to him on her eighteenth birthday, but they were the rules, and the rules were the price of being in one of the most exclusive and secretive schools in the world. Miley was even more excited about the fact she'd be able to get to see her dad and Chloe in a few days. It needed a boat and two planes to get to London's Heathrow airport, but it was always worth it.

She loved the school; loved the power and energy that came with being in the place every day. At the same time, it was hard being so far from her dad and not able to speak to him whenever she wanted. Miley knew how hard he'd taken her leaving despite being in total agreement with Uncle Jake's plan.

It was also difficult being apart from Chloe. In the short time they'd spent together since escaping from the house where both of them had been held, the two young women had become firm friends.

Miley even missed the guys from Uncle Jake's crew after the two months of intensive training they'd given her before she came to the school a year and a half ago. While her dad had been reluctant to allow his brother to teach her some of his tricks, with Alex still free in the world was threat enough to persuade him.

In those two months, she'd developed from a soft English teenager to what Miley considered to be a battle-hardened badass capable of taking on all the villians in society. While it might not be strictly true, it was how Miley liked to think when she was feeling low or vulnerable. Learning to shoot like a sniper was the part she'd most enjoyed. Miley had shot before, having gone with her dad to the firing ranges in England. But what she'd been taught at the training camp felt like a Hollywood movie. Martial arts, fitness, and weapons training that made her feel like Black Widow.

Miley had loved being on the range, lying in the prone position, and carefully monitoring her breathing as she peered down the scope at a target hundreds of metres away. There was an intense adrenalin burst after gently squeezing the trigger and watching the target burst apart.

Uncle Jake had told her she had a natural aptitude for rifle shooting, even though she only seemed to hit the target with every other shot.

After typing in her username and password into the computer, Miley hit the dial button, and a few minutes later, her dad's head filled the screen.

"Wow, you look older." A broad smile crossed his face.

"Don't be silly, Dad." Miley laughed. It was great to see him.

"Happy birthday, hun. Did you have a good day?"

"It was okay, sorry I couldn't Skype; you know the rules."

"Only on your allotted days, I get it. You still have a leave pass?"

"Of course." Miley beamed. "Can't wait to come back and see you all. Maybe I'll show you some of my mysterious skills."

"Unless they've taught you how to fly, I'm demanding our money back."

"Don't be stupid, Dad. We aren't even paying any fees." Miley flicked her hair behind her ears and couldn't help glancing at the timer. They were only allowed ten minutes for security reasons. The school was set on an island in the middle of the Atlantic, which apparently, classed it as residing in international waters and not under the jurisdiction of any country.

It was a special school, and the owners didn't want it to be known outside of their circles of influence. While it would always be difficult to hide its existence, they tried to keep as much of it a secret as possible. This meant the communications with the outside world were kept to a minimum. Each pupil was allocated a slot every week in which they could speak to a family member.

None of the students felt it was enough, but neither would any trade going back to an ordinary school. Miley knew many of the students came from affluent families and could probably afford to go to some of the best schools money could pay for, but that didn't seem to be what the island school was about. It recruited the brightest and the best from anywhere in the world, regardless of ethnicity, language, or wealth. They wanted to turn every student into citizens that would make society a better place, or so declared their mission statement.

"How are things, Dad? You turned into Sherlock Holmes yet?"

"Sadly, no." Zack shook his head and swallowed. "Things are okay though. We're getting by."

"I can tell when you're lying to me." Miley could see it on his face.

"It's okay, honest."

"Another lie right there." She shook her head. "I'm a copper's daughter. I'm your daughter, so I know when you're lying."

"Ex-copper," Zack reminded her.

"Whatever. I'll get the truth out of you when I get home. You do know that?"

"Uncle Jake taught you some interrogation techniques, did he?"

"Well, after I've pulled all your teeth out, I've heard peeling off the fingernails is the next best thing. Though, Uncle Jake wouldn't let me practise."

"I'm going to have a word with my brother when I next see him." Her dad tried hard to bring some levity into the conversation, but Miley knew he was hiding the truth. When she'd last been in London, she'd done some snooping and found out the agency was failing. Her dad blamed himself for her being kidnapped and felt responsible for not finding Alex, so her dad still classed Miley as being a possible target.

She'd also found a bottle of pills with the label Xanax, and when she'd looked it up, she realised her dad was suffering. If given a chance, Miley was going to try to talk to Chloe about it.

"I worry about you, Dad, and I miss you." It broke her heart to see her usually strong father hurting so much.

"I miss you too, honey." Zack touched her face on the screen. She glanced again at the countdown timer and knew their call was about to be over.

"I've gotta go, Dad. You got the flight details?"

"I'll be there to get you. Love you, honey."

"Love you too, Dad."

The screen went dark.

7

"I would like to talk to you about this policeman." Chloe was putting her coat on, ready to leave the office, when her mother floated in from the other room using her disapproving tone. Her mother was visiting from their constituency office in Oakwell.

"He's not a policeman anymore, Mother. He resigned."

"Well, exactly. It's about him and this silly agency." She could see her mother was flustered. The one positive effect of the horrific events in their hometown was Chloe was determined to take control of her own life. When offers came in for her story about the abduction in Oakwell, she'd negotiated hard and got one hell of a deal.

After her father finally won the by-election and needed to set up a London office, Chloe got involved on her terms. It worked out well they'd decided London was the best place to open their detective agency. The idea had been conceived in Zack's brother's Spanish Villa while they were all escaping the horror of what had befallen them. Though, she had to admit it was more her idea than Zack's. There were times when Chloe wondered if he went along with the plan because he couldn't think of anything better to do.

After collecting the money from her media deals, and with

a small revival in her old modelling career, she ploughed the cash into the agency. Their ultimate goal was to expand, so they would have the resources to track down Alex, and if he ever surfaced again, go after him. They'd tried to locate him in the early days, but it was as though he'd ceased to exist.

"It's not a silly agency. It's decent work, and it helps people who the police sometimes can't."

"I bet there are a lot of sleazy people round there all the time. I've seen it on the TV." Her mother was starting to tut now, getting into her stride.

"Yes, Mother, that's exactly the type of clientele we encourage." Chloe knew there had been one or two cases that bordered on sleazy. Hiding behind a tree waiting to picture an unfaithful spouse in the embrace of another was not what Zack had signed up for when they'd started the agency.

Chloe was on her way to see Zack as he'd said there was something they needed to talk about. Having hung up the phone, she'd tried to shed the despondent mood that had fallen over her. Her partner might believe he was hiding the agency's decline from her, but she knew.

"Zack's a good man. If it weren't for him, I probably wouldn't be here now." It was always Chloe's trump card, which had her mother tutting again.

"I know dear, I know." Her mother's tone went defensive. "And your father and I will always be thankful to him for keeping you safe. But, you should be with men more your age Chloe. We are having a dinner party tonight, and there will be some very eligible, single men there."

"Not this again, please Mother. I think I've had my fill of men for a long time. At least Zack doesn't try to get me into bed every time he sees me." Chloe started to button up her coat determined to end the pointless conversation. "More's the pity." She added half under her breath.

Smiling inwardly at her mother's shocked expression, Chloe took the opportunity to slip out the door. There was a time when she'd wished Zack wanted to be with her, but of late, he seemed so distant, and he had lost the powerful aura of the brave hero who'd led her through the burning cellars to freedom. She knew he missed his daughter badly, but it didn't seem he wanted anyone in his life. Chloe still hoped he might come around one day. She wanted him to be happy and believed he could be happy with her. But, she could only wait so long.

"Looks like rain, Miss Evans. I'd be taking a cab." It was the doorman Clive who spoke as he opened the door for her. With all that had happened in the past, her father's London office had decided upon some security. Not that she thought middle-aged Clive the doorman would offer much defensive if someone like Alex came calling. He might have been ex-army, but the days since had not been kind to his waistline.

"Thanks, but the tube is good." She finished buttoning up her coat as she passed through the door and into the busy London street.

The chilly afternoon was quickly turning into a cold evening. Chloe hurried down the road, joining the mass of commuters making their way home for the evening. It would be good to see Zack again, even if it was unwelcome news about the agency. She knew he'd tried his best, but his heart wasn't in it after his daughter had left.

When Miley went overseas for her training before going to the exclusive school, Chloe had noticed Zack seemed less than enthused about being a private detective. It probably didn't help because of the mundane cases they were getting rather than the glamorous world of private detectives seen on TV.

At least Chloe had her role with her father, as well as the modelling jobs. Though they too were drying up, old news together with her ageing looks meant the money that had helped tide the detective agency over wasn't there anymore.

She wondered what Zack would do once the business folded.

The Evening Standard caught her eye as she was standing in the queue for the escalators down to the Underground platforms. Its banner headline indicated that there had been a flash crash on the New York stock exchange.

Chloe wondered what the hell a flash crash was.

8

"Take a seat, gentleman," Zack smiled. "I'd offer you a drink, but my secretary has left for the day." The truth was Amy had left for the day five months ago and never came back. Hardly surprising since she'd been told there wasn't enough money to pay her salary anymore. But Zack had to at least try to make out to the two professional gentlemen Adam had brought to the office that they were a thriving business.

The men had the city look and the city suits. The older one certainly had the confidence, bordering on arrogance, of a man with the experience of making billion-dollar deals. His younger colleague, in the slightly less expensive charcoal suit, didn't look as comfortable in his city skin. He kept adjusting his glasses as if he felt his hands needed something to do.

Zack felt embarrassed welcoming them into the office with its dowdy look and worn furniture. He'd found a vacuum and duster to try to make it look more presentable, but anything was going to be inadequate compared to the offices of a top finance house these two gentlemen belonged to. He thought one of their suits was probably worth more than all the furniture the agency owned.

"Gentlemen, I'd like you to meet Zack Carter, the owner of the Angel Detective Agency." Adam introduced them as the men took their seats. "Zack, this is Brandon Walsh, Senior Associate of Risk Tracking at Global Money here in London, and Terry White, a data scientist in the same department."

Zack nodded to them both while Adam took a seat next to him. He wasn't quite sure what a data scientist was. While Zack had spent years in military intelligence sifting through data to find critical information to assist the troops on the ground, it had never been known as a type of science. "It's all software driven nowadays, I take it?"

"For a long time." Brandon nodded. "But more than you'll ever realise. Global Money was one of the first to move into automated trading powered by very sophisticated artificial intelligence. It does a lot of our work as it's far better at spotting trends than most humans."

"Most?"

"The algorithms will still take years to perfect, if they ever can be, and until then, we adopt a hybrid model where there are human inputs and assessments of trades to see if we need to tweak things. While the software learns from its mistakes, it's only as good as the data it learns from. New variables need to be considered all the time. This is where my department and Terry get involved."

"You said you were the first." Zack was mostly following what Brandon was saying. "Are the other banks doing the same?"

"Many have started programs, but none have reached the level we have." Brandon exuded pride at this, and even his junior seemed to sit a little straighter.

"So, what can I do for you today?" Zack used what Chloe called his winning smile. She'd made him use it when they posed for photographs for the small media campaign they'd done when opening the office in London. Zack had hated every minute.

"I want you to find out who was behind the pub bombing." Brandon pulled at his well-trimmed beard that was showing signs the latest colouring was wearing off.

Zack was taken aback. "Don't you think that's a job for the police and security agencies? Wasn't it a terrorist incident?" He'd heard a little-known branch of the Islamic State had set up in the UK and claimed responsibility.

"We've reason to doubt this," Brandon said. "And a lot of our staff, people from our floor, were killed in the attack. Terry would've been if he'd not stayed in the office working that night."

Zack glanced at Terry and saw the pain in his eyes. The guilt of being glad he'd not been out with his colleagues that night. "It must be traumatic. My sympathies for the loss of your friends."

"The bomber was an ex-employee," Brandon continued. "He was let go a few months back. We need fewer traders as the software improves. He was one of the weak ones, and as a US company, the weak ones soon find themselves looking for other jobs. He was born to a Muslim family but never seemed to be aligned with extremist values."

"You think it was a revenge attack?"

"My information is that the police have found evidence on his computers which show he's been visiting radical sites and communicating with an organisation that provided him with the equipment he needed. He'd also been known to visit a local mosque on occasion on the pretext of working with the poor. His wife however, doesn't appear convinced he'd been turned by religion or radicalised in any way. She'd never heard him talking in that manner. Right up until the moment of the bomb, he was mad at Global Money, but there was nothing to suggest that he was going to kill himself."

"You've got good information," Zack said.

"It pays to in our business," Brandon replied. "This will soon become public, which is why I can share it with you. I have papers prepared for you to sign. Non-disclosure agreements. You understand? Few people know what I am about to tell you, and the company we work for would rather it was kept that way. There is something more to this case that directly affects Global Money. I cannot divulge anything further until you've accepted the assignment?"

Zack was puzzled. If this were a terrorist case, there would be little he could offer.

"Why did you come to us?"

"We started looking for someone suitable, and Terry has a friend." Brandon nodded to Adam.

"We shared a house in Uni," Adam interjected. "Proper den of geeks."

"I knew he'd gone on to work with the police and thought I'd seen on Facebook he was with a detective agency in London," Terry said. "He has the sort of skills that we may need."

"As do you." Brandon looked at Zack. "Not just from what happened at Oakwell. From before."

Zack nodded. He knew Brandon was referring to his time in military intelligence.

"We believe those particular skills will be needed in this case," Brandon said. "If you'll take it."

"So, is this a type of computer fraud, hacking?" It was the only reason Zack could think would have brought them to this office.

"Will you take the case?" Brandon said. "We've seen your rates, and they're fine, and we encourage you to engage as many people as you need. We'll pay an extensive retainer, and all we ask is that this investigation is kept confidential."

"You had me on extensive retainer." Zack smiled. It wasn't a total lie as he was hooked by the intrigue. "Though, I should get my lawyers to check any documents."

"Mr Carter, we're here to help, not hinder. I understand the financial predicament your company is in and how much you need the retainer. I'm not here to quibble; I'm here for your skills." Brandon pulled open his laptop case and produced a sheaf of papers. "All I need is for you to sign these, and we can begin. I understand you won't get started until the retainer clears, so this will be concluded by bank transfer today. Will the sum of twenty-five thousand be sufficient?"

"That'll be fine." Zack tried not to show his hands were shaking as he took the papers.

9

"Daddy says everyone is going into meltdown over the crash." Lilly began rubbing Darren's shoulders through his black polo top. As usual, he was at his computer writing the incomprehensible hieroglyphics he called code.

"But pleased it didn't affect Global Money."

"Oh, yes." Lilly's father was James Goldstein, CEO of the third largest bank in the world. Or soon to be first as her father kept telling her whenever she went round for dinner. Lilly worked in the company's media department, putting her much-maligned journalist degree to effective use. "I've already sanctioned the press release telling the world, and our investors, that our systems behaved perfectly and there was no risk to client investments. Wouldn't like to be in the PR departments of those banks where the shit hit the fan. Rumour has it JP Morgan got walloped. Guess they'll be looking for new software now."

The flash crash had been blamed on high-frequency traders operating out of some of the finance house's dark pools, though the experts were questioning this. High frequency traders made fast trades for tiny amounts of profit, but doing so many meant the gains were huge. Only this time, the movement had been so massive the markets had flashed down for a few minutes before the system recovered.

"Which will be why our share price has gone up." Darren flicked his screen onto the share prices, highlighting Austin Trading Services had jumped three percent.

"Nice." Lilly nodded. She appreciated how much work her boyfriend had put into his software company and how much that was helping Global Money become the giant it was. "The markets are expecting more of them to be knocking on your door. At least the exchange safeguards kicked in and suspended trading, but there's still a lot of panic. Everyone is checking their software." She draped her arms around his neck, loving the feel of the solid body underneath. "Maybe you'll make enough money one day for Father to approve."

"I'm surprised he's not worshipping at my feet after today."

Lilly laughed and threw herself into the comfortable chair near the desk Darren was sitting at. She liked to curl up next to him working on her tablet while Darren immersed himself in a complex web of code and financial transactions. Even though few words would pass between them for hours, it was comforting to have him close.

"That's because he believes you only exist because of his company," she continued. "No funding from Global Money, no Austin Trading Services. Ergo, you owe him more than he owes you, and that makes you unworthy of his only daughter."

The two of them had met after Darren had been invited to one of the many social affairs her parents attended. As usual, Lilly was along in her role as head of media relations. Her father had wanted a piece recording how they'd worked with the latest artificial intelligence trading software to help push Global Money ahead of the competition.

The two of them had met privately, and sparks had flown.

Only it wasn't the sort of matchup her father approved of, so for the most part, she'd kept the relationship out of the limelight. That had suited Darren. He'd only agreed to the media piece if his picture and details were kept out of it. Despite his confident persona, Darren was shy around other people, shunning some high-profile invitations in favour of a cosy night in. It was something Lilly found refreshing after dating a string of men hungry for fame and money who looked to use her connections to achieve their ambitions.

"I seem to recall the class system in England was similar." Darren stretched his back and rolled his shoulders. "I need a drink."

"You making?" Lilly said looking hopeful.

"Strawberry or banana?"

"Ooh, strawberry." Lilly loved his milkshakes and had never known a man to be so into them. "Do they know the real cause of the flash crash?"

"Greedy companies with fraudulent algorithms in place taking advantage of exchanges that haven't got their act together," Darren said.

"Their safeguards did kick in," Lilly pointed out. It was something the trading platforms were continually espousing in the media.

"Should've been able to stop them in the first place." Darren re-entered the room carrying two large glasses. He handed one to Lilly.

"Lovely," she said sucking up the smooth strawberry flavour like she was a teenager again. "Phoebe has got tickets for the game at the Garden tonight. Do you want to come?"

Darren threw out his best smile. "Love to."

"I don't believe you." She chuckled stirring her shake with

the straw. "You never like basketball." It was a game Lilly loved, but then, she was a fan of all sports, which was probably because her father had always been able to get free tickets to the best events.

"I'm always happy to be where you are, beautiful." He stepped across the room and kissed her tenderly on her milkshake coated lips. Lilly's insides tingled as he drew back and returned to his chair. She was tempted to jump him there and then.

"But I have got to go to London in a few days."

"Again?" That shattered her mood. "We've only just come back."

Darren shrugged and annoyingly turned back to his computer. "We've got some good deals in the pipeline. It's still a new office and needs my help."

Lilly knew there would be no discussion on this. Darren was terrific, but when he wanted to do something, he did it regardless of how she felt. Maybe that decisiveness was something she liked about him, but at times, it really upset her.

"But before then, we might have a little trip."

"Ooh, where to?" A previous trip had been to a beautiful lakeside cabin in Oregon where they had spent most of it in a bed that overlooked the stillest lake in the world. Lilly felt aroused just thinking about it.

"Now, that would spoil the surprise."

After seeing his wicked grin, Lilly couldn't resist it any longer. Rising from the sofa, she peeled off her sweatshirt and began to slowly push her leggings down.

Darren swung his chair and watched her. "And would your Daddy approve of this behaviour?"

"He'd call me a dirty little slut and disown me," Lilly said climbing naked on to Darren's lap. "And as long as I'm fucking you, I don't give a shit."

10

"When do we close?"

"I'm sorry?" Zack was taken aback by Chloe's direct question. They were sitting in the office, Chloe with her feet curled up under her on the sofa opposite, nursing one of the bottles of cold lager they kept in the fridge.

"I've felt it coming, Zack. And I assume you didn't get the rest of the money for the William's investigation?"

"Worse."

"Worse?" Chloe raised an eyebrow, bottle pausing midway to her lips. "How so?"

"He's going to sue us for the money he's already paid."

"What a gentleman. So, we're screwed?"

"You think I should have done differently?" Her tone ruffled Zack. She sighed, stretched her legs out on the sofa and took a long drink of lager before turning to look at him again.

"No, I don't. It's a shit world out there Zack, but at least a few of us need to try to keep some morals."

"Bad day with your mother?"

"Got it one. Tried to have the same old you are spending too much time with that loser and the silly agency conversation as I was on my way over."

"Do you want to talk about it?" He tried to ignore the tag

of a loser as it was an accurate description of how he'd felt as the agency collapsed around his ears. Chloe swivelled on the sofa, so she was lying down.

"How much do you charge for a session, Doctor Carter?"

"It depends on what sort of session you want." Zack couldn't help himself, and Chloe burst out laughing before pushing herself back up to a sitting position.

"Maybe that's the therapy I need, and perhaps a selfie I could send to my mother."

Zack laughed and took a swig from his bottle. "I'd pay to see that."

"What, the session or the selfie? Or maybe it's a session with my mother?"

"Chloe, wash your mouth out."

"You laugh, but I'm convinced she's got a crush on you."

"Ah, that's why she never wants to see me. In case she can't resist tearing all her clothes off and throwing herself at me."

"Got it one." Chloe pointed her bottle at him. "Anyway, I take it that's it then. No more money. I've haven't told Mother yet. I don't think I can take the endless I told you so."

"Well, that's not quite it."

"Ooh, now you've piqued my interest." She leaned forward. "Do tell."

"We've had another job come in this evening. A big one with a hefty fee and nice fat retainer."

"How fat?"

"Twenty-five grand."

Chloe spluttered on her drink. "Are you serious? What the hell is it for?"

"To investigate the circumstances around the bombing the other night." Having dreaded telling Chloe the agency was going to have to shut down, the assignment from Adam's contact had made the conversation a whole lot easier.

He'd already let Chloe down by not making a success of their business. By not being the friend she wanted him to be. By letting his grip on things slip so severely he was staring into the dark abyss of despair.

"The terrorist attack?"

Zack nodded.

"Who the hell is paying us for that?"

"Global Money."

"Who lost people in the attack," Chloe's face was screwed up as she tried to make sense of it. Zack couldn't help but notice who cute it made her look. It reminded him of the opportunity he'd let go by.

"Sort of figures. But why us when the police will be all over it?"

"The employees were from a department keeping tabs on the trading. Apparently, there's some high-tech software doing a lot of the grunt work for them. They've uncovered the possibility someone has been trading with client money and syphoning off the profits without it ever appearing on the books."

"And they think the bomb was to cover it up?"

"It's a possibility." Zack lifted his bottle in acknowledgement. Having a few hours ago been facing an uncertain future with no job or prospects, the hope of the previous meeting had given him a lift and made the sweet lager taste so good. He felt like a night on the town. He felt like getting smashed.

"So, it wasn't a terrorist bomb?"

"It's still the most likely explanation. Which is why I wanted to talk to you." Zack sucked back the last of his lager before rising to his feet. "It's possible the same people behind the bomb are effectively harvesting money off Global Money. All the company wants us to do is find out what we can. If it's really being taken and by whom. Anything after that will get handed over to the relevant authorities. We'd get paid and would be out of the game."

"I sense a but."

"Not so much a but. It's just this may mean going against the terrorists. We might be probing areas they don't want us to. If they're behind the trading anomalies, there's a possibility it opens us up to being targets."

"We've been there before." Chloe shrugged.

"One crazed individual. This could be an entire organisation."

"We're not trying to bring them down, just get to the truth of where the money is going. And what's the alternative for our company if we don't take it?"

"We'll be shutting down," Zack admitted.

"Proving my mother right." Chloe shook her head. "I can't have that. ISIS seems almost tame in comparison to a lifetime of I told you so. Shit, let's take the money, do what we can, but bug out if anything looks like it could spill back on us."

"We'll need Adam, too. He's already down because it's one of his Uni friends who found the issue. He's checking into a hotel."

"Small world." She relaxed back into the sofa as Zack drifted into the kitchen to retrieve another couple of bottles from the fridge.

"Will you have time for this?" He handed a fresh one to Chloe. "With all our other help gone, I'm a little short-handed."

"The modelling jobs aren't exactly queuing at the door right now, and unless I want to do the round of reality TV shows, it's helping out at Dad's London office. And there's only so much I can do there."

"Offers for reality TV?" Zack was surprised, but then again, you didn't seem to need much media exposure to be considered qualified for most of the TV shows.

"Believe it or not, I still have what it takes." She flicked her head melodramatically making him smile. "But the thought of being cooped up with a bunch of wannabees doesn't appeal anymore. I know what a pretentious bitch I was before all of this, and I don't want to be around that sort anymore."

"What do you mean were a pretentious bitch?" Zack sat back down, narrowly avoiding a cushion hurled in his direction.

"Cheeky bastard."

"Don't think your mother will like you playing detective again?"

"No, but if I offer the alternative of going on Big Brother, I know which will win. I'm tempted to go on just to see if she stays in the country. And either of those options is still better than being married off, which is what she wants for me. Let's give Adam a call. We can get some food and talk about it."

For the first time in a while, Zack felt he was doing something useful again.

11

Harvey watched Francine's cute arse wriggle provocatively as she made her way out of his apartment. She stopped at the door, blew him a kiss to make sure he didn't forget her sweet embrace, and then pulled the door closed while giggling with her colleague. Harvey doubted Francine was her real name, and frankly didn't care if she kept coming over for their regular sessions, especially if she kept bringing her hot blonde friend with her. It might cost him double, but it was worth it.

As the sound of their heels on the hard floor of the corridor faded, so too did Harvey's happy feelings. The euphoria was dissipating, and his body was spent after a full night with two high-class hookers. Reality seeped back into his world, and Harvey didn't like it. He considered a line of coke, or maybe a couple more blues to keep his mood going. But Harvey knew it was too late to stave off the mood swing.

He looked forward to the weekly sex sessions. It was a reward for the countless hours spent piecing together the multi-million-dollar deals which had made his company a shit load of money for twenty years. There were nights when he was able to score girls who didn't have a set of rates for each sexual activity, but he'd always liked to have a regular session with a sense of familiarity. And fuck it, he'd made so much money, why not spend an evening with the best hookers, booze, and drugs money could buy?

His mood swing was because there was a deadline on his ability to spend cash at the rate he had been. The money was fast running out. In fact, who was he kidding, it had already run out, and he was relying on the credit he'd built up over the years. His moneylenders thought he was using the loans to enhance his fortune. Only Harvey was using it to keep his habits going while the rest of his life turned to shit. He needed to show people he still had it, even if most knew he was on the way down. They saw him as a burned-out trader who'd lost the edge. What pained Harvey was watching young, arrogant pricks flashing their cash as their chips were coming in and laughing at the old guy who was probably about to be canned.

Harvey looked at his dwindling stash of pills on the table and knew he'd need more to get him through the week. That meant having to restock from Alphonse, a dealer he was already in massive debt to. He'd considered a new supplier, but who else would give him a line of credit? And how long before Alphonse decided to call in his debt? Harvey knew the time was near, and that made the need for a drug-fuelled oblivion even stronger.

Tina Turner blasted out on the smartphone on the black table next to the bright blue pills and discarded wine bottles. Francine loved expensive red wine.

Who the fuck was messaging him this time of night?

Harvey automatically glanced at his wrist before realising the smartwatch was probably on the bedroom floor. He grinned for a moment, trying to recall the moment it had been ripped off during his fuck-fest with the girls. He thought of ignoring the message, allowing himself to slip into a peaceful oblivion fuelled by vodka and pills, but there was a nagging thought at the back of his head. Something told him the message was important. He leaned over, stretched out to grasp the phone, and thumbed the slider.

How badly do you want to get back in the game?

Harvey read the words a few times. He didn't recognise the number, and while it could be dismissed as junk, he was drawn in by the prospect of something that could improve his lot.

Who is this?

Do you want to get back into the game?

Yes.

Check your email.

Was this for real?

Harvey dragged himself from the sofa to his solid oak table in the kitchen diner. Every surface in his kitchen was made with the finest material he could afford in an ostentatious display of his wealth. Recently, he'd wondered how easy it would be to sell it and clear his debts to Alphonse. Only Alphonse though, the others he owed money to could fuck off and die.

Flipping open his MacBook, a shaky finger brushed the screen allowing him to check his email. At the very top was one with the title "Back in the game." Still expecting it to be a scam, Harvey opened the email.

He took a sharp intake of breath as adrenaline surged through his body.

With this information, Harvey Gibbons was very much back in the game.

12

It reminded Chloe of the exciting times when they'd first set up the agency as she looked around the office. Printouts were piled high on a large table; other pages considered significant were pinned to a board on one of the office walls. Chloe was entering information about the bombing and Global Money found on the Internet in a spreadsheet, so it could be catalogued and cross-referenced.

When they'd first moved in, Zack had been caught up in the enthusiasm of preparing the new office as they printed business cards and figured ways of getting their name out better known. Zack had fancied himself as a Private Investigator, even though he knew the real police detectives looked down on them like pond scum. Adam had been there in the beginning, too. Head into the numbers as usual, trying to work out how far their budget would stretch for advertising.

Having seen Zack slip into a morose state over the last months, and knowing how much he missed his daughter, Chloe had begun to worry. While she had other things going on outside the agency, it was all Zack had. Now, her friend was sitting at the end of the table, a mug of steaming black coffee in his hand and a glint in his eye. This was the man she loved to be around.

"When did Brandon say we can get the rest of the information Terry had?" Adam said, swiping a hand through his wavy blond hair. Chloe thought he carried a greater air of confidence than when he first worked for them.

"He's going to come by tonight," Zack said. "Terry will join us to help you make sense of it. He's doing his own research today, visiting a few mates elsewhere in the city to see if something similar is happening."

"Good." Adam nodded. "Did you ask Brandon about access to the Global Money network? It's the only way I'm going to get a good look at what could've happened. Might need to drop some tools on there too, if I'm allowed."

"He's asking, but getting your software on there is a no-go through official channels," Zack said.

"Unofficial ones?" Chloe raised her eyebrows.

"Well, I can't ask him. It's something we'd have to do ourselves. Can you avoid detection?"

"I'd need access to the server rooms." Adam didn't look confident. "If they have them, as a lot of their stuff might be in the cloud, but we can try to get something in place."

"Could you make it look like an external hack?" Chloe said, "So it can't be traced to us?"

Adam shrugged. "Possibly. I'd need to call on some friends." She wondered what sort of friends he was mixing with.

"Okay, if he can get us in the room at least, then let's do it," Zack said. "Otherwise, let's keep hacking off the table until we know it's a must. What do we know about the bomber?"

"An Asian male, thirty-six years old with two children." Chloe looked through her notes. "No previous connection with terrorist or radical organisations, can't see any evidence he was on the watch list. He was a training to be a social worker in Tower Hamlets after being canned from Global Money six months ago. There is a chance he could've been radicalised at the local mosque, but it's not known for that sort of thing. His wife has said he spent time there, even though he wasn't a practising Muslim. She thought he was helping out in the community."

"Can people go from zero to suicide bomber that quickly?" Zack asked.

"I'll do some research." Chloe made a note. "Regards, the attack itself, he travelled by tube to Bank underground station then walked into The Lamb Tavern where he set off the device. A woman on the train remembered him because he looked as though he was going to puke."

"Can we get hold of CCTV?" Adam was typing furiously on his black laptop.

"I'm trying," Zack said, "but it's still being linked to terrorism, so not easy to get released. A splinter group of ISIS has claimed responsibility, stating the man was one of their agents of Allah. Authorities are still waiting on confirmation of a direct link to ISIS."

"I'll see what's on social media," Adam said.

Zack turned to look at the board where seventeen pictures of the murdered victims were pinned. Twelve were from Global Money's risk department, as well as a further fifteen of the thirty seriously injured. "Nothing yet to suggest this was a cover-up of the money scandal?"

"Zip," Chloe said. "Global Money has garnered some sympathy for bankers for once. Though not too much." She'd seen the news shows where certain groups saying the money men deserved all they got. It was a message from God to clean up their act.

"Adam, can you get a profile on as many of the co-workers as you can, starting with those still alive?" Zack asked. Adam nodded without looking up from his screen. "Then, I want all the personnel in their IT department. If someone is running a money scam, there must be people on the inside. Anything significant on the systems they use?"

"Software from Austin Trading Solutions," Adam read from the notes he'd typed up. "A hi-tech company that writes auto trading algorithms to cut humans out of the loop as much as possible. It uses some sophisticated AI. Global Money was one of the first to implement the programs and it's propelled the bank to the third biggest in the world. It's left others desperately trying to catch up."

"You're checking on the company?" Zack asked.

"Sure am. Interestingly, Global Money was not affected in yesterday's flash crash. They claim the state-of-the-art software protected their investors from any spurious trades. I've printed off the release."

"You think this software is involved in the anomalies?"

"It's where Terry was finding them," Adam said.

"Okay, you concentrate on the software and Austin Trading Solutions. Chloe, can you find out more about where the bomber worked and see if you can talk to anyone he would've been linked with? I know the police have probably been all over it, but you can be subtler. There has to be a connection between the money and the bombing."

"Right you are, Sir." Chloe gave a mock salute as she rose, already armed with a list of names to visit. It was surprising what people would say to a stranger they wouldn't to the authorities.

"I'm going to chat with some contacts," Zack said. "A few

of my old colleagues when I was last down here are in Anti-Terror. I might be able to tickle some information out of them. Brandon is due here at seven, so let's meet back then."

Chloe grabbed her coat on the way out the door feeling a surge of adrenaline she hadn't for a long time.

13

Brandon felt sure he'd be caught transferring files to the memory stick attached to his key ring. Security performed cursory searches as you entered and exited the building. But they hadn't spotted his tiny drive disguised as a Chelsea football on the way in, and he was hoping it would be the same when he left for the evening.

Following Terry's instructions, Brandon had located the data they needed. Extra auditing had been put in place the morning after the explosion, and the agency expected the logs would reveal the source of the secret trades.

Brandon knew the career risk he was taking by smuggling sensitive data out of the company. But, the clandestine way he'd hired the private detective agency was already breaking company policies. As he had complete control of his department's budget, the retainer Brandon had already authorised wouldn't be questioned for a while. By then, he hoped to have concrete results to justify his actions.

His actions might cost Brandon his career and lucrative pension, but it was nothing compared to the lives already lost.

The atmosphere in the office was strange, even without his subterfuge. Already, the desks were left empty by the dead analysts, and assessors were occupied. Some staff had flown over from the US office, and others had been transferred from elsewhere in the building.

Perfunctory counsellors had been hired for the employees to talk to, so the company could ensure it was complying with its duty of care. But while compassionate leave seemed to be freely offered, everyone at Global Money knew the effect that prolonged time off had on your career.

Brandon and Terry had been offered the chance to take a leave of absence, only he'd seen it in his own bosses' eyes that while it was okay for Terry to take a day or two, it was not something they expected from a department head. Brandon was supposed to suck it up and get on with his job of making money.

Could it really be that they didn't know about the funds being syphoned away from the company? Or was this part of some internal fraud certain people in the organisation were aware of? So many questions made Brandon feel very unsafe in the company he'd been at for over thirty years. He twitched whenever his phone rang, expecting it to be one of the directors summoning him for a conference. At least, if they wanted to get rid of him, then the payoff would be good. More than once during the day, he considered that might well be the best option.

His own direct line manager, Jan Helmund, had been dismissive of the possible fraud. While Brandon understood he might not have followed the complex calculations put in front of him, he should at least have listened to those who did. Instead, Brandon had been told to get back to work and rebuild his team.

The searches being more thorough on the way out of the building, Brandon's nervousness increased as the time to leave neared. Despite his seniority within the company, Brandon wasn't convinced they wouldn't pick up on his newly acquired accessory. Reaching into his holdall he retrieved his phone, slipped it into his trouser pocket, and headed towards the toilets. He checked they were empty before stepping into one of the cubicles and sitting down.

He plugged the flash drive into the Windows phone and waited for it to boot. While unsure if there was any software monitoring, which would detect sensitive data being transferred out of the building, Brandon decided it was a risk worth taking. When the phone sprang to life, he connected to his personal email, attached the zipped file on the drive, and sent it to two private emails. He then deleted the sent items from his account and shut down the phone.

For a few minutes, he waited in the cubicle, expecting security to burst through the door and apprehend him. When nothing happened, he eased from the toilet seat and slipped back into the central office to say his goodbyes as others were leaving. At least, if he were caught, the data would be available for the detective agency to examine.

Taking deep breaths to calm his nerves, Brandon pulled his jacket off the rack and headed for the lifts. Once again, he thought about trying to forget about the nightmare Terry had brought to him. Brandon could work out his final few years in ignorant bliss, take his hefty pension, and live an excellent life far away from the corruption of the money world. He already had enough to live a wealthy lifestyle in retirement.

Taking these risks could only bring him trouble. But good people had died, and Brandon wanted to know the truth.

14

Zack let his call ring through to Brandon's voicemail before hanging up. He'd already left a message.

"Have you tried his personal number?" Chloe asked.

"Straight to voicemail, too." Zack glanced at the clock on the wall. It was nearly eight in the evening. Brandon was an hour late.

A loud banging on the office door attracted their attention.

"This has to be him." Chloe rose from the sofa and pulled open the door.

"He's dead." Terry staggered inside. Chloe caught hold of his arm to prevent him from falling over.

"Bring him through here." Zack rushed to help. Terry was a deathly shade of white. "Adam, get him some water."

Zack and Chloe steered Terry into the office and onto a couch.

"Stay with him." Zack moved out of the door and onto the landing. Their offices were on the third floor of a small complex shared with mainly accountants and lawyers. He looked around the spacious hallway that served as a stopping off point for the lift and stairs. If Terry had been followed, he couldn't see anyone, and he already knew the workers had left the accountancy firm opposite for the night.

Terry was on the couch sipping water with Chloe next to him, one arm around his shoulders, while she also held his hand. She looked up at Zack as he returned, closing and locking the door behind him.

"It's Brandon. He's been killed."

"How?" Zack perched himself on the opposite sofa next to Adam.

"Hit as he was walking away from the office." Terry's voice was shaky. "A van mounted the kerb and struck a load of people. Brandon was one of those killed."

Adam flipped his phone from his pocket and brought it to life. "It's in the news. Three killed. The driver jumped out and attacked people on the pavement with a knife while shouting "God is great" in Arabic before running off. Apparently, the media are speculating it was a Christian prayer group on the street corner he was aiming for."

"I want any footage that's on the news," Zack said, "and any phone images as soon as they are uploaded."

"On it." Adam jumped off the sofa.

"It's not random," Chloe whispered.

"No chance." Zack shook his head. "Fuck, this just got very real. Brandon was supposed to bring the data for us to examine, and he never made it, which tells me that whatever he was bringing was the real deal." He paused for a moment, trying to collect his thoughts. "We need to get hold of that data."

"I've got it," Terry said. "He sent it to my personal email before he left in case anything happened." His voice cracked as he fumbled in his pocket before handing his phone to Chloe.

"Adam, new priority, get the files and then delete them. In fact, trash his phone. Shit, it could already have been traced here. Is there anything we can do?"

"Drop it in the back of a taxi." Adam moved off towards the other office and his laptop. "But it will still have signalled as being here. Assuming it was tracked."

"Can we slow down a minute?" Chloe asked. "What are you saying, Zack?"

"They knew Brandon was carrying sensitive data. So, they could also know Terry had been emailed the files, and it could make him a target."

"I'm scared," Terry stammered.

Zack looked sympathetically at the young man. "You need to stay with us until we figure this out. I'm just calculating the worst- case scenario. The reality is anyone tracing us here would need access to some very sophisticated law enforcement technology. And if they did, they'd already be knocking on our door."

"Should we go to the police?" Chloe asked.

"I think we're going to have to." Zack nodded. "Let's see what more we can piece together tonight, and we'll take it to them in the morning."

"Guys, I've already got some aftermath footage that's been posted online," Adam shouted through from what used to be the secretary's office.

"Thank you for the voyeuristic public," Zack said. "Bring it here."

Adam returned and sat on the sofa, allowing the others to crowd around him and see the screen. As usual, there was a litany of professionals espousing their opinion on what happened and speculating if the attack was related to the bombing a few days ago. The screen flicked to shaky mobile footage as the person holding the phone tried to zoom into the scene. They could hear people screaming in the background.

"There he is." Zack saw a man in a hooded coat carrying a knife in his gloved hand. He ran to the bodies, and there was the sickening sight of him stabbing the first victim, which appeared to a woman, before moving on to a body in a business suit. The man plunged the knife into the businessman's chest.

"Oh my god, Brandon," Terry wailed before Chloe buried his head in her chest to muffle his sobs. Out of the corner of his eye, Zack saw she was giving him a questioning stare at showing the footage to Terry, but it had served its purpose in him identifying the body. Plus, Zack needed to see what happened next. It was only a subtle movement of the attacker's hands, but Zack saw it.

"Adam, stop and replay the last twenty seconds."

"Zack, don't."

Zack held his hands up against Chloe's protests. "Play it back a quarter speed."

"Zack."

"Chloe, you have to see this."

All eyes turned to the screen again as the film played just after the first stab penetrated Brandon's upper body.

"Do you see it?"

"My god, he's searching the body," Chloe exclaimed.

"And he's taking things, look." The figure appeared to have grabbed something from inside Brandon's jacket. Then he was up and gone.

"He knew exactly what he was looking for." Zack rose and began to pace the room. "It confirms what we suspected. This was no random attack by a lone terrorist. This was a targeted hit."

15

The stiff breeze buffeted Chris's body. He nearly lost his grip on the cold metal railing behind him. Steadying himself, Chris felt his oversized belly clench with fear. He was shivering, too. It wasn't the temperature to be so high up on the roof in a standard company shirt and tie.

Despite the amount of coke he'd snorted, Chris hadn't been able to follow the instructions. His hands had been shaking so much he couldn't hit the right keys at his workstation. It wasn't as though he couldn't remember what he'd been asked to do; that had been etched into his mind along with the images on the emails.

How had the bastard got them?

When would the torment stop?

The first few tasks he'd been asked to perform had been simple, and Chris hadn't been able to understand how it would benefit anyone. Giving up his login details were useless unless you were already inside the network due to the security of the systems he worked on. But he knew the servers processed millions of stock trades every day for some of America's largest exchanges, and that information would be valuable to someone.

Chris even recognised some of the trading numbers he'd

been requested to send to his tormenter. Yet, if the data was acted upon, the traders would be flagged as insider deals, and the authorities would be hammering at their doors.

Only now, it was different; now, they wanted unrestricted access to virtually all the system, and while Chris had argued he didn't have the correct permission to do so, it was clear these were the type of people who didn't take no for an answer. They'd exploited his relationship with Eamon to get him to do what they demanded; they knew everything.

He could feel his heart hammering as the coke high flooded through his system. While the wind whistled passed his frozen ears, it seemed so peaceful high above the Manhattan streets. The building was tall; anyone looking up from the street might think it just a bird perched on the edge of the roof. And, if anyone could see him from other buildings, they were apparently too busy with their own pathetic lives to give a shit about him.

His fingers were numb. His whole body was losing feeling, and Chris imagined what it was going to be like when he let go. Would he be able to fly like a bird? Would he be free?

Tears rolled down his cheeks. Chris knew he should've been in control of himself, especially at work. His job paid for an impressive New York apartment even his parents had struggled to criticise. But the reality of his sexual preferences he'd kept secret from a fundamentalist Christian family while growing up had emerged when Eamon had started working in their small computer team a year ago. It wasn't an exclusive relationship. Chris accepted that Eamon liked to play both halves of the field. But it was dangerous and exciting, and most of all in a Christian upbringing—forbidden.

It was Chris who'd suggested they did it on Eamon's

night shift in the server room. Letting his desire for sexual excitement run away with him, they'd created a temporary glitch in specific security cameras to hide what they were doing, a glitch that also masked Chris introducing the exploit he'd been given via a flash drive. Eamon hadn't seen him do it either as he'd been puffing on a joint near the air vents, talking about how fucking incredible it had been.

It was what Chris loved so much about his strange IT colleague, his enthusiasm for life defied the company's attempts to tame his wild personality and turn him into a corporate clone. They wouldn't get rid of him, though; he was just too damn good at his job for that.

They'd eloped for a weekend at a ski lodge, which ended up with very little skiing. When they did go out, Eamon had been a wild daredevil on the snow, demanding they go off-piste or on the most challenging runs. It was a shame the weekend had ended with a fight when Eamon went off with a chalet girl. Eamon had an insatiable sex drive and didn't want to be tied down to any sort of meaningful relationship. It was something Chris found hard to handle.

Perhaps it was Eamon's way of dealing with the rejection from his parents. It was something Chris hadn't suffered because his didn't know. But they would soon. Whoever was hounding him wasn't going to stop until he did everything they wanted. It would always mean having to do one more thing, or the truth would be outed and the videos released.

He was supposed to go to his parents for Thanksgiving, go to their fundamentalist church and hear the pastor spout on about sin. No doubt, he would mention how evil the type of sexual activity Chris yearned for was and how he was sinning against God. When he was sitting beneath God's gaze, Chris felt like running to the front of the church and prostrating himself in front of the pastor, begging forgiveness and asking to be led to a better path.

But then, he imagined the looks of disgust and disappointment of his family. They would turn their backs, walk away, and never speak to the sinner in the family again.

Chris couldn't face that.

And he didn't want to be relieved of his sin.

Eamon didn't believe in God anymore. He said that if a God was going to condemn him for who he was, then he could just fuck off. Eamon was colourful like that. Chris wished he could be as strong as his friend.

But he couldn't face it anymore. He couldn't go on living with the pain that tore at his gut every day.

The cold air sent a wave of shivers across his body.

It was time for him to stop being manipulated.

It was time to take control.

Glancing round, Chris saw there was no one near him on the roof. His absence went unnoticed by anyone who worked with him. Or, if it had, they didn't care. This was the summation of his life. No one cared. Not even God.

Chris loosened his grip on the railing. His fingertips held his body steady now. Another gust buffeted him, he tilted forward with the momentum, and just for a moment, his hands moved instinctively to let himself get a better grip.

Then he let go.

He was free.

16

The banging on the door sounded distant at first, as though it was somewhere else in Zack's apartment block. There seemed to be a rhythm in tune with the banging in his head. Opening his eyes, the bright autumn sun streamed through his bedroom window. He hadn't bothered to close the curtains before climbing into bed. Just pop the extra pills he knew he'd need to sleep.

Hearing muffled voices at first, Zack realised it was the police. Opening his eyes, he jumped out of bed.

"Jesus, I'm coming." There was a crashing sound, which meant they were coming through the door whether he opened it or not. It also indicated they had a warrant. What the hell did they think he'd done? Still in the previous day's shirt and boxers, he found the trousers he'd abandoned on the floor, and he hauled them on.

"I'm coming." Standing upright, he felt dizzy as pain throbbed across his temple. Throat-parched Zack glanced around to see if there was any water.

They'd worked through most of the night, going over every scrap of information. Adam was working with Terry on the data from Global Money, and it was clear from the audit logs that Terry's suspicions had been correct. Someone was using

Global Money accounts to trade before syphoning off the profits. Adam had been in awe at the sheer genius of the idea, comparing it to Lex Luthor in Superman, taking just the pennies off bank transactions so no one noticed. And like Lex, whoever was behind the scheme was making millions.

But by the end of the night, they'd been no closer to finding out who was responsible or how they were doing it. Adam had taken Terry to the hotel he was staying in, where Zack suspected they would continue working. Terry's place wasn't considered safe, though they promised to swing by today and pick up some things. Zack was going to go with them just in case.

"Step away from the door, Sir."

Zack knew the drill, and as he reached the compact hallway of his two-bed apartment, he stopped. The door burst open, revealing two uniformed and two plainclothes officers.

"Mr Zack Carter?"

"Yes, what's this about?"

"Mr Carter, you are under arrest on suspicion of theft of company property. You do not have to say anything, but it may harm your defence if you do not mention, when questioned, something which you late rely on in court. Anything you do say may be given in evidence."

17

It wasn't the first time Zack had been on the other side of the table in an interview room, but even when the Independent Police Complaints Commission had investigated the events in Oakwell, he hadn't felt like he was in trouble. There might have been some awkward questions about his conduct, and the fact he'd been carrying a gun his brother had brought back from Iraq, but this interview smacked of them having something tangible on him.

He'd waived his right to a solicitor, more interested in what had brought them to him. Zack knew the system well enough to know the interview could be stopped at any time and a legal representative summoned. He also hoped being an ex-copper might stand him in good stead.

The two detectives were cordial as they'd introduced themselves as DI Knight and DI Kyle on the way to the custody suite.

"Mr Carter, have you in your possession data removed yesterday from the offices of Global Money by a Mr Brandon Walsh?" Detective Inspector Knight was straight to the point as he started the digital recording. He appeared a no-nonsense guy with a smart suit, short trimmed black hair, and a respectable beard. While the DI next to him looked about five years younger, his face showed the signs of a severe case of acne in his adolescence.

"Not in my personal possession, but the agency has a copy, yes."

"This is," DI Knight looked down at his notes, "the Angel Detective Agency?" Could Zack detect scorn in his voice? He knew how most coppers felt about Private Detectives; he'd pretty much felt that way himself until Chloe had persuaded him otherwise.

"That is correct."

"When did you come into possession of this data?"

"Last night at about eight, when one of the employees of Global Money brought it to us. He received it via an email."

"Were you aware the data was stolen earlier in the day?"

"Incorrect." Zack shook his head.

"You weren't aware?" DI Kyle said.

"It wasn't stolen by him. I'm referring to Terry White, an employee of Global Money. The data was sent to him by his boss, Brandon Walsh."

"Sent to him?" The DI looked genuinely puzzled, which intrigued Zack as to where they'd received their information, as it was undoubtedly incomplete.

"Mr Walsh sent the information to Terry via email as a precaution before he left the office. He was on his way to bring the data himself."

The two detectives looked at each other, and Zack knew they were already finding out new information. He relaxed a little more in his chair as DI Knight examined his notes again. It wasn't rare that the investigating detectives had a whole load of blank spots in their knowledge. After all, it was a detective's job to tease out what they could during interviews without giving away how much information they had. Only, Zack was savvy enough to pick on the subtle shifts in body language that gave away their position.

And the two detectives were already getting uncomfortable.

"Right before he was killed," Zack added.

"Killed?" DI Knight looked startled, and Zack knew the interview was going south. He'd been there. Zack knew what it felt like when, as an interviewer, you realised just how much you didn't know.

"By the van driver last night. You might have seen it on TV." DI Kyle bristled at that comment, which Zack regretted, but he was irritated they'd arrested him with very little evidence or information.

"You've proof he was bringing you the data? Would it still be on him?"

Zack wasn't sure how much to tell them. "We've the money deposited by Brandon as a retainer for our services."

"The money you were blackmailing from Global Money because you had sensitive information you were threatening to release."

Zack was even more confused about the intelligence that had led to his arrest. Was that what they'd been told? It smelt of an anonymous tip offering just enough factual evidence to get them a warrant. But it had apparently missed out the juicy details the detectives needed, as well as throwing a few untruths to muddy the waters. The detectives were being played.

"He'd asked us to investigate anomalies in some of the transactions going through the system and was bringing us the data to help us."

"But the management in the office knew nothing about it?"

"Brandon Walsh knew," Zack said.

"But, as you have pointed out, Mr Walsh is dead," DI Kyle put in.

"Do you have emails?" DI Knight asked rubbing his fore-head.

"No, we got rid of it and trashed the phone." Zack could see DI Knight was struggling, and he suspected the detective realised things weren't adding up. Which was good news in Zack's eyes as it made him a smart cookie. There was nothing worse than a detective doggedly refusing to move away from a conclusion he'd already reached. "But I'm sure if you got forensics onto the accounts with the right warrant, you could still get them." Zack knew deleting emails was only any good after so many days when they'd been overwritten on the servers. Until then, they were fair game if you could get the right legal authorisation.

"Why would you delete them, Mr Carter?" DI Kyle asked.

The younger detective wasn't so smart. "Because we suspect the bombing in the pub and the killing of Brandon Walsh was an attempt to cover up what had been happening within the company. And we were trying to reduce the chance of the same people finding us."

"Can you prove that?" DI Knight looked interested in what Zack was saying.

"We've only just started investigating."

"This all sounds very fanciful, Mr Carter." DI Kyle took over. "Are we to believe that Global Money has been killing its own employees to hide financial irregularities?"

"Never said that. We don't know who's behind it, but we suspect there's a link to the bombing. Terry White, who found the anomaly, should have been at the pub that night."

"So, the terrorists are also ripping off Global Money?" DI Kyle said.

"Possibly, we don't know," Zack answered.

"But, why didn't Mr Walsh take this to his own management?"

"He went to his boss, who told him the numbers were obviously wrong as nothing like that could happen at Global Money."

"We've spoken to Mr Helmund, Mr Walsh's boss, who had never heard of these allegations but was alerted to someone tampering with the data files late yesterday afternoon. He then discovered there had been an unauthorised payment to your company. Knowing Mr Walsh, he could only surmise the man was being threatened by somebody taking advantage of the unfortunate circumstances of the terrorist attack. The information Mr Helmund received indicated fraud on a massive scale."

This was why they were able to get a warrant so quickly, Zack realised. He'd learnt more from this interview than the detectives. Someone had raised the alarm, and Brandon's boss had passed on the information, as well as his own little lie. Throw in a possible terrorist connection, and the police weren't going to hang around. He was going to have to look at Mr Helmund more closely.

"And you think it's us?" Zack asked.

"The trail leads us to your door," DI Knight said.

"Why the hell would we do that? We're just a small-time detective agency."

"Because of the financial trouble your company is in," DI Kyle put in. "And I hear your daughter goes to school abroad; that can't be cheap."

Zack took a deep breath. Miley was due in later that night, and the way the interview was panning out, he was still going to be inside a police station answering questions.

"We looked at the data last night. Brandon had instructed his IT department to add extra auditing on the quiet. We caught some transactions in progress until they ended five minutes after the new auditing kicked in. We didn't get much, but it was enough to prove everything Terry White had suspected. Did you search Brandon Walsh's body, know what was on him?"

"That's with the anti-terrorist branch."

"Then go talk to them because I think you'll find Mr Walsh's keys and phone were missing."

"How could you possibly know that?" DI Knight seemed more interested in what Zack had to say than his colleague.

"Examine the footage. Look at what happens when the driver gets out of the van. Especially at what happens to Brandon Walsh. You can find it all on YouTube."

The two detectives looked at each other, and Zack could see the uncertainty in their eyes.

"I may be financially in the shit gentlemen, but I'm not the sort of person who would steal money as a way out. Never have, never will. I would have thought my record of service should have put that doubt in your mind before you knocked on my door this morning."

DI Knight reached over to the tape recorder. "Interview terminated at eleven seventeen."

18

James swivelled towards the three people sitting in his office. He'd re-read the latest chilling message he'd received boasting about the death of another member of the London branch. While James hadn't heard the name Brandon Walsh before, the image of his dead body on a street corner was etched in his mind. Whether the sick bastard was using the terrorists to add to the hate, or he was directly involved in the attacks, James was terrified.

If that was not enough, James had been informed about the tip off the London office had received about money being stolen. Using their extensive contacts, Global Money had managed to get the police involved straight away.

"Do we know if there's any truth in it?" James directed the question towards the large woman wearing a cream pants suit sitting between Brad and Marian. She adjusted her glasses as she looked at her tablet.

"We are investigating. People are being sent over to assist."

"I need more than that." James tapped his fingers on the desk. Underneath the table, his foot was shaking back and forth. He made a note to see his therapist later. Things were getting out of control.

The woman looked uncomfortable. Liz Holden headed up

the maintenance of the trading software, a crackerjack team leader who made sure everything ran smoothly. And usually, it did. "It appears there is a chance this might be true."

"Jesus Christ." James tossed his phone onto the dark wood of his desk. "Right under our fucking noses." His gaze bored into Brad Reynold's face at first, but he knew this was something outside the security chief's remit. Marian seemed to lean ever so slightly away from the larger woman as if she knew there was a barrage coming and didn't want to be in the line of fire.

"How could this happen?"

"We don't know at this time." Liz took a deep breath. "We believe it may involve personnel within the company."

"Someone like Mr Walsh?" James asked.

"Possibly." Liz shrugged.

"Who is now dead. Very convenient. So, were they stealing data or money?"

"The tip-off received informed us of data being stolen and smuggled out to an outside agency." Brad Reynolds took over. "Which turned out to be a private detective agency. But when we saw the data, we realised it wasn't quite so straightforward, and the detective agency is saying that they were asked by Mr Walsh to investigate anomalies in the trading algorithms."

"How true is that?"

"We just don't know, at this point," Brad confessed.

James tapped his fingers on the desk in frustration, but they couldn't have been expected to figure this out in such a short space of time. He wanted to fire Liz just to make himself feel better about the whole thing, but that wasn't a prudent action in the current circumstances.

"Then go and find me the answers. I want to know the facts and how much this is costing the company. Marian, go with

ANGEL OF MONEY

her and give her all the help you can. If anyone gets in the
way, you have my full authority to deal with it."

James knew Marian wouldn't suffer any nonsense as his
Human Resources enforcer. She was part security guard,
part lawyer, and no one in the company liked her, which
was just the way Marian preferred to operate. "I have a board
meeting in four hours," James continued, "and they're going
to demand answers. So, get me something better than 'we are
investigating' before then. Do I make myself clear?"

Liz and Marian nodded.

"Then go."

"I want Liz out of here at the end of the week." James waited
until they'd both left before continuing. He sat back in the
chair and interlocked his fingers to keep calm. "She's good,
but if this is true, then she's fucked up big time, and the board
will need a head."

"It will be done, Sir." Brad sat straighter in his chair as if
acknowledging the seriousness of the request.

"What do you think?" Despite his failure to track down the
person behind the messages, James knew you couldn't get
much better than Brad Reynolds. Everybody in the industry
had told him that.

"I can't see how they are connected. The money and the
bomb. But." Brad left it hanging as though reluctant to speak
freely.

"Go on."

Brad took a breath. "I don't believe in coincidences either.
We're gathering as much as we can from our sources on all
the events in London to see what we can find, see if there
is something that links them. Two terrorist attacks killing
our people." Brad shook his head. "It's too much, and for the

attack on Mr Walsh to have been pure chance while he was carrying stolen data."

"It's too fucking scary to contemplate." James felt sick and needed a drink. Rising from his chair, he began circling the main area of the office. "Have we been used by fucking ISIS to fund their operations? We need to find out, Brad. Because if we are, this company could go down overnight. If a sniff of this gets out, our share price could tank."

"I know, Sir. We're pulling in every contact and every favour to find out what the police know."

James nodded. He expected nothing less. "What about this detective agency? Where do they fit in?"

"We think Mr Walsh contacted them," Brad said looking down at his tablet. "A Zack Carter was arrested on suspicion of receiving the data and questioned. He's got some pedigree. Was involved in an incident a few years ago where some nutter was targeting a town and tried to burn most of the politicians on election night."

"Doesn't sound like a nutter to me," James said, and Brad gave a nervous laugh.

"Yes, well, Mr Carter helped stop it while rescuing his daughter and another woman. A lot of dead bodies, a lot of fall out, and he resigned from the police. The agency was set up with the woman he rescued, a Miss Chloe Evans. She'd been stalked by the killer before being kidnapped." Brad stopped pacing and looked up. "From what we can gather, she received a lot of messages from the killer before she was taken. Messages that couldn't be traced."

"Interesting." James continued his pacing. "I want to know what they know. Can I meet them?" He tried to think why Brandon would have gone to an outside agency and not dealt with it internally? Did he already know something was rotten inside the organisation?

"You mean to tell them about the messages, don't you?" Brad looked uncomfortable, and James knew he was taking things personally because of his failure to find the person cyberstalking him. "Is that wise?"

"We need all the help we can get, Brad," James said. His security adviser nodded. "But we need to do this on the quiet. I don't want the authorities to know anything. I don't want fucking anybody to know anything."

Brad nodded. "I'll make it happen."

19

"Can I have a word?"

"Do I have a choice?" Zack was in the reception area leading away from the custody suite when Detective Inspector Knight approached. He was sat waiting his turn to retrieve the belongings he'd given up when the detectives had brought him in. They'd released him without charge pending further investigation. But, it had meant a few tense hours locked in a custody cell while they made their decision and processed the paperwork.

"Yes, you do, as a matter of fact. I'm Mike Knight, financial crimes." The DI held his hand out, offering a genuine smile. Still suspicious, Zack took his hand, wondering why they were suddenly on first name terms.

"We've already met."

"But I'd like to start again. You are free to go with no charges. But we'd like you to stay around London in case there are any further questions you can help us with." Mike moved over to the door and held it open.

"And this isn't questioning?" Zack stood and passed through the door.

"No." DI Knight followed Zack into the corridor that led down to the Custody Sergeant. "I'd like to talk to you off the record. I've looked at the video with Mr Walsh getting hit. You're right. Something was taken from him. I also believe your story."

"It wasn't a story. It was fact," Zack pointed out. "And your colleague?"

"He's not in financial crimes. Doesn't have the same way of looking at things."

"Then why were you with him?" Zack knew it wasn't standard practice for the detectives from different departments to be doing the questioning.

"Request from my boss who is good friends with his. You know how it works. And the possible link to terrorism has garnered everyone's attention. There was talk of you being held under the terrorism act."

Zack certainly knew how the system worked. One of the best ways to get anything moving in the police was tapping into the old boy's network they always denied existed. That and making out it was linked to terrorism. If that had happened, Zack would've have been spending days in custody. He turned to face the DI.

"Look, Mike, it's been a shitty day so far, and my daughter is arriving in the country later, so why should I talk to you?"

"Because I think you're right; I don't think it's terrorists, and I think Global Money is trying to cover it up."

That got Zack's attention. "You mean there's no connection?"

"That would seem too implausible given the way we know organisations like ISIS work. For them to conduct a sophisticated financial crime of this magnitude is unprecedented. If they are, then we need to work out how the hell they've got into the system pronto because they'll be moving into a whole new league, which scares the hell out of me."

Zack nodded. Walking up to the Custody Sergeant, the paperwork was presented, giving him time to think while he glanced through and signed. All his belongings were returned, and Zack noted there was no attempt to put any restrictions on his travel despite what the DI had requested. He passed through another door into the heart of the public area of the police station.

"There's a lot about this that doesn't add up." Zack headed over to a cooler and poured a plastic cup of cold water. He didn't offer to get the DI one; Zack was still wondering what his angle was. There'd be no problem with getting the lowdown on Mike once he left the station. Zack wanted to know what kind of copper he was.

"Does DI Kyle know you are talking to me?"

"No." Mike's mouth showed the hint of a smile. Zack had a feeling DI Knight didn't like his colleague much. That was good because Zack thought DI Kyle was an arsehole. "Lunch break. Look, there's only so much I can say. You know how it is."

Zack could accept that.

"DI Kyle thinks private investigators are scum who should stick to divorce cases; he thinks even less of those who are ex-coppers."

"And what do you think?" Zack drained his cup and tossed it into the recycling bin next to the cooler.

"I don't much like private investigators either and think they should stick with divorce cases." Mike attempted a smile. "But you were a good copper and a damn fine soldier, so anybody who doesn't court your opinion is an idiot."

"Including DI Kyle?"

"As I say, there are things I can't tell you."

Zack gave a chuckle; he was beginning to like the guy. "Can you give me a lift to my office?"

"Might be awkward," Mike said.

"Okay, then meet me there at seven to give me time to get my daughter, and we can talk."

"Thank you."

"No problem, Detective Inspector."

Zack shook Mike's hand again before turning towards the entrance to the police station just as Chloe entered through the revolving doors. She spotted him, and her welcome smile warmed his heart.

"Christ, are you okay? They said they were letting you go, so I came over." Chloe threw her arms around his neck. It was good to feel her embrace after a morning in the cold station.

"I could murder a coffee." He needed a damn site more, but caffeine would have to do until he got back home.

"There's a place across the street, but we need to get on the road because I've also got news."

They stepped out into the brisk but bright day.

"Mr Carter, Mr Zack Carter of the Angel Detective Agency?"

"What the hell is it now?" Zack turned, expecting to see DI Kyle coming to arrest him again. It was a man in a suit carrying an envelope and with a stern look on his face.

"Yes, that's me."

"Then I hereby notify you that my client is suing you for failing to carry out the services you've been paid for." The man thrust the brown envelope at Zack.

20

"The fucking cheek of it." Chloe pulled her blue Ford Fiesta out of the large multi-storey next to the police station. It was an hour before rush hour, but the commuter traffic was already building.

"I suppose we didn't do what he paid us to do." Zack was in the passenger seat, the envelope having been tossed in the back.

"You did the right thing, and you still did the work before you knew what a total shit he was. It's one thing to not pay the rest but to go after us like that. Doesn't he know we're broke?"

"Were being the operative word." Zack stirred the takeaway coffee Chloe had bought. "I expect all he really wants to do is shut us down because we weren't his little lap dogs."

"What are you going to do?" She was seething. The man was a nasty son of a bitch who'd wanted to chuck his wife on the cheap. "We could just give the money back. Get it off our plate."

"Fuck that." Zack shook his head. "I'll instruct the solicitors tomorrow; now we've got a bit of cash, we can at least string him along. Anyway, you said you had news."

"I'm flying out to New York to see the CEO of Global

Money," Chloe said as if it was something she did every day when the truth was she was bubbling over with excitement. This is what she dreamt owning a detective agency would be like.

"Sweet Jesus, how did you arrange that?" Zack stopped drinking his coffee.

"I didn't. They called a couple of hours ago for us to go over. They're paying expenses."

"Do the police know?" Zack asked.

"Global Money wants to keep it between us for now."

"Jesus, where is this heading?"

"I know." Chloe pulled out of a side street and onto the A40, her main route to Heathrow. "One minute, Global Money has you arrested, and the next, there's a first-class ticket to see their head honcho."

"First class. Why aren't I going?" Zack went back to his coffee. "I thought I was the boss."

"Only when I let you." Chloe smiled. "And there's the minor matter of needing to meet your daughter."

"Some visit this when we are knee deep in an investigation."

"She'll understand, Zack, and she'll be pleased you're not moping around. She's worried about you."

"And of course, it's okay now we could be on the path of terrorists." Zack gave a huge sigh. Chloe thought his face looked drained, and it was as though he was struggling to hold his coffee still. But as he'd been dragged out of bed and spent the better part of the day in police custody, it was hardly surprising. "I want to see her, but I wish she was safe at school while all this is going on."

"You think it's that bad." His concern gave Chloe pause for thought. Things had been happening so fast since Terry and Brandon first brought the case to them. The call today, after Zack being arrested, was extraordinary. Brad Reynolds, Global Money's head of security, had insisted on someone going to see the boss right away. No expense was spared to get her on the first possible flight.

It had felt good telling her mother she was off to New York to meet the head of Global Money, something that had finally managed to impress her. There was a rare missed call from her father too, no doubt wanting to get the lowdown on the meeting. Chloe knew he had a few contacts in the financial giant and suspected they'd been lobbying him on the quiet. She didn't know the finer details of politics, but it seemed as corrupt as the world of modelling from what she'd seen.

"I have no idea," Zack continued, "and that's the problem. The police think its implausible for there to be a link between the bombing and the money because of how we know ISIS operates. But we can't deny the coincidence. And who tipped off Brandon's boss to try to halt the investigation? If it was the terrorists who tipped him off, weren't they attracting more attention to themselves?"

"The police didn't say who it was?" Chloe asked.

"No, and I'm not sure they know. I want to speak to Brandon's boss. I've messaged Terry to find out where he is, so I can pay him a visit. Terry says Brandon had been told that the data issues were nothing to worry about when they came to us, but Brandon wasn't convinced."

"Stalling tactic." Chloe navigated around a red London bus that was clogging up the traffic on the inside lane.

"Exactly. And why would you do that?"

"Because you don't want the truth to come out."

"And that's because either you fucked up royally and are

clinging to your job, or you're implicated in some way."

Traffic remained solid on the main trunk road to the airport. Chloe glanced at the clock. She had plenty of time. Going through her mental check list, Chloe made sure she had the essentials. The ticket would be at the airport, and anything she'd forgotten she'd be able to get in New York.

"What are you doing with Miley tonight?"

"Taking her to the office first."

"Zack, no way." Chloe threw him a stern glance. "Can't you let Adam and Terry work on it tonight?"

"The DI wanted to speak to me off the record. I told him to go to the office when he finished his shift."

"Mr Carter, you are a thoughtless idiot."

"Do you think she'll be mad?"

"No, because she dotes on you, and she kind of likes you being a private detective. As long as she imagines you're doing the sort of exciting things she sees on TV."

"So, I'll have great stories for her now. Take the next turning." He pointed off to the left. "It's quicker down the back roads from this bit."

Chloe nodded, ignored the satnav's commands to keep straight on, and followed Zack's directions. The gloomy London sky was darkening as dusk approached, and a light drizzle forced her to flick on the wipers.

"If you drop me off, you can take the car for Miley."

Zack nodded. "You take it easy on your trip out there. Try not to blow all our profits shopping."

"Babe, I've got a first-class luggage allowance to come back with. You just watch me go."

21

As they reached the first floor of their office block, Zack saw smoke in the stairwell above them. He put his hand out to stop Miley.

"Call the fire brigade. We've got a problem."

His daughter pushed past his arm and stretched her neck to see the smoke for herself before pulling out her phone. "Are they still up there?"

"I guess so." Zack used his phone to call Adam.

"Hey, you got Miley?" It was Adam's chirpy voice.

"You still in the office?"

"Of course, DI Knight is here."

"You need to get out of there. We're on the first floor, and there's smoke between you and us."

"Shit, okay, we're on our way." Zack heard him shout to the others in the room. He carried on up the stairs.

"Fire crew's on their way." Miley followed once she'd hung up from the emergency services.

"Stay back, I'll take a look," Zack commanded.

"Really, Dad. I don't think so." His athletic daughter bolted ahead while tying her bouncing auburn hair into a ponytail. "There might be others in the building; we have to let them know." She headed straight for a fire alarm on the landing and smashed the glass. "What the hell." Miley struck the alarm again, but there was nothing.

"No wonder the rent was cheap," Zack muttered.

"Or it's been disabled."

"Shit, Zack, we can't open the door." Adam was still on the phone, his voice rising in panic. "We didn't lock it when we came in, but it won't budge."

"Where's the key?" Zack asked.

"I think we might have left it on the outside."

"Okay, I'll come and get you." Zack hung up. The office doors were heavy wooden affairs with solid key locks. Feeling in his jacket, he recalled his own set of keys was still in his apartment.

"The door's locked; I'm going to try to get them out." He didn't add that it meant the fire was more likely deliberate. "You need to get out of the building."

Miley shook her head. "I'll check the other offices and make sure there's no one else."

He would have preferred his daughter went back downstairs to safety, but Zack knew that wasn't going to happen. Instead, he nodded his acknowledgement and hurried up the stairs.

Reaching the second floor, thick, acrid smoke billowed from the gaping entrance of one of the offices. The office was directly underneath theirs.

Flames danced out of the door, trying to gain a foothold in the corridor. Pulling an extinguisher off the wall, Zack pointed it into the doorway and let loose a stream of thick, white foam. While it temporally beat back the fire, the flames had such a hold on the furniture in the office a single extinguisher wasn't going to make much difference. Abandoning his efforts, Zack headed to the next floor.

"Miley, you good?" He leant over the stairs. Her face appeared below him.

"No one here. What do you see?"

"Office on the right is on fire, and I've not seen anybody in the other. You better stay down there."

"Go and get the others; I'll keep checking for anyone else."

Before Zack could say anything, her head vanished, and he knew she would be coming up the stairs.

We can't get the door open.

Zack read Adam's message and raced up the next set of stairs as the fire, recovering from his attempts to put it out, poured more smoke into the stairwell.

Having hoped he'd find the brass key in the outside of the door of their office, Zack's saw an empty keyhole. At least the door opened inward. It gave him a better chance to break it down.

"Stand back, guys." Taking a deep breath, Zack charged the door. Pain exploded through his shoulder as he bounced off the solid wood. He hadn't moved it at all. Ignoring his injury, Zack stepped back before he kicked the door between the keyhole and the frame. For a moment, he thought there was give, striking it again and again, until his leg was wracked with pain.

"Can you get us out?" Zack heard the panic in Adam's voice from inside the office. He was forced to stop to wipe the sweat from his eyes and try to regain some breath. "The smoke's coming in here now. It's really bad."

"I need to find something else," he said as much to himself as those behind the door.

"Can we do anything?" Adam was coughing badly.

"Just try not to breathe in the smoke." Zack knew it wasn't

going to be easy as his own lungs started to suck up as much smoke as fresh air. His exertions were only making it worse.

Spotting another pair of extinguishers on the landing, he rushed to grab the largest. Back at the door, he took a swing and sent a painful judder through his arm at the impact against the frame instead of the door. He swung again, this time hearing the satisfying sound of splintering wood.

Gasping for air, it took two more tremendous blows to smash the lock. Zack dropped the extinguisher before hurling his body against the door.

It burst open.

Adam caught him as Zack stumbled inside the hallway. The smoke was thick, and he could see the desperation and relief on the three faces that greeted him.

"Come on," Zack urged them. "The floors below are on fire. We haven't got much time. Grab extinguishers. Anything that might help."

The four men made their way to the stairwell before descending into the grey smoke. Having already been exposed to the choking air, the other three were continuously coughing. While it wasn't as bad for Zack, he could feel his lungs getting overwhelmed.

Down on the next level, the carpets and floor fittings were alight, allowing the flames to spread more rapidly. He could feel the intense heat as more sweat poured down his face. Both office doors were open, and peering into one of them, Zack saw a shape of a person.

"Miley, is that you?" he shouted.

"Help me, Dad. I've got someone."

"Shit, I'm coming." Zack turned to the others. "Get down the stairs and get out." He raced through the smoke into the office where his daughter was desperately trying to drag the body of a middle-aged woman across the floor. Miley's face was streaked with grime, strands of brown hair soaked and matted against her face. But her determination to help the woman was evident in her expression.

"I got the other lady out." Miley stooped, letting go of the woman for a moment as she endured a bout of coughing. "But she fainted."

"Come on, let's lift her together."

Miley nodded, helping Zack lift the woman to her feet before each of them threw an arm around her shoulders.

"Just like old times," Miley shouted as they passed through the office door and onto the landing.

"Yea, welcome home."

As he spoke, the flames on the landing powered across the ceiling. Zack realised the fire was overhead, and the heat forced them back from the stairwell they needed to reach. He was sure his bare skin was blistering as they backed away. One more flare up, and the flames would consume them.

"Not good," he muttered checking their options and trying to suppress the rising panic.

There was a burst of thick white foam from below.

Two figures moved up the stairs, laying down the contents of their extinguishers.

"You need some help?" Adam shouted out as he and DI Knight reached the landing. Their efforts provided enough of a safe passage for Zack and Miley to sprint across the floor to reach them.

A few moments later, they were on the street sucking in fresh cool air as fire appliances and ambulances screamed to a halt in the road.

Zack looked at his daughter.

Miley smiled back at him. "And you told me being a private detective was boring."

22

Alex could hear Lilly's soft snoring from the bedroom as he logged onto Snapchat. He used the alias Mohammad al-Sharif. A specific user created for communications with a single contact. Having seen the news of the fire in London, Alex was livid and didn't care what time it was in England. The leader of the small group that hailed themselves as Islamic warriors seeking to bring down the English infidels answered straight away.

MOHAMMAD: I thought you were going to take care of them?

AHMED: We wanted it to look like an accident. Others turned up.

MOHAMMAD: You used an accelerant, you idiot. How would that make it look like an accident?

Alex wanted to get his attention. The group had become cocksure about their actions because of their minor successes to date. What they had forgotten is those achievements were orchestrated and funded by the man they knew as Mohammad al-Sharif. While they thought he was an agent of the main branch of ISIS, Alex had been pulling their strings ever since he'd contacted them online. While not being the brightest, which was why the real ISIS probably didn't want to go near them, they'd given Alex another dimension to his plan.

AHMED: You can't speak to us like that. We are doing Allah's work.

MOHAMMAD: Then you don't need to deal with me anymore.

Alex waited, knowing this would elicit the response he wanted. As much as Ahmed thought of himself, he wasn't such a fool as to not know what he'd be throwing away. Ahmed had been contributing online to various public forums that would have brought him to the attention of the security services if Alex hadn't intervened. He'd taught Ahmed how to keep off the grid, so the authorities wouldn't be on to them. He'd given them the resources to turn their ideological fantasies into reality.

It had been Alex who'd orchestrated the bomb attack on the pub. While Ahmed and his group had found the ideal candidate, applied the appropriate pressure, and delivered the vest, everything else had been put together by Alex. The excitement level had reached fever pitch in Ahmed's group forcing Alex to calm them before they did anything stupid that would get them.

AHMED: We are with you, brother. Allah wills it.

MOHAMMAD: Allahu Akbar.

AHMED: Allahu Akbar. I sent you what we found on the agency.

Ahmed had sent a document over with their findings, but it was nothing Alex hadn't been able to discover himself in minutes. He'd sought information about the agency as soon as its name had come up and been shocked to discover the identity of the people involved. It seemed an impossible coincidence when he saw Chloe and Zack's profile on the website, sending a shiver down his spine.

While he didn't believe there was any sort of deity controlling the world, when Alex witnessed these moments of serendipity, it gave him pause for thought. Despite having given up on Miley ever being a replacement for Angel, occasionally, Alex would find himself trying to find out where she was in the world.

After they'd sent her away with her uncle, Miley had become almost impossible to track. There were only minor glimpses of her digital presence because she'd no doubt been using some of the tricks Alex had taught her. In the beginning, he'd first contacted her online using yet another alias and tapped into the fact she was a keen programmer with excellent skills. It had been Alex who introduced her into darker areas of technology, where sometimes even the authorities were blind.

It made him smile to see she was growing up. Alex was sure it was how Angel would have turned out: sassy, confident, and beautiful. The only reliable data as to Miley's whereabouts was when she visited her father in London.

It was disappointing to see that Zack had not stepped up his game since they'd last met or that Chloe's flame had only briefly flickered back into life. They'd both seemed almost worthy adversaries in Oakwell, deserving of his respect. But they hadn't been able to keep even a small-time detective agency going profitably from what Alex had seen. He knew they'd tried to hunt him down. He'd expected nothing less, and while they'd made more progress than the useless authorities, they had no clue where he was. Or even who he was.

AHMED: The police don't believe them. We will get another chance.

MOHAMMAD: If the police don't believe them, then why

was there a police detective meeting them in the office?

Alex glanced from where he was sitting on the sofa towards the bedroom. Lilly had stopped snoring. He listened to make sure she wasn't awake.

AHMED: They know nothing.

MOHAMMAD: No matter. It will cause confusion, and that is a good thing.

AHMED: We need more money.

MOHAMMAD: Don't you have enough?

Alex was sure they were blowing most of the cash he gave them on very western sins.

AHMED: Allah's work needs a lot of the infidel's money.

MOHAMMAD: How much more? Are there not enough rewards waiting for you when this is over? Or do you and your friends like the local white girls too much to make the ultimate sacrifice?

AHMED: We are dedicated to the cause. We have suffered at the hands of the infidels, and we will enter the afterlife to help create a new Caliphate.

Alex wasn't so sure. But he'd made sure his plans didn't rely on the group. There were enough others under his control to give him the opening he needed in London when the time came.

MOHAMMAD: Forget the agency. I'll deal with it. Keep to the plan; keep to the date. The shipment will arrive tomorrow with everything that you need.

AHMED: Allah has provided.

Alex snorted. Allah had provided nothing. His genius had provided the know-how and contacts to get the money and equipment they needed for the operation.

MOHAMMAD: Let me know when you have it, and keep

up the reading.

AHMED: And the funds?

MOHAMMAD: They will be there tonight.

He was such a greedy little bastard. Alex knew Ahmed's group would more likely be on top of some young white teenager they'd groomed than reading the scriptures, which were supposed to get their spirits in the right place.

Alex decided he was going to make them martyrs to the cause. Whether they wanted to be or not.

There was another group he needed to speak to. Alex stretched his back as he let out a long breath; for a moment, he wondered if he'd taken on too much by dealing with so many people. Especially when that had agendas he didn't give a fuck about.

This, of all the missions he'd planned to show the changed world, was fraught with the greatest danger. Rising to his feet, Alex drifted into the kitchen to make a milkshake. He needed to go for a run to clear his head. Others may not be as dedicated to their cause, but Alex Ryan was determined to see every one of his plans to the very end.

The world had to open its eyes to the horror ordinary people suffered while a few enjoyed the riches at the top of the pyramid. Youngsters like Angel were thrown to the dogs because they weren't important enough to be cared about. Alex had cared for her. He'd loved her. And Alex Ryan was going to make sure the world was taught a fundamental lesson about what happens when you leave people on the scrap heap.

23

Alex could hear Lilly's soft snoring from the bedroom as he logged onto Snapchat using the alias Mohammad al-Sharif. Having seen the news of the fire in London he was livid and didn't care what time it was in England. The leader of the small group that hailed themselves as Islamic warriors seeking to bring down the English infidels answered straight away.

MOHAMMAD: I thought you were going to take care of them?

AHMED: We wanted it to look like an accident. We did not know the others would come back.

MOHAMMAD: You used an accelerant you idiot. How would that make it look like an accident?

Alex knew that would get his attention. The group had become cocksure about their actions because of their minor successes to date. What they had forgotten is those achievements were orchestrated and funded by the man they knew as Mohammad al-Sharif. While they thought he was an agent of the main branch of ISIS, Alex had been pulling their strings ever since he'd contacted them online. While not being the brightest, which was why the real ISIS probably didn't want to go near them, they had given Alex another dimension to his plan.

AHMED: You shouldn't speak to us like that. We are doing Allah's work.

MOHAMMAD: Then you don't need to deal with me anymore.

Alex waited, knowing this would elicit the response he wanted. As much as Ahmed thought of himself, he wasn't such fool as to not know what he'd be throwing away. Ahmed had been online contributing to various public forums that would soon have brought him to the attention of the security services if Alex hadn't intervened. He'd taught Ahmed how to keep off the grid so the authorities wouldn't be on to them. He'd given them the resources to turn their ideological fantasies into reality.

It had been Alex who'd orchestrated the bomb attack on the pub. While Ahmed and his group had found the ideal candidate, applied the appropriate pressure and delivered the vest, everything else had been put together by Alex. The excitement level had reached fever pitch in Ahmed's group forcing Alex to calm them down before they did anything stupid that would get them caught.

AHMED: We are with you brother. Allah wills it.

MOHAMMAD: Allahu Akbar.

AHMED: Allahu Akbar. Did you get the information on the detective agency?

Ahmed had sent a document over with their findings, but it was nothing Alex hadn't been able to discover himself in minutes. He'd sought information about the agency as soon as its name had come up and been shocked to discover the identity of the people involved. It seemed an impossible coincidence when he saw Chloe and Zack's profile on the website, sending a shiver down his spine.

While he didn't believe there was any sort of deity controlling the world when Alex witnessed these moments of serendipity it gave him pause for thought. Despite having given up on Miley ever being a replacement for Angel, occasionally Alex would find himself trying to see if he could find out where she was in the world.

After they had sent her away with her Uncle, Miley had become almost impossible to track. There were few glimpses of her digital presence because she used some of the tricks Alex had taught her. In the beginning he'd first contacted her online using yet another alias and tapped into the fact she was a keen programmer with good skills. It had been Alex who introduced her into darker areas of technology where sometimes even the authorities were blind.

It made him smile to see she was growing up. Alex was sure it was how Angel would have turned out. Sassy, confident and beautiful. The only reliable data as to Miley's whereabouts was when she went back to the UK to visit her father.

It was disappointing to see that Zack had not stepped up his game since they'd last met, or that Chloe's flame had only briefly flickered back into life. They'd both seemed almost worthy adversaries in Oakwell, deserving of his respect. But they hadn't been able to keep even a small-time detective agency going profitably from what Alex had seen. He knew they'd been trying to look for him. Had expected nothing less, and while they'd made more progress than the useless authorities they had no clue where he was. Or even who he was.

AHMED: The police don't believe them anyway. We will get another chance.

MOHAMMAD: If the police don't believe them then why

was there a police detective meeting them in the office?

Alex glanced from where he was sat on the sofa towards the bedroom. Lilly had stopped snoring. He listed to make sure she wasn't awake.

AHMED: They don't think they have enough proof.

MOHAMMAD: No matter. It may well cause chaos and confusion among the authorities and that is always a good thing.

AHMED: We need more money?

MOHAMMAD: Don't you have enough?

Alex was sure they were blowing most of the cash they had on very western sins.

MOHAMMAD: How much more do you need? Are there not enough rewards waiting for you when this is over? Or do you and your friends like the local English girls too much to make the ultimate sacrifice for your cause?

AHMED: We are dedicated to the cause. We have suffered at the hands of the infidels, and we will enter the afterlife to help create a new world of Islam.

Alex wasn't so certain. But he'd made sure his plans didn't rely entirely on this group. There were enough other people under his control to give him the opening he needed in London when the time came.

MOHAMMAD: Forget the agency. If anymore action is needed, I'll deal with it. Keep to the plan, keep to the date. The shipment will arrive tomorrow. It will have everything that you need.

AHMED: Allah has provided.

Alex snorted. Allah had provided nothing. His genius had provided the know-how and contacts to get the money and equipment they needed for the operation.

MOHAMMAD: Then let me know when it's here and keep up the reading.

AHMED: And the funds?

MOHAMMAD: They will be there tonight.

He was such a greedy little bastard. Alex knew Ahmed's group would more likely be on top of some young white teenager they'd groomed with the riches Alex had provided than reading the scriptures which were supposed to get their spirits in the right place.

Alex decided he was going to make them martyrs to the cause. Whether they wanted to be or not.

There was another group he needed to speak to. Alex stretched out his back as he let out a long breath, for a moment he wondered if he had taken on too much by dealing with so many people. Especially people with their own agendas that he didn't give a fuck about

Of the missions he'd set himself this was always going to be the toughest. Rising to his feet he drifted into the kitchen to make a milkshake. He needed to go for a run to clear his head. Others may not be as dedicated to their cause, but Alex Ryan was determined to see every one of his plans to the very end.

The world had to open its eyes to the horror the ordinary folk suffered while a few enjoyed the riches at the top of the pyramid. People like Angel were thrown to the dogs because they just weren't important enough to be cared about. Alex had cared about her. He'd loved her. And Alex Ryan was going to make sure the world was taught a very important lesson.

24

Even the view from the waiting room was exhilarating. Chloe had been to New York a few times, but the offices of Global Money were something special. When she reached the heights of the executive floors, Chloe saw they looked over Central Park, while the buildings opposite had the backdrop of a clear blue sky. It made her wonder if it was the size of the offices that made bankers such pretentious arseholes.

Though Chloe had to admit she'd been treated exceptionally well so far. It was clear she was the special guest of the CEO. After a relaxing flight in first class, she'd been whisked from the airport in a Limo that had taken her to the Plaza Hotel for the night before collecting her that morning. Despite the time zone difference, the flight had been so comfortable Chloe felt rested. She hoped the Angel Detective Agency would one day be able to afford first class as standard.

Sitting outside the CEO's office, she suddenly felt she didn't belong among all the finery. They were small-time. No other clients and being sued by their previous one. It was hard to imagine the CEO realised this and still wanted to bring her all the way to America. With all the money they had, surely they could afford far more upmarket investigators.

The office door opened, revealing a well-built man with a

crew cut who smiled and beckoned her over.

"Miss Evans, if you would."

Chloe nodded, her heels clicking on the marble floor as she walked across the room. The inside of the office was as magnificent as she'd expected. A man Chloe estimated to be in his mid-forties and wearing it well stood beside an imposing desk. He stepped over, taking her hand with a firm grip as he flashed an expensive looking smile.

"You are Miss Evans, partner of Zack Carter, the former police detective. I understand he couldn't make it."

"No. Your company saw fit to have him spend the day in a custody suite."

"That was unfortunate but necessary." It was the man who had shown her in. "The London office was doing its job when they received a tip-off."

"I'm sure they were. I'm Chloe Evans, a former model." She added plenty of sarcasm to her tone. On first impressions, she'd seen nothing to shake the thought they were pretentious arseholes.

"Pleased to meet you, Miss Evans; I'm James Goldstein, and this is Brad Reynolds, Head of Security here at Global Money."

To be fair, for a CEO, James didn't look as cocky or confident as most of the people she'd met in the building. But she couldn't be sure it was because of why she'd been called over to America or it just was his natural demeanour.

"Would you like something to drink, Miss Evans?" James led her towards the sofas, where he sat on one with her, while Brad sat opposite.

"Call me Chloe, and no thanks. To be honest, I'd like to find out why you wanted to see us. Your London office seems very conflicted with regards to our investigation. Brandon Walsh hired us before he was killed, and the next thing we know, Zack was arrested."

"They need to be careful," James said. "It's not good for outside agencies to be prying into the affairs of the city. People in such organisations as ours can have nefarious intentions. We like to deal with them internally, discreetly. Outside agencies tend to get over excited and speak to authorities or worse, the press."

"You think this is an inside job?" Chloe asked.

"We are investigating the matter," Brad answered. "But I'm sure we'll find it was someone from the London office in due course. And we aim to keep it out of the press."

"After all," Mr Goldstein opened his hands as though there was nothing to worry about. It was the kind of gesture Chloe knew meant there was plenty to worry about. "Nobody's money was stolen, just borrowed for a while by someone making a little extra cash."

"Oh, so it was all legal then?" Chloe said. "That's good."

"Well, not quite. But this isn't the reason we asked you to come. It's of a more personal matter."

"Go on." Chloe tried to keep up the type of demeanour her mother insisted on when they were in polite company.

"From what Brad tells me, you have past experiences that might be able to shed light on my current situation."

"I'm sorry; I'm afraid I have no idea what you are talking about."

"Your Agency is doing an excellent job in the investigation. But, I hear you were also involved in a previous incident, and you were personally cyberstalked by the man behind it."

"You mean Alex Ryan?" Chloe was shocked at the turn in the direction of the conversation. "Yes, that's right. He was stalking me at first, goading me."

"You had no idea who it was?"

"No, and nothing could be traced. Again, I'm sorry; I don't see how this is all relevant." Chloe saw James glance to his Head of Security who shrugged.

"Your call, Mr Goldstein."

"I'm currently receiving threatening messages," James said. "Now, in my position, this is not out of the ordinary. I often receive threats from those who would like to see the end of bankers or the demise of capitalism. But, these threats are of a personal nature and stem from my time working in the London office. They refer to activities few people are aware of. To be perfectly blunt, I thought there was no one of consequence who knew about them."

"Are they threatening to kill you?"

"No, just ruin my family and me."

"What are they asking for?" Chloe asked.

"Nothing, which is even more disturbing. Apparently, I have a reckoning coming, and I will suffer for my past and present crimes. I need you to investigate these messages and find out who's behind them before the threats become real.

"I'm an influential man, Miss Evans, but I seem powerless to stop this individual. I would like to think it has nothing to do with current events in the London office, except this person has inside knowledge."

"We've interviewed everyone in New York who came over from London but found nothing," Brad said. "I want your agency to interview the personnel in London. We're giving you full clearance, provided you agree to keep this discreet. We're hoping you might be able to bring some insight we've been missing."

Chloe could see how much it pained the Head of Security to utter those words. "Is there anything common about the messages, the timing, the way they're delivered?"

"Sometimes email, sometimes messenger, even a Skype Account normally used by my wife. The only thing in common is the way they are signed off."

"And how's that?" Chloe asked.

"Always the 'Angel of Money.'"

For a moment, Chloe was sure her heart had stopped beating.

25

"Boys, it's Alex." Chloe climbed into the Limo, nodding to the Latino driver holding the door open. Her heart was still racing from what she'd heard, and she kept looking at her phone as if expecting to see messages from Alex. Just the thought of his being involved had her reliving those moments when he had her running all over Oakwell in a desperate attempt to stop her family from seeing her naked modelling pictures. After so long of trying to hunt Alex down, it was hard to believe he had finally surfaced.

"We suspected," Zack answered.

"Really, how?" Chloe was a little deflated at not being the originator of the news. She settled herself into the car as the door closed, and the driver climbed into the front next to Marian, one of Global Money's security operatives who was going to stay with her.

"Angel's father worked for Global Money. During the crash, her father lost his money and his job. He killed himself."

"And set Angel up to be exposed to the world that abused her," Chloe said.

"Exactly. But how did you know?" Zack said. "What's happened over there?"

"The CEO has been getting similar messages to the ones

I used to get from Alex. Some talk about when he ran the London office. James Goldstein helped turned Global Money around by being ruthless. The headcount was cut to save money, and he was at the heart of it. My betting is, if you check, he was there at the same time as Angel's father, probably fired him."

"I'll get right on it," it was Adam's voice from the conference phone.

"But that's not the kicker," Chloe went on. "The messages are signed off as the 'Angel of Money.'"

"No way." Zack whistled. "That nails it for me."

"I know. I almost fainted when they told me. With what you have, it all fits."

"Except the terrorist angle," Terry pointed out.

"He uses other people to get what he wants," Zack said. "Maybe he's even gotten in with an ISIS cell."

"Especially if he gave them access to all that money."

"Bingo."

Chloe could virtually hear the cogs going around in Zack's head. It was good to have him back.

"But they don't normally work well with others, especially people they consider infidels," Mike put in.

"It's a good point," Zack said. "Can you find out from inside what they've got on the terrorist cell? Have they traced the man who ran Brandon down for instance?"

"I'm not sure how much they'll be willing to divulge," Mike said. "But I can try. I'll have to tell them what you know."

"That's fine," Zack said. "There's nothing they can do about the messages on this side of the Atlantic anyway. Let them know to keep it on the quiet, so we can stay in with Global Money. Nice work over there, Chloe. How do you feel?"

"Like we're finally going to get him," Chloe said.

"Damn right." Zack was almost whooping. "What are you doing now?"

"Going to the hotel to get my head down before dinner with the CEO and his family. He's sending all the information and messages to you guys."

"Dinner with the CEO," Zack said. "Boy, you work fast."

"Hey, what kind of a woman do you think I am?"

"A woman who wants to buy more shoes."

"Cheeky bastard. Anyway, he's married, and his wife and daughter will be there."

"I hear these bankers are into some kinky stuff," Adam threw in, and Chloe heard the others laugh.

"You be careful over there," Zack said. "I don't think your mother would want an international scandal."

"Jealous, Mr Carter?"

"Just concerned for your safety, Miss Evans."

"Well…"

The colossal impact jolted Chloe forward. The seatbelt tightened, squeezing her chest before her head smashed back against the back of the chair. The sound of crunching metal came from behind. "Jesus Christ, what was that?"

A second impact threw her forward again. The Limo crashed into the car in front. Chloe glanced out of the rear window to see a dark SUV with tinted windows right up against the back of the Limo. It was feeling like an accident.

"Stay down, miss. I'll see to it." Marian had recovered quickly, and Chloe watched her climb from the car, gun in her hand. The driver's head was still lying on the airbag. Turning to get a better look at what had hit them, she saw someone getting out of the SUV. A hooded man with a machine gun.

As the first shots were fired at the back window, Chloe was already diving into the footwell shouting for the driver to do the same. More shots discharged from near the front of the Limo she assumed were from Marian. Looking up, Chloe saw cracks in the rear window where the SUV shooter's bullets had struck but not penetrated. She was thankful the rich only bought the best.

Another two shots. Someone fell past Chloe's window. Was that Marian? The Limo driver started screaming and scrambled to get out. Bullets ricocheted off the windows again. She hoped they'd hold long enough for help to arrive.

"Lock the doors," Chloe screamed at the driver. "We'll be safe in here if you lock the door."

"Fuck that, I'm getting out of here." The driver pushed the last of the airbag out of his way before tumbling out of the door. Chloe heard shots. Crimson sprayed across the white airbag the driver had pushed aside. There were screams from outside the car. Tyres screeched as other vehicles ground to a halt.

With the door open, Chloe knew she was vulnerable. A figure appeared in the window beside her dressed in blue.

"NYPD, freeze."

Her heart leapt at the thought of the police. There were more shots, and the figure vanished. More cries. People were running. Was her attacker down? Was the policeman down? The car moved again, and Chloe looked out of the back window to see the SUV backing up with a passenger hanging out of the window, firing at someone on the pavement. People on the sidewalk dove to the ground.

The relief at the SUV pulling back gave way to the horrific realisation it was about to ram the Limo again. She plunged herself back into the footwell, trying to make herself as small as possible as she heard the crash.

26

Opening her eyes, Chloe glanced about her. It was obvious she was in hospital. She couldn't help noticing it was exactly as she'd seen on the American TV shows. The instruments beside her flashed and beeped, while more than one set of wires were attached to her body.

Remembering she was in New York, the images of the attack flooded into her head. She gripped the bed, feeling a sense of panic. Had she been badly hurt? The beeping sound increased with her elevated heart rate, but as she scanned her body and noted the lack of pain, she began to relax.

She'd only been awake a short while when three people entered the room. The first was easily identifiable as a nurse with her green smock and her black hair tied back in a bun. The other two consisted of a tall black man with keen brown eyes and a woman dressed in a calf-length pencil skirt and dark blue jacket who had an equally astute gaze. Chloe didn't think they were doctors, noticing they held back to allow the nurse to carry out her checks.

"How are you feeling, Miss Evans?" The nurse, Emma, from her name badge, retrieved a clipboard from above the bed and began jotting down some of the readings from the machines.

"Fine, I think. What happened? I don't remember getting

here."

"You were bounced around in the car and knocked unconscious. Some cuts and bruises but no real physical harm. You got lucky."

"The driver?" Chloe looked at the coloured man in the suit who was standing just inside the door. "And the security lady."

"'Fraid they didn't make it." The man bowed his head.

"Oh god." Chloe let the air escape from her body. "Who were they? The attackers. Why did they do it?"

"That's what we're here to find out." He looked towards the nurse. "May I?"

"Yes, she's fine. Take sips of your water, Miss Evans, and remain lying down. If you feel faint or dizzy, stop right away and call us. You may have a concussion." The nurse turned to the other two. "Not too much, you understand?"

"I know the drill." The man stepped over to Chloe and held out his large hand. "Special Agent Leon Bennet. This is Special Agent Mandy Smith."

Chloe shook the offered hand. "I need to let my family know I'm okay."

"Your family has been informed." The nurse smiled reassuringly. Chloe wondered what her parents were thinking. How much had they been told? After the events in Oakwell, her mother had been continually fussing over her safety. While her father might have given in to the pressure and had security 'round him, Chloe had point blank refused. She couldn't imagine her mother taking no for an answer when she got back.

Chloe tried to relax and recall the earlier events. "I heard shouting in a foreign language. Not French or Spanish or anything like that."

Special Agent Leon pulled up a chair and sat beside Chloe, while his colleague kept further back, as though she was watching the corridor. The male agent had a broad, friendly face, but there was a look in his brown eyes of someone you wouldn't want to mess with.

"They were speaking Russian. They escaped by ramming other vehicles before fleeing on foot. We're combing the CCTV footage, and we'll find them."

"Russians?" Chloe's head throbbed as she tried to shake it. "What did they want with me?"

"Well, to be honest, we can't be sure you were the target. The Limo belongs to the CEO of one of the biggest banking corporations in the world. And someone who's been getting threats."

"You've been told about them?"

"Powerful men have a habit of becoming very honest when they think they need our help." Chloe detected the sarcasm in Agent Mandy Smith's tone.

"Why would the Russians be after him?"

Leon shrugged. "We don't know; they may have only been hired guns. Are you able to provide a description of your assailants?"

"Only the one who was shooting. The SUV had tinted windows, so I couldn't see anyone inside. The one I saw shot straight at the window, but the glass held."

"Mr Goldstein's Limo is bulletproof."

Chloe closed her eyes, trying to recall the man. "He was tall, taller than the roof of the SUV, and wearing dark clothes and a balaclava; it's about all I remember." She opened her eyes. "Sorry, not much to go on."

She noted the female agent was scribbling down some notes,

but she couldn't imagine it was anything they didn't already know.

"Of particular interest is your reason for being in New York. I understand you were asked to investigate the threatening messages."

"Because I'd suffered similar threats in the past." Chloe saw the inquisitive look in his eyes. "We think we know who's behind them. Well, the messages at least."

Leon looked surprised. "Go on."

"Three years ago, I was harassed by email and phone messages. It turned out, I wasn't the only one, and the man behind it, Alex Ryan, killed over twenty people in separate attacks. He used others to carry out some of his plans. Blackmailing them into doing horrible things. It ended with the town hall, where an election count was being held, being blown up."

"And this Alex Ryan got away?"

"Vanished. He'd been in the same year as me at school, but after he left, there's no history of Alex ever existing until he went back to Oakwell. Then, Alex ceased to exist again, despite all the efforts to track him down. It's the reason we formed the agency. He kidnapped me and my business partner's daughter, and we don't feel safe knowing he's still out there."

Leon whistled and looked at his colleague, who was writing furiously on her pad. "What makes you think he's back?"

"For one, he signed the messages to James Goldstein 'Angel of Money.'"

"I saw it. How's that significant?"

"Alex's childhood sweetheart was called Angel; it was her life of abuse and brutal murder that triggered his desire for vengeance. The coincidence is too strong."

"But just a coincidence?" Special Agent Smith suggested.

"Angel's father worked at Global Money; after the financial crash of 2008, he was fired, and he killed himself."

Leon nodded. "Circumstantial but interesting. You think he could have hired the Russians?"

"Anything's possible. I'll need to speak with the boys back in London to see what they've found since I've been here." Chloe glanced around. "How long have I been out, by the way?"

"About four hours," the nurse said, hovering at the door. Leon didn't look impressed she might have been listening in. "And I think that's enough for today. You've suffered quite a trauma, Miss Evans. You need to rest."

"I need to speak to my friends in London." Chloe looked pleadingly at the Special Agent rising from his chair.

"I'll get it sorted. Meantime, get some rest; we might have more questions soon."

27

Zack hung up, sliding his phone back into his jeans pocket.

"She's okay," he said to the expectant audience. He didn't hide the relief in his voice. "Shaken up, some bruises, but she should be out tomorrow."

"Is she coming home?" Miley asked.

"Well, that's what she wants us to decide. She's for staying, now there's something tangible stateside."

"I think she should come home."

Zack reached out and squeezed his daughter's shoulder. "She's okay." Miley gave him a weak smile, but he could see the concern on her face. "The CEO of Global Money has sent some security to be with her. Chloe says he looks like The Rock."

The group were in their new office. It was less impressive than their old one, which Zack thought would have been impossible. Consisting of a single large room, it had a wide shelf running around the walls providing a platform for the various devices and displays Adam had set up. The centre was dominated by an old table coupling as an eating station and another workspace. The table reminded Zack of an old school desk with names and dates etched into its surface by bored students. But it was a private space with abundant, secure internet access, which Adam had insisted was a priority.

The office Adam had found through his contacts was nestled in what appeared to be abandoned lockups when you first drove up. A bearded gentleman with an eighties Motorhead t-shirt manned the crude reception desk. When they'd first arrived, Zack had wanted to walk away until Adam had assured him this was the right place for them. As they'd walked down the corridor towards their designated space, it became apparent these were no ordinary set of shared offices. It was a space for companies who wanted to keep their projects off the radar until they were ready. Adam claimed even Alex would find it difficult to trace them here.

"You think he's operating on both sides of the Atlantic?" Terry asked. He'd become one of the team. Global Money didn't seem over eager to welcome him back while the investigation was ongoing but seemed happy enough for him to assist the agency.

"Without a doubt," Zack said. "Everything points to it. And he's stepped up his game with who he's using. It's not just troubled individuals anymore. It's professionals. But if we're right about his end game, then how is he going to do it?"

"Bringing down the CEO of Global Money and the company itself won't be enough." Adam looked up from his laptop.

"It'll be bigger than that," Miley said. "He thinks bigger than that."

"So, it's the whole system," Adam added, and Miley nodded her agreement. "The system that nurtured evil corporations like Global Money."

"That's it," Zack said. "So, we need to figure out how he plans to do it."

"What are the police saying?" Terry asked. Mike hadn't been

with them since the fire, but Zack had briefed him on what had happened to Chloe. They'd already handed over all they knew about Alex Ryan, a relatively thin file with significant gaps in the timeline where there was no evidence of his existence.

"His bosses aren't buying it. Not shutting him down completely, but to them, it sounds too far-fetched for one man to be behind a terrorist cell and possibly a Russian mob attack."

"Put like that, it does sound a bit out there with alien abductions," Terry said.

"He's a one-man conspiracy." Adam nodded.

"That's right." Zack looked at the bottom of a Styrofoam cup hoping there would be a few more dregs of coffee. He'd been pleased to see there was a vending machine in the communal area of the building. It wasn't what he needed to keep his nerves under control, but it helped. Finding time to replenish his supply of pills while Miley was around was proving difficult. "It means the UK police aren't taking the threat seriously because they are understandably more concerned about possible terrorist attacks from an active cell. Mike has heard they'd received a warning that talked about how 'the infidels of the city will suffer the wrath of Allah if they do not change their ways.'"

"Do you think it's true?" Adam asked.

"Misdirection," Zack responded. "He's got the authorities looking the other way to hide his plans. And can you blame them after what's happened? We haven't got any closer to working out what has happened with the strange trades and disappearing money Terry detected. Dead bodies and the threat of even more carnage has to be their priority."

"Does Mike believe us?" Terry said.

"Yes, and he has permission to continue to work with us, but we have to make our own plans on how to find Alex and stop him." The others around the table nodded their assent. Zack had started the meeting by allowing anybody who wanted to walk away from the ever-perilous investigation to make it known. No one left, and Miley continued to refuse to go back to school.

"Okay, Adam I want you to run searches on anything unusual linked to the financial sector here and in New York. You know the score, suicides, scandals, sackings or unexpected resignation. Cast your net to other foreign exchanges if you can, and let's see what shakes loose."

"That's a lot of processing." Adam put his head down.

"Can you get what you need?" Zack knew Adam would come good.

"I think there'll be some guys here that can help, but it's going to cost."

"Then do it because Global Money is footing the bill. But we need this to be covert Adam; we don't want to alert Alex. He might already know we're involved, but we need to keep what we have away from him."

"If we've got the money, then it's no problem. The folks here don't like strangers, but money talks. They need it for their own research projects." Adam threw out some air quotes.

"What is this place?" Miley asked.

"Sort of a dark Silicon Valley," Adam said. "Can't you tell from all the glamour? White hat coders who flirt with the dark side of the web but for ethical reasons."

"Cool, but I didn't think something like this would have existed in London," Miley said. "I thought most worked out of countries with less enforcement."

"Times have moved on, Miley." Adam smiled. "London is the place to be. It's the place where the not so respectable geeks come to do work that might be on the fringe of the law in most countries and beyond the law in some cases. The signals coming in and out of here are bounced all around the world and encrypted to make it virtually untraceable."

"But I don't see many servers," Terry put in.

"You won't. Most are held elsewhere; otherwise, the power drain would give the place away. Over the years, servers have been added to existing data centres to spread the network far and wide. But only from these walls can you get access to them. It's like the darknet within the darknet but heavily controlled. No sick shit goes on here. It's about research and cutting-edge stuff they don't want the world to know about yet. I know one of the girls in the room three down from us. They're paid to penetrate test network security, and doing it from here keeps them invisible."

"This is almost cooler than my school," Miley said. "I've got to see some of the what they do."

"Well, you already know the effect a pretty girl who knows her way around code affects these people. From the little you've told me about where you've been through, this doesn't even get close to the top of the cool board."

Miley laughed, and Zack saw his daughter redden.

"Will they help us?" Zack asked.

"If we are not doing anything immoral and can pay for it, then sure, they'll say bring it on. They only take cryptocurrency though. These guys don't like to use banks, consider them pure evil."

"Sure, they'll be keen on us trying to save them," Terry laughed.

"Oh, they are pragmatists, too," Adam replied. "They'd like to keep their jobs."

"I still feel we need someone on the ground in New York," Zack said. "This is going to be played out on two fronts, and we need to be on top of it."

"I'll go," Miley said. "Chloe shouldn't be on her own out there."

"No." Zack shook his head.

"There's no other way, Dad," Miley protested. "You need to run things here, and Adam needs to work with Terry. I can add the tech skills over in the States with Chloe, and I can handle myself now."

"I can't, Miles." Zack reached over and placed his hand on her bare arm. It was hard in front of the others to say he didn't want her in harm's way when he was willing to send someone else.

"Dad, I'm not that fifteen-year-old anymore. I'm different; I'm prepared and better trained than anyone here if things get rough. And I've already handled a case."

Zack couldn't deny what she said was true. The girl he'd rescued from the cellar three years ago was a trained young woman now. Jake had seen to that; it frightened Zack to see how quick she was and how casually she talked about weapons. Jake had managed to get her into the school because the owners had wanted some suspicious activity among the pupils investigated. Like Nancy Drew, she'd uncovered the mystery.

Zack had been furious at the time and rowed with Jake about putting his daughter in danger. Not that she came to any harm, instead becoming a significant part of resolving the issue and earning free tuition for the rest of her life.

"I can go," Adam said quietly. "The work can be done remotely. Plus, I've heard it's first class all the way."

"Thank you, Adam."

Zack tried to ignore his daughter's angry stare.

28

It was exhilarating to observe the CEO of one of the biggest financial houses in the world while knowing that inside he was screaming in terror. Alex could see the anxiety on James Goldstein's face and in his body language, and the arrogant bastard twitched every time his cell went off. James had insisted they still made their dinner reservation despite the day's events. He'd told Lilly they couldn't give in to scum trying to threaten them.

However, a brute of a man had been posted outside Lilly's apartment that afternoon a few hours after the attack on the Limo. Alex hadn't approved of the hit. The Russians had killed the driver and one of the security team because they'd heard somebody had been brought in to help Global Money with their investigations.

As with the team Alex was using in London to further his ends, it was becoming harder to control them, to keep them on his agenda. Alex cursed his ego for convincing him he'd be able to manipulate units on either side of the Atlantic so easily. It wouldn't be a mistake he'd make again.

Lilly had informed him there'd been someone else in the car, a woman from England who'd met with James, and there was a rumour it was his mistress. Lilly dismissed the talk as nonsense, and if James's wife knew about any infidelity, she wasn't showing negative emotions towards her husband.

Alex would have to persuade Lilly to do a little more digging to discover the identity of the mystery woman. Having known this mission would be his most significant challenge, Alex was finding it difficult to keep the plates spinning. He'd been laying the foundations for Global Money's demise well before his actions in Oakwell, but now the plans were nearing their conclusion, he often had to stop his hand from visibly shaking with excitement and trepidation.

Sometimes, when he looked at James Goldstein, Alex wondered who was under the most strain.

"Not for me, thank you," he said as the waiter offered him wine. They were eating in the Goldstein's opulent apartment only a short walk from the offices.

Lilly frowned, but she knew Alex didn't drink, despite the number of times she'd said it would loosen him up. Gaining access to Lilly Goldstein had been a bonus. It hadn't been his original intention to court the CEO's daughter, the opportunity having arisen when she'd been asked to do a piece on his company. He'd turned on his exceptional charm and quite literally swept her off her feet.

She was beautiful, dynamite in bed, and while the offspring of a man Alex considered pure evil, Lilly had a tender side so different from her father. It was a pity what would happen to her. A shame she'd be in the hands of those who wouldn't show her lithe body any respect. But Alex had been distracted once before by a beautiful girl. He wasn't going to let it happen again.

It was a match frowned upon by her doting father, which made it all the sweeter. Knowing that with the software he'd designed, Alex was inside the company, and with Lilly, he was inside James' family, added an extra kick. He'd wondered if Global Money's security team had done any background checks. If they had, they should be fired. While Alex had meticulously created the persona of Darren Anderson, a Texas whizz kid who'd built a software company from scratch, there were anomalies that he'd feared would catch him out if inspected closely.

Austin Trading Services was one of many companies Alex owned and his most profitable. Only his film production company was more prominent, but that rarely turned a profit, and its funding coming from other investments.

The software he'd devised for auto-trading was a piece of technological artistry which made the companies who used it, including Global Money, billions of dollars. Of course, his real piece de la resistance was the complex code within the program he'd used to generate his own fortune, enabling him to fund other ventures. It was unfortunate the keen analyst in London had noticed the anomalies when he did.

Alex smiled as the waiter carefully placed the first-course pate in front of him. Lilly squeezed his knee. James was hogging all the chat, talking about the lack of security and how democracy had to prevail over thugs and terrorists.

Alex knew he really meant how capitalism needed to prevail. He wanted the rich to make even more money, regardless of what it did to the ordinary person trying to get by. The James Goldsteins of the world didn't know what it was like to go without. He didn't know about the little girl who found her father hanging from the neck because the banking system was so greedy it issued loans people had no hope of paying. He didn't know what it was like to hold that girl's hand as she breathed her last because some motherfuckers had killed her for drugs.

All because James had fired Angel's father. All because the system didn't give a fuck about the ordinary people.

"Darling, you're not on the steak yet." Lilly chuckled, and Alex realised he was driving his knife into the pate with alarming aggression.

"Just wanted to make sure it didn't get away," he beamed back.

"Could've done with that sort of spirit today." James attempted a lame joke that only brought polite smiles from those around the table. Lilly's mother, Rose, was sitting opposite Alex, wearing an elegant blue dress that clung to her body as if sculptured to her contours. Her auburn hair was tied back in a severe bun, accentuating her sharp features.

"I'm not sure the joke was in good taste, dear." She admonished her husband. "Good people died today."

"Yes, quite." James dabbed his mouth with a serviette.

"It's a good thing you weren't in the limo at the time." Alex decided a little probing was in order. "Was it just your security guard?"

"A poor girl from England, I heard," Lilly said.

Alex noticed she glanced at her mother to see if there was a reaction.

"Yes, she was going to dine with us tonight, but instead, she's recovering in hospital," James said. "I've never had any problem with the Russians, so it's hard to imagine it was them."

"Who was she?" Alex tried to sound nonchalant as it could hardly be James's mistress if she was going to dine with them.

"She's from a private investigation firm in London. I've been getting threats, and we thought they could help as they'd been working on a case for the London office. Probably nothing as I get threats all the time." The waiter hovered over his shoulder, and James nodded before turning his attention to the wine glass itself.

Alex kept his composure as thoughts whirled through his head. It had to be Chloe. It was too much of a coincidence that he'd only recently discovered Zack and Chloe were investigating in London. Maybe the Russians had done him a favour, or he could well have been unmasked tonight. Even with his altered appearance and Texan accent, he didn't think he'd fool Chloe a second time if they were sitting at the same table.

"I hear you're going back to London soon?" James was apparently keen to change the subject.

"Yes. Business is really taking off there." Alex regained his composure. "Explosive plans for some of London's financial houses."

29

"Mike, have you got any contacts who can get the passenger manifests for flights to New York today?" Zack shouted into the handsfree while simultaneously honking the driver in front for the crime of being in his way.

"Come on, Zack, you know that's not possible without a warrant. What's wrong?"

"It's Miley; she's on her way to New York. Left me a note saying she'd be the best person to help Chloe."

"Jesus. Do you know which airport?" Mike said. "I could make some calls and see if the security can spot her."

"There's a flight out of Gatwick in an hour; I'm heading there now."

"I'll see what I can do."

"Thanks Mike."

Zack rang off and drove between two cars on the slip road to the M23 towards Gatwick airport. He'd tried Miley's phone several times, only receiving a message telling him she'd be okay and not to worry. He cursed himself for sleeping so long and not checking on his daughter as soon as he'd awoken. They hadn't gone to bed until near dawn after returning to his apartment, and Zack had been more than happy to let Miley sleep late considering she'd only just recently arrived back in the country.

When she hadn't responded to any calls or knocks, he'd entered her room only to find a note on the bed informing him she was going to New York to help Chloe. After a few frantic phone calls and web searches, Zack was betting on a flight out of Gatwick.

Undertaking two middle lane hogs, Zack increased his speed as much as he dared. Cursing his brother for putting such a spirit of adventure into Miley, he couldn't help also being proud that she was so empowered after all that had happened. Zack also wanted to know how the hell she had the money to get to the US.

He'd tried to contact Jake, but his brother wasn't answering either, which wasn't unusual, and he was only ringing for someone to shout at for the reckless actions of his daughter.

After negotiating the final few miles to the airport parking zones, Zack abandoned his car in a drop off point not caring about the consequences.

Ignoring angry shouts from a car behind he'd blocked, Zack ran into the departures area. His rushed entry drew the attention of two armed officers, and it probably wasn't the wisest move to reach into his pocket and start making a call at that moment, but he had to do it. The two men strode towards him as Mike picked up.

"Anything?"

"I've made the calls; they're looking, and we may have something."

"Are you a Mr Zack Carter?" one of the approaching police officers said.

"Thanks Mike, I think I've got help." Zack killed the call and turned to the two officers. Their weapons were tucked under the cradle of their arms and pointing downwards. "That's me. Have you seen my daughter?"

"She's heading for security. There's a bitch of a delay, so you might get lucky. Once she's airside, we can't let you through."

"I understand."

"We'll escort you, so you don't attract any unwanted attention."

Zack understood shouting and racing around an airport wasn't a good idea if he wanted to keep his liberty and so hurried with the two officers towards the security gates. The area was crammed with disgruntled passengers desperate to get on with their journeys. Zack wasn't hindered by any security as he made this way through the lines and scanned the crowds for his daughter.

The first lone woman traveller he saw with auburn hair was somewhat startled by his sudden appearance. Zack apologised and moved on. He saw the woman glance around at the policemen who'd stayed back at the entrance. They raised a hand in acknowledgement to the woman and nodded to Zack to carry on.

The second time he got it right.

"Miley."

"Dad, what are you doing here?" She turned, a shocked look on her face, but it probably wasn't as stunned as Zack's at her round spectacles and demure makeup making her look ten years older and a lot more sophisticated.

"Taking you back."

"No way, dad; I'm best over there, and it would be better if you don't make a scene."

"It's too dangerous, Miley. You're too young to handle this."

"Oh, and Adam and Chloe have all the age and experience."

The line of people shuffled forward. She was nearly at the point of scanning her passport, and Zack wouldn't be allowed any further.

"Miley, please come back with me, and we'll talk about this. I know my brother has put ideas in your head, but you're only eighteen. You don't have the kind of training he has."

"Uncle Jake didn't make me this way, dad." It was Miley's turn to scan her passport. "It was Alex. I don't want to be a victim anymore. I don't want to be scared. If he's out there, I want to find him, and all that Uncle Jake did was give me some tools to make it happen."

Zack opened his mouth to speak, but Miley shushed him with a finger to his lips. "Dad, I may be eighteen, but I've been through more than most forty-year-olds, and I've got yours and Mum's toughness. I'm going because there's nowhere safe from Alex until he's caught."

"The tools were to protect you, not go chasing after him."

"I'm not going to be stupid, dad. Chloe is my friend, and she needs my help."

"Miley, you take this flight, he'll know where you are. What if he's tracking your name?"

"Then he won't have a clue." Miley flashed her passport, and Zack saw the name Bel Powell and a date of birth that made Miley twenty-four. "I love you, dad." She reached up and kissed him. "But I've got a fashion event to attend."

Zack was so shocked at seeing the passport he could only stand in a daze as his daughter scanned the document before the gates flipped open to allow her through. She turned, blew him another kiss, and was then swallowed up by the crowd.

He'd never been so scared or proud in his life.

30

Clenching and unclenching his fists, Harvey stared at the numbers in front of him. They were all within the parameters he'd been given by his benefactor. The instructions demanded he stay within the prescribed limits, and Harvey understood why. In fact, he'd marvelled at how well they'd been calculated to keep the transactions from raising red flags. The chances are they would be caught in a company audit, but one of those was a long way off, and his benefactor had promised he would be out of the game before then.

Only Harvey didn't want to wait.

Harvey had fucked up.

The money he'd already stashed from previous deals had been enough to clear his debts had he not got high with a couple of his favourite hookers and stumbled back into the casino. Now, he was broke again, and time to pay the debt was fast running out. He needed access to a lot of capital pronto and was holding a golden ticket. Only he wasn't allowed to cash it in.

Up until then, he'd traded as instructed. He'd understood there'd be consequences if he broke ranks. Reaching towards the keyboard, Harvey changed the figures to see what it looked like if he did his own thing. The numbers looked good. Life changing kind of good.

Traders saw these projections on their screens every day. Fantasy figures if everything went well, a moment to dream of the massive bonus they'd receive when their best-case scenarios came in, and the company showered them with money. There were two differences. The first was Harvey knew these were not fantasy numbers. Every morsel of information he'd been fed had been one hundred percent on the money. The second difference was the figure was what he would make, not the company he traded for. He might be borrowing the money to complete the trades, but he was looking at his profit margin. The surplus would allow him to live like a king for many years. Longer if he picked the right destination.

There was nothing to keep him in London, apart from some of the best hookers he'd ever known. But it was about time he travelled the world and sampled all manner of foreign ladies. Harvey knew he'd have to get out fast if he pushed the button on these trades. It might be a few days before they were investigated, but the flags would be raised, and they'd be calling him in.

They'd know he was trading on insider information. They were always looking for people making large profits when companies announced their quarterly results. While many brokers would bet on those results blind, there would be some in the know wanting to make a quick buck. If they did, and they were caught, they could end up in prison.

He changed the number again, dialled it back. Not enough but it would give him more time. The tips had been coming in at the rate of two a day. In his head, he calculated three trades at the lower price might go undetected. Enough so he could stay in the country.

"You okay, Harvey? You look a little peaky." He felt the large hand of the floor boss on his shoulder. "What are you looking at now?" The bespectacled man peered closer at his screen. Harvey held his breath. "Wow, you're betting on those; the results are out later today. You know something we all don't?"

"Only what I see in the data, Jonny, but firms like this are turning profits better than expected."

"Well, your record over the last couple of days tells me you might have got your old mojo back old chap. I might not get to fire you after all. So, don't blow your winning streak with some crazy arse trades." Jonny nodded at the numbers Harvey was speculating with. "Unless you're in the know, of course." Jonny gave him a wink and slap on the shoulder before going off, his voice booming as he taunted another trader whose performance put him on the brink of being let go.

Harvey felt his heart rate settle. For a moment, he'd thought he was about to be busted.

Did his boss suspect he was insider dealing? Even if he did, he probably didn't care if Harvey was bringing home the bacon for his department. After all, if Jonny didn't know, then he'd be able to accuse Harvey of being a rogue trader during any subsequent investigation.

Harvey changed the numbers back to the higher figure. He needed to do this and get the fuck out of dodge. He wasn't supposed to be working with his own money either. The instructions had been explicit about that because he'd receive a substantial bonus when it was over. A bonus big enough so he'd never have to work again for the rest of his life, the messages had said.

But it sounded too good to be true. There'd been a deposit

in his account as promised. Small enough not to trigger any alarms with the banks, but Harvey had learnt to mistrust everyone he met in the city. It's why he preferred the beds of hookers where he knew they could only be trusted as far as the next dollar he was paying them.

Making his decision, Harvey executed the trades; he'd only have to wait a few hours for the expected results. Logging through a proxy he'd been provided with, Harvey checked a Dropbox account to find there was already another tip. Looking around, Harvey smiled at the ignorance of the poor suckers trying to work the markets. He entered another set of trades and sat back to watch the money roll in as he fantasised about which exotic islands he would visit first.

31

Seeing his daughter travelling as an older woman with a false passport had been a surreal experience. Where was the innocent girl who'd begged him to go to Disneyland? Zack wished her mum was alive to see the tough little madam their daughter had become. Mary would have been so proud. The tears had streamed as he made his way back to the office, forcing him to pull into a motorway services.

After mainlining coffee and aspirin, Zack managed to get a modicum of control over his emotions. He missed Mary so much. After the shit he'd witness in Iraq and Afghanistan, settling down with the most wonderful woman in the world and starting a family had changed his life. Only Mary had known he couldn't get to sleep without popping some pills. Or that he woke so early not even the birds were singing. But in his time with her, all that had receded, and he felt like he was a normal human again.

When cancer gripped her, the slow descent returned. If it hadn't been for Miley, Zack didn't know what he would have done. He knew why his brother did what he did, taking on jobs where he could deprive bad guys of their breathing privileges. It wasn't for the money, he no doubt had plenty of that; no, his brother couldn't live with the things he had seen, and he knew that one stray bullet could at any moment end the nightmares.

Zack could empathise with that.

But he had to work harder than ever to nail Alex and prevent him from causing further chaos. Miley and Chloe were in the firing line once more of a very dangerous killer.

Before pulling into the compound on the outskirts of Clapham, Zack did a final check of his mirrors to ensure he wasn't followed. The ticket he'd acquired for parking in the drop-off zone at the airport still flapped on his windscreen.

At the compound, there was space to park in an abandoned section of the warehouse; it was undercover and away from the prying eyes of satellites. The location was ideal because being so close to the Heathrow flightpath meant other aircraft, and most drones weren't allowed to fly over. The noise of the planes meant it was hardly a piece of prime real estate, even in London. Once Zack had shut the large metal door behind him, it was difficult to hear anything outside. The outside might look like shit, but the sophistication of the interior must have cost thousands.

Down the long corridor that led off to other offshoots like their own, Zack made his way to the office they'd been allocated, always hoping he would see a door open, so he could get a glimpse of what the other companies were up to. He was sure one of the rooms was a secret Dungeons and Dragons club from the dress of the people he saw entering and leaving.

"She good?" Adam looked up from his laptop on the desks that ran down the left side of the room. It was hooked up to two larger monitors with incomprehensible code scrolling on each.

"Miss Bel Powell is on her way to New York for a fashion

show to choose the latest line of clothes for her new business venture. Jesus, Adam, I barely recognised her. She had a false passport that made her look like a businesswoman."

"That passport must be top work. The guys here can't even get hold of stuff like that."

"That's my brother for you." Zack poured some coffee from the machine Adam had brought in. The younger man liked his caffeine and thought the stuff from the vending area tasted like mud. "He knows some of the lowest, dirtiest people on earth."

"Nice."

"But to be fair, he spends a lot of time killing them."

Adam chuckled. "Sounds like a fun guy. Anyway, here's a new phone and laptop."

Adam stepped over to the main table where Terry was sitting using an identical laptop to the one pushed Zack's way. "For now, we only communicate on WhatsApp; I've set up accounts for us all with one-time only email addresses. When this is over, we ditch them. With the computer, don't use them on the net until the VPN is logged in, then you are good to go. It will be slower but secure."

"Is all this cloak and dagger stuff really necessary? It's creeping me out." Terry looked around the small room. "I'm just a risk analyst, guys; I'm not sure I'm cut out for all this."

"You're a damn good analyst, Terry," Zack said. "If it weren't for you, we wouldn't know anything about Alex's plans, and we wouldn't be on the trail of the sick bastard. This time, he's got some nasty friends, Terry. Right now, I'll take every precaution to keep us safe."

Terry took a few gulps from the can of Coke next to his laptop before he wiped his brow. "Are we safe here?"

"Safe as anywhere, pal." Adam gave him a reassuring thump on the shoulder. "Alex showed us before he's able to move around networks undetected and tap into areas we thought would be impossible. You've seen his power yourself. But here, we're behind layer upon layer of protection."

"I know." Terry nodded. "I'm scared but feel safer with you guys."

"Hardly the Fast and Furious family, though, are we?" Adam flexed his muscles, which only served to move his black T-shirt a little.

"And the quicker we can find him, the faster we can stop Alex, and this can all be over," Zack said. "You got anything?"

"Just maybe," Terry said looking back at his screen. "I've got a friend in Reuters who I'm taking out to dinner. I was talking about some of the data I'm looking at, not saying I'd found a problem, and he said we should catch up and go out. I'll also have the figures later to tell us exactly how much he might have made from these secret trades. Oh, and I need to get Chloe and Miley to look at some suspicious order types in the US. A dark pool over there has been disbanded, and there is talk of fraudulent trading."

"Dark pool?" Zack asked.

"Yes, a lot of high-frequency traders work out of dark pools within the big finance houses. They start the day with no position and end the day with no position, using fast trades throughout the day to make money. It's all about the tech with them, front-running the exchanges to try to get their deals done ahead of their competitors. Turns out, there were special order types these guys were using which gave them an edge. A couple of new ones have appeared that SEC is finally calling foul on, which most folk think they should've done it a long time ago."

"I'm not sure I get it but okay. Get them looking."

"There have been suicides stateside too within the banking sector," Adam said. "Few they could look into, though one stands out, an IT guy. It could have given Alex an in."

"Anything on the Russian connection?" This was the area that concerned Zack the most while Chloe and Miley were in New York.

"No, but a lot of the code on the exchanges was written by Russian programmers who were used to programming on shit hardware. It made their stuff super-efficient. A long shot but maybe some of them were involved."

"It's rumoured they tried to rig the US elections; do you think they could be after something else?" Zack said.

"Well, they must be pretty pissed at the outcome since he's been in office, so who knows. He's not exactly been very friendly towards the Russians."

"Just too much we don't know." Zack looked at the pin board that had been pushed up against one of the walls to act as his incident board. Despite the myriad of technology at their fingertips, it was reassuring to have as much information physically pinned to a timeline as possible, so he could sit back and examine the evidence while mulling things over in his mind.

"We need to figure out how he's going to do it, and how many people he's going to hurt along the way.

32

"Jesus, Miley, are you a spy or something?" Chloe circled the hotel suite Miley had checked into, astonished at the opulence. It made her accommodation look like a cheap bed and breakfast.

"They probably won't be expecting a small-time detective agency to be hiding out in this sort of place," Miley said.

"Er, no, are you charging this all back?" Chloe ran her hand over the satin sheet on the bed.

"It's coming out of an emergency fund Uncle Jake set up for me. Though, I'm not sure he'd class this as an emergency." Miley smiled at Chloe as she pulled up a gold-coloured chair to the large desk in one of the rooms. "We better not meet your FBI friend here or let him check my real identity."

Chloe flopped down on the huge bed deciding this was the sort of lifestyle she could aspire to. "That might not be too clever."

"You should have seen my dad's face when I showed him my passport." Miley flipped open her laptop. "I think Uncle Jake is going to get it in the neck when he and my dad next speak. I was going to try to call on him for help."

"Can you?" Chloe propped herself up on her elbows. She liked Jake even though they had only met briefly on holiday after the events in Oakwell. He'd emerged from his mysterious world of adventure before melting back and taking Miley with him. Finding out what he did was like getting blood from a stone. But she knew he was no travelling salesmen.

"I've left a voicemail, but Christ knows where he is. Once the training camp was over, and I went to school, I've only had a few messages."

"So, is it a spy school? Or Hogwarts? Are they teaching you magic, and that's why it's on an island? So the dragons can't get loose."

Miley looked up from her screen and laughed. "I wish. No, it's a school for rich or gifted kids. Of which I don't appear to be either. It's sort of creepy and cool at the same time."

Chloe's phone buzzed.

"It's Adam; he says they've got some names to have a look at. He's sent it through."

"Got it." Miley glanced at the large TV on the wall. "I can display the info on the big screen. We can go through it while we eat."

"Now that's an excellent idea." Chloe rolled over to the side of the bed and lifted the phone. "I wonder how much every dessert is?"

As they waited for room service, Miley connected her laptop to the TV and brought up Adam's work.

"Adam has looked at every suspicious death or activity he could link to Wall Street or any other financier." Miley opened the list, which had links to further details on each case. "Shit, that's a lot. Twelve suicides alone in the last three months."

"Stressful job." Chloe settled down next to Miley and began

to scan the list. "What's the number to the right?"

"Not sure. Oh, it's a weighting. Adam has added a probability of it being of interest to us, so we can start with the top ones. Even got contact details and police reports. Nice."

When there was a knock at the door, Chloe had almost forgotten about the room service, she'd become so engrossed in the data. It was astonishing how many people had either committed or attempted to commit suicide. The information also showed the deviance from the standard suicide rates, which was high, but it seemed it had been no different in the finance sector in the last few years.

As the food trolley was wheeled in, Miley brought up the information on three people that they'd decided were most interesting.

"There's number one." Miley pointed at the screen with a chubby-faced guy, who Chloe saw had worked in IT until he'd thrown himself off a building.

"But not into the money side," Chloe pointed out.

"No, but he has the means to influence. Passwords, keys to the entire system of a major exchange, and possible contacts to the rest." Miley brought up some tech forum she knew about where Adam had found links to and from the guy. She pointed to some of the posts. "This is him." The username was TopNetW0rkAdmin. "A tech who talks about his city contacts. Playing it big on the forums as though he gets stuff from the big financiers."

"And he threw himself off a building," Chloe said.

"Probably because of this." Miley brought up some other of his posts, which suggested that he was gay.

Chloe read through the posts and then looked back at his bio. "Shit, yes. He came from a devout Christian family. Looks like he didn't go much by the religion himself, but the shame it would have caused him at home if it came out might have been enough for some leverage."

Chloe remembered an old school friend who had thrown himself in front of a train rather than let his family know he was gay. It had been Alex's doing. Taunting him through social media. Telling him the world would be a better place without his kind. It reminded Chloe what a sick bastard Alex was.

"Who's he talking about, some work colleague?" Chloe read the post Miley pointed to. It looked like one night he decided to lay bare some of his emotions. Pity that many of the replies he received were telling him to fuck off and kill himself. It appeared there was a shit load of homophobia in the boards he frequented. Chloe wondered if one of them was Alex; it might be worth Adam trying to see what he could find out about the users who'd taunted him.

"I think so." Miley tapped on the keyboard before dragging a browser window across. "I've grabbed the public personnel records. It will take longer for Adam to get the private ones. These two worked in the same department."

"Unrequited love tragedy," Chloe murmured. "Yes, I wonder if he came out to his colleague, and it didn't go well." She leaned forward. "No, I might be wrong." She brought up the colleague's social feeds. "Okay, so he's a top dollar geek who's into his sheek, and from what I can see, he likes to play the field. Loves himself, too."

"Any gender will do," Miley commented. "I think you should talk to him."

"Err, why me?"

"Because of his Tinder profile."

Chloe looked at his preferences and groaned. "Loves his girls and boys blonde-haired and blue-eyed. It says mid-twenties."

"I thought you might be able to get away with that." Miley smiled.

"Now, that's a cheap shot but very flattering." Chloe hurled the cushion she had been resting her plate on at the teenager. "Okay, that one's for me, but let's find someone for you to chat up. Perhaps a forty-year-old fat bloke with bad body odour."

33

Ahmed started monitoring the container's movements from the moment it had been unloaded in the docks. The software their mentor had provided gave astounding access to the CCTV cameras they needed. There were blackspots, of course; it was not sophisticated enough to hack police cameras, but it allowed Ahmed to follow the progress of their delivery to the location where his two colleagues were waiting.

Even in the safety of his flat, rented under false names and paid up front, Ahmed was forced to wipe the sweat from his palms. It was becoming real now, their goal; their target was in sight. He looked at the picture on the wall of the small bedroom they used as an office and threw insults at the building epitomising all he hated about western society. Soon, it would be no longer; it would be ashes and rubble.

Are they close?

A message from Syed. He and Bhavik had taken the van to the lockup where they would pick up the crates from the delivery truck before transporting them to another anonymous lock up on the other side of the city. They needed to make sure no attention was drawn to them. Ahmed was relying on the paperwork to be correct. They were having machine parts delivered, but among them were the guns and munitions that were going to bring them glory. Fail now, and everything they had dreamed about would be over.

Just pulling into the yard.

He messaged Syed, keeping a close eye on the cameras.

I see it. Can you see us?

Yes.

Ahmed's role was to keep an eye on everything from afar. On a second screen, he monitored the cameras covering the approach to the yard. As night fell, it had become increasingly difficult to observe anyone lurking in the shadows, but it still gave them a chance to see if there was any sign of a double cross or if the police had been tipped off.

So far, everything was clear.

The half-sized container was loaded into the yard. He watched Syed hand over the cash to buy the silence of the driver. Most disreputable hauliers who did this kind of work assumed it was drugs or counterfeit goods in the containers. Few would comply if they knew they were transporting weapons or people. Ahmed was aware all you had to do was lie and offer a large enough bribe, and people didn't ask awkward questions.

The container was lowered into the yard, and as the truck pulled away, the two men set to work. Even in the gloom, Ahmed could see them pry open the wooden crates to sort through the useless parts until they reached what they wanted. The smaller boxes were extracted from the containers before being transferred into the back of an anonymous, white van they were using.

This was the moment Ahmed feared most. He half expected to see the police charge into the yard once the exchange had been made. Despite the amount of money they were paying for the driver's silence, Ahmed had no idea if he could be trusted to keep his mouth shut. But as the transfer of boxes neared completion, there was no sign of trouble.

Are we clear? Syed messaged.

Ahmed checked the cameras once more.

All good.

He saw the two men close and secure the door of the lockup. They wouldn't be returning to it. Sitting back in the chair and nodding with satisfaction, Ahmed started to relax a little.

They hadn't checked the goods yet. That would be done at the other warehouse across the city, but the transaction had been brokered by their mentor, and so far, he hadn't let them down. Ahmed knew it must be the will of Allah for their mentor to have recruited them to the great cause.

Ahmed had been to the websites that told them of the true glory of Islam and had attended the more private gatherings at a mosque where Imam Hassain had raged about their duty to bring Islam to all corners of the country. There was a new Caliph coming, and those who helped its rise would be rewarded in this life and the next.

He would also show his parents how wrong they'd been about their son. Ahmed was not a loser warped by western culture. He was a warrior of Islam.

It was their mentor who'd shown them the true path to glory. They were going to rip out the heart of the capitalist system and crush the infidel's institutions.

It would be a new Caliph, and its followers would offer hope and assistance to the impoverished people of the west discarded by the disgraceful capitalist bastards.

And only a favoured few were born for this mission.

Ahmed would go down in the annals of his Islamic history.

It's all there. Fuck me, you should see it. Bhavik wanted to start shooting now!!

Well done, brothers. Ahmed was pleased with their enthusiasm.

Shall we drop the items at the address?

Yes, our first statement will be tomorrow as planned.

Tell him we are on our way.

Doing it now.

He sent another encrypted WhatsApp message to Emir, who was part of another location in London closer to their target. Emir had been to a training camp in Libya two years ago, and their mentor had suspected he may be on a watch list and should remain as separate from the others as possible. Emir had gone to ground a month ago, living out of the lock up the white van was heading to, and he would prepare the weapons for the great day.

Ahmed returned his attention to the computer, logging into TOR before accessing a site through the dark web that was never tagged by search engines. The forum was in glorious Arabic, and there, Ahmed could read the inspiring stories of followers making fantastic sacrifices for the cause. He navigated to the correct board before flipping his screen to notepad, so he could copy the pre-written text into his post.

He smiled, hitting the post button and knowing this would get the attention of the British authorities as Mohammed wanted. In the flat, there was a camera set up, and in a few moments, he would make a video to be posted where anyone on the internet could view it and learn the truth about their future.

34

Alex climbed from the bed, ignoring Lilly's complaints.

"I need to speak to the London office, babe."

"At this time?" Lilly turned over, holding his hand with her head on the luxury pillows. A frown replaced the expressions of ecstasy of only a few moments ago.

"Always work to do, honey. And I need a drink."

"Can't you just hold me until I go to sleep?" Lilly's eyes pleaded. He leaned down and kissed her on the head.

"I'll be back soon, babe."

Her face clouded, and she spun 'round, turning her back on him. A few weeks ago, he would have complied, making sure Lilly thought herself the best-treated woman in the world. It didn't matter anymore. Her role was nearly complete. There was only one more part for her to play.

Alex padded into the kitchen and made himself a blueberry shake. He limbered up, trying to keep his energy levels high. There hadn't been much chance to exercise the way he preferred over the last few months, and once this was over, he might attend a boot camp to sharpen his physical skills. There was another role he had to play, which meant mixing with the most beautiful people on the planet. It wouldn't be good carrying excess weight.

His film production company thought he was away on some secret shoot and weren't expecting to see him for a while. He would be back soon enough, and from the desperate emails, he knew was needed. Or at least, his financial investments were by some desperate producers who thought the only way to create works of art was to throw money at it. Even if only twelve people were ever going to pay to see the film.

Alex was going to miss the abundance of wealth he'd created over the last few years through his computer company. But there was plenty squirrelled away in offshore accounts to see him through the next task, and he had other projects smouldering away that might yet make a decent return on his investments.

Devouring his milkshake, Alex powered up his laptop, positioning himself so he could see if Lilly emerged from the bedroom. There was plenty he could bring up on the screen to fool her into thinking he was working. Alex double tapped an innocuous-looking icon on the desktop and entered his password.

The screen filled with feeds giving instant data on his current activities. He was pleased to see Ahmed had gathered the weapons they needed for the London attack. Each task they completed gave Alex more confidence they would fulfil his plans. Checking, he saw the note claiming there would be a reckoning for the infidel bankers was posted. It would have the British security services scrambling for any hint of a terror cell in a desperate attempt to stop the attack.

There was a message from his Russian contacts agreeing to meet face to face. The tone was terse, as always. They didn't like working with him; Alex knew they considered him beneath them. However, he had the data they wanted to release regarding the president, and they believed his promise of financial Armageddon would aid their cause in the destruction of the American economic muscle.

The group of Russians he worked with hoped to be once more reunited with their motherland after being ostracised for over twenty years. He doubted it would happen. The US President may have gone against some of his promises to the Russians, but he was considered a joke by most foreign powers. The Russians hoped his presidency would be enough to weaken the US influence on the world, while Alex thought it would do the opposite. Not that he cared who was in power. It made no difference to any of his plans.

Moving on, he saw there was excitement on some of the forums about the imminent cyber-attack Alex had been orchestrating. Nearly three hundred people had downloaded the necessary software. Typically, this would be good news, but it only took one of them to blab on some open forum to attract the attention of the National Security Agency. Checking, he couldn't yet see any posts that would give the attack away so remained satisfied.

Trying to get information on the members of the Angel Detective Agency was proving more difficult than he'd anticipated. He knew Chloe was still in New York and had been tempted to contact her. It gave him a stir of pleasure to think of the woman once again reading his messages and quaking with fear. But, if they hadn't worked out Alex was the mastermind behind them, then he didn't want to give himself away just yet.

Miley had vanished. There were no records of her travelling and nothing he could see of her in London with her father. He surmised she may have been packed off to where she spent most of her time. Alex had an inkling she was at some sort of school. There were murmurs in corners of the web about certain institutions that managed to stay hidden. Most of the stories were wrapped around conspiracy theories and tales of the Illuminati. But Alex had dug a little deeper and found whispers that tied up with real world objects or events. If there had been more time, he would have gone even further and sought to find them. There was always the option of following Miley if she popped up again to see where she went. It was a thought that stirred his emotions and brought forth a longing that he knew would only detract him from his work at hand.

He had let the Angel do that to him before. He wasn't going to allow it to happen again.

While Alex knew Zack and the others were still in London, he hadn't been able to source their location. They had to have new premises, and though Ahmed had tailed Zack a couple of times, he'd been unable to stay with him. Even their online trace had dwindled to virtually nothing. That meant they were learning how to keep hidden, and it made Alex smile.

As he was so close to the end game, Alex doubted they could have an impact now. Even if his plans were disturbed, he only needed to melt down the software Global Money, and some of the smaller banks were running to cause massive financial disruption. The knock-on effect from that alone would be enough to send waves of panic around the world's markets.

At Oakwell, Alex had learned you didn't have to win every battle to win the war. While most of Oakwell's finest had survived the explosion at the town hall because one of his operatives had gotten cold feet, enough damage had been done to change the town forever.

Logging off, Alex smiled before heading back to the kitchen. He needed another milkshake before he returned to bed, and perhaps he would pleasure Lilly one last time before handing her to his Russian friends.

35

It seemed tragically stereotypical to be talking to the IT guy in a KFC. Once Chloe had created her fake tinder profile and swiped that she liked him, it hadn't taken long for him to reply and set up a date.

"You're new to New York then?" Eamon asked as they grabbed a table. It seemed to be quietening down from the early evening rush.

"Just a few weeks," Chloe poked at her anaemic looking fries and tried to work out how she was going to be able to drink the bucket of Diet Coke that was part of the meal. She'd forgotten in America large really did mean large. "I'm nannying for a trade manager from Global Money."

"Not had a chance to see much of the city." In contrast to his slim build, Eamon seemed to have a huge appetite.

"Only the nursery school and park," she said. "It's my first night off since I've been here."

"Then we'll have to make it one to remember."

Chloe tried to work out if he intended the double meaning as he bit a sizable chunk out of his Zinger sandwich.

"What made you like my profile?" Eamon continued.

"Curious."

"Oh, I see. And yourself?"

"Not so sure, been tempted." She nibbled on some of the fries.

"Well, you're in the city where anything goes."

Chloe almost laughed the way waved his arms and only took in the KFC.

"I thought I'd better make the most of my time here and get to know the place. Too many nannies come back having not seen a thing. I'm not going to be like that."

"Looking for a true New York experience then." Eamon was obviously trying to look seductive while chomping on chicken. Chloe was changing her mind about him being a stereotype.

"I suppose you know some places?"

"Maybe one or two."

"But I thought you were an IT geek." Chloe decided she needed to steer the conversation where she wanted. "Don't the bright city lights and loud music hurt your senses?"

"Jeez, it's not the nineties, babe. Geek is the new sheek." He quoted the line from his profile.

"Apart from the fact both babe and sheek are still from the nineties."

"Touché." He smiled taking another mouthful.

"What sort of work do you do?" She kept picking at her fries as the people continued to thin out from the KFC. She was facing the street and could see there was plenty of life in the city. The buzz of New York always filled her with energy. It seemed something was happening whatever time of night. She wondered if Zack would mind if she took Miley out for a night in a few bars. Chloe was sure she'd be up for it, even if she wasn't allowed to drink. Not that it would be a problem with her fake passport.

"I look after the servers for three of the largest exchanges in the city." He puffed his chest out. "Top role. Trillions of dollars flow through my machines every day."

"Impressive. Do you do it on your own?"

"There's three of us." Eamon's face fell. "Well, two for the moment."

"Oh really, has someone left?" Chloe tried to remain nonchalant.

"Sort of." He didn't offer anything more.

"Were you close?" She knew she had press home now if she was going to get any information.

"He was a good friend." Eamon put his cob down and took a deep breath. "A really good friend, if you know what I mean."

"What happened?" She reached across the table and put a hand on his arm that was holding his drink.

"Went the way of a lot of city guys and dived off the building. Though it's normally the traders, not techs."

"Christ no. For real?"

Eamon nodded. "When you have strict Christian parents, then being gay has its problems."

"I'm so sorry, Eamon. That must have been hard."

"Yes, well, we keep up the good work, got to keep the data moving and the cash flowing." He rattled his fingers across the desk as if it was money. "I was pretty choked up, though. Still am."

He put a pained expression on his face. Chloe could see the cogs whirring as he worked out it might be a good idea to play the sympathy card.

"Will they replace him?"

"They have to, but it takes so goddamn long, all the security clearances the SEC need because of what we run."

"I'm surprised it's in the city," she said. "I thought most of the data was stored in big centres away from it all these days. All I hear about is everything is stored in the cloud."

"Quite the nanny geek you are."

Chloe cursed herself for not realising a nanny probably wouldn't know what she knows. "I still read the news."

"Well, yes, the bulk of the servers are in a farm up north in Maine; that's where the real gold is, but we have machines close by so people can trade as quickly as possible."

"It makes a difference?"

"Yup." Regaining his composure, Eamon finished off his sandwich. "Milliseconds can be the difference of a few billion dollars the way these guys work. They pay top dollar to get their machines the closest to the fastest network."

"Sounds impressive; I'd love to see it."

"It's not that cool. But I could take you if you want." His eyes lit up.

"I thought it was super secure."

"It is, but I know a few people." Eamon tapped the side of his nose. "You can watch trillions of dollars flow right between your legs." He gave her what was supposed to be a seductive wink. She almost choked on her drink with laughter.

"Then I'd love to sometime. Though, I don't suppose I could just hold my hands out and grab some of it."

He laughed. "No, you can't. Finish up, and we'll go." The man slugged back the last of his drink.

"What now?" Chloe wasn't expecting it to be so sudden. Her mind raced with possibilities.

"Sure. It's only a fifteen-minute walk."

"Well, then I better pay a visit before we go."

She slid from the plastic chair and headed past the serving

counter where bored adolescent faces counted down the minutes until they could knock off.

"You get that?" Chloe pulled her phone microphone from underneath her jacket as she entered a cubicle. "Can we use this?"

"I heard," Miley answered. "I'm on with Adam, and I've got something you might be able to get onto their network. Have you still got your memory stick?"

"The small one on the keyring, yes."

"Plug it into your phone." Chloe retrieved the keys from her handbag, detached the tiny silver USB key, and slipped it into the bottom of her phone.

"Okay, I'm controlling your phone; give me two minutes."

"Watch what you are looking at."

"Then you shouldn't be such a slut, girlfriend."

"Hey, that's out of order, young lady. Where are you?"

"Starbucks across the street pretending to do some work. Okay, it's done; if you get the chance and find any USB port, then plug it in. You'll probably have to leave it there, so make it look inconspicuous."

"I'll do my best."

"Be careful, Chloe. I'll watch your back."

36

Zack rolled off his bed after once again being awoken by banging on his door. His phone told him it was two in the morning, and the last time he'd been disturbed in the early hours, he'd been dragged down to the police station. He remembered seeing one in the morning on his phone as he kept checking it. Another night of little sleep.

Answer your door.

A message from Adam. Pushing himself upright, Zack reached over to the window sill for clothes before pulling on his t-shirt and shorts. A few minutes later, he opened the door to Terry and Adam.

"I take it you have something good."

"Terry got word from a friend." Zack could hear the excitement in Adam's voice. "The Financial Conduct Authority is investigating possible insider trading."

"Okay, I get insider trading, but explain to the simple-minded who just got out of bed what that means to us." Zack ushered them into the kitchen before he busied himself filling the kettle and retrieving some cups. Caffeine was badly needed.

"Okay, so it's illegal," Terry said. "But we know it goes on all the time. It can be disguised, so it's difficult for the FCA to crack. But they come down hard when they have proof, and they're always on the lookout."

"Something's been triggered?" Zack asked.

"Yep, and Terry says they're moving pretty fast." Adam nodded for Terry to reveal his information.

"Transactions by one trader have aroused suspicion, and it only took a short time for them to then realise his recent trades, while under the thresholds, had all the hallmarks of someone in the know. It's profits declaration season, so a lot of lesser known brands on the stock exchange are releasing figures."

"What do you mean thresholds?" Zack leaned against one of the white kitchen units as the kettle boiled.

"The authorities are constantly looking at trading patterns to see if anyone is working with inside information," Terry said. "A large spike in profits raises red flags, and if a trading floor manages it multiple times in a brief period, the FCA investigates. But if you are smart," Terry let the thought hang.

"Anyone with crucial information can make a killing," Zack said. "The guy was trading clever, staying below the limits," Adam put in.

"Until yesterday." Terry took a seat at the small kitchen table. "Olly, my friend, has emailed some information over."

Adam retrieved his laptop from his rucksack and placed it on the table among the plates Zack hadn't bothered to clear away from his takeaway dinner.

"Chinese. Nice." Popping the lid, Adam swung his computer around, open for the others to view.

Terry pointed out some of the numbers on a spreadsheet. "He upped his game by about twenty-five percent making a very nice profit and enough to send the alarm bells ringing at the FCA."

"But that's one guy with a mate on the inside somewhere." Zack was leaning against the kitchen counter while the kettle boiled. "So why all the excitement?"

"Because Olly cross-checked against other trades for the same companies, and this guy wasn't alone," Terry said. "Some of the transactions other brokers were doing were almost identical. Only not exactly because they'd kept it smart."

"And they'd traded in the last two companies that triggered the alert." Adam added.

Terry nodded. "However, they stayed with the same pattern as before. It looks like this guy broke ranks."

"So, someone is not only feeding them the numbers but how to stay undetected." Zack could see where this was going, and it had the genius of Alex Ryan written all over it.

"That's right." Terry looked pleased.

"So, they'd never have been caught otherwise?"

"Not strictly true," Terry said. "There are a number of internal audits that companies do to protect themselves from rogue traders, and these deals would have unravelled in the end when the analysts at the FCA looked at historical trends. If a trader starts performing above average, even by a small deviation, there is normally a check of all their deals to make sure things are on the straight and narrow. The companies themselves do the same, so they can protect themselves and lay the blame at the trader's door. They don't like the backwash and fines."

"So, this would have come out anyway? What timeframe are we looking at?" Zack queried.

"Could take weeks, months even. If they stopped and went back to normal, the traders could get away with it. If they hadn't already escaped to a tax haven."

"Interesting." The kettle having boiled, Zack poured three mugs of coffee while he mulled over what he'd just learnt. He sat down at the table after pushing the coffees to the others. "Alex."

"It's what I'm thinking," Adam said.

"It fits, but what would be the benefit?" Zack asked.

"To get them in his pocket," Adam replied. "They'll owe him."

"But to do what?"

"Two possibilities." Terry took one of the mugs. "He needs more people inside the system to do his bidding," Terry suggested. "Or he's setting them up for when the bigger company announcements are being made in two days' time, even though those figures are usually well under wraps."

"Or not," Adam exclaimed and started typing on the computer. "Fuck me, look." He turned the screen towards the others showing breaking news on the BBC website. Zack read the small description of Worthington Accounting admitting there had been a hack several weeks ago.

"And this is important because?"

"Worthington Accounting would have been doing audits on some of the companies on the exchange," Terry said. "They could be the source of insider information."

"What will the FCA do about the trader already identified?" Zack asked.

"They are monitoring him now," Terry said. "But they'll move against him soon as they want his source."

"Can we get to him first?"

"If we want to." Adam swung the laptop 'round to him. "He's gotta pretty up to date social media account, and it tells us he was at Callooh Callay bar about fifteen minutes ago."

"No doubt celebrating his good day," Terry said.

"How far?"

"Twenty minutes by taxi this time of night."

"Then it's worth trying to get hold of him." Zack drained the rest of his coffee wishing there was time for more. "Get an Uber, and I'll get dressed; if we can get to him before he's lifted by the FCA, then we might find something on his source."

"We won't be able to track it." Adam looked up. "If it's Alex."

"No, but it helps us build up a picture." Zack moved into his bedroom and swapped his t-shirt and shorts for shirt and trousers before splashing on some cologne to at least appear a bit more respectable.

"Zack, Miley's on," Adam shouted. "They're onto something."

Zack rushed back into the kitchen carrying his shoes.

"What does she say?"

"Chloe's met a contact in one of the exchanges, and they're going for a look. There's a chance we might be able to get something on the network to have a snoop. Shall I stay and help?"

Zack nodded. "Yes, and keep me posted. Terry, come with me.

Can you get a photo of our guy so we can identify him?"

"Is Alex finally making mistakes?" Adam asked hopefully.

"Not necessarily," Zack said. "Not of all of his plans worked out in Oakwell, and he still managed to cause devastation. For all we know, these could be mistakes, or he has us chasing our own backsides."

37

Chloe glanced at her phone to read Miley's message.

There's a tail.

She resisted the urge to look 'round while listening to Eamon play tour guide by pointing out the many things that interested him about the city he was obviously proud of.

Shit, how do you know?

I clocked him waiting outside KFC. He's following you. I'm behind him.

Be careful.

Chloe still resisted the urge to look. They'd left the KFC five minutes earlier as Eamon insisted it was only a short walk and would let her see some of New York. He continued babbling on for a few more blocks before they stopped outside the least impressive building she'd seen so far and declared it as his place of work.

"It's what's on the inside that matters," Eamon said reacting to her look of disappointment. "Come on, I'll need to sign you in."

Chloe allowed herself to be steered into the lift. She noted how close he was standing as they ascended to the seventh level, which he called his domain. The guards had seemed more concerned about watching that night's basketball game than who Eamon's new conquest was.

He was right about the inside of the building being impressive. Everything gleamed in silver or white, and there didn't seem to be a speck of dirt or any scuff marks on the walls.

"Robot cleaners," Eamon pointed to the small round object that appeared, rotating slowly, moving down one side of the corridor as the lift doors closed.

"Tommo should be there now." They were deposited on the twelfth floor into another long corridor with plain white flooring. It was colder than downstairs, and Chloe gave an involuntary shiver. "Yea, that gets you." He put his arm around her waist and pulled her close as they walked the short distance to a door he opened. The way he gripped also gave Chloe the shivers, but despite wanting to pull away, she allowed his arm to remain. At least it gave her a clear indication of his expectations.

Stepping into an office, she saw an actual image of computer geekdom hunched over a console in the compact space. Sporting a Big Bang Theory jacket and a dreadful ponytail, the man gave them a disapproving look. Chloe suspected it wasn't uncommon for Eamon to bring his acquaintances to his workplace.

"She wants a look around, TJ." Eamon smiled and winked. TJ stayed silent, shook his head, and returned his focus to the screens in front of him. "Is everything good?"

"Fine," TJ mumbled as he adjusted his glasses.

"Cool, let's have a look."

On the opposite side of TJ's desk was a set of double doors. Eamon fished a plastic card from his pocket and swiped the lock. The keypad turned green, and when the door opened, Chloe was struck by a blast of frigid air that made the rest of the building seem tropical.

"There's some serious GPU's in here." Eamon closed the door behind them before steering Chloe towards banks of rectangular boxes displaying a myriad of flashing lights and countless cables erupting like tentacles before stretching off to various corners of the room. She was surprised at how roomy and clean it was; even the air felt purer.

"Not what you expected?" He was clearly enjoying his role.

"Very different." Chloe looked around to see if there were any machines with suitable ports for her USB key. There was another workstation in the room holding two computers. She could see lights blinking on one of them and moved towards it while still pretending to be impressed.

"I see you've spotted my desk." Eamon pressed his hand against the small of her back, propelling her towards the workstation. "We only use it when there are problems where we have to be close. I find it very intimate. You're cold. Let me warm you up."

His attempts at seduction were making her retch, and Chloe was surprised she hadn't heard Miley giggling. Despite her distaste when Eamon pushed her against the desk, she didn't resist. Instead, she flicked the USB key into her hand before sliding her arm towards the computer. Turning to face Eamon, her backside pressed up against the ceramic workstation.

"Of course, this is only part of the system," he said. "The real magic is at the data centre in Maine."

"Is it bigger than this?"

Eamon pressed himself against her while moving his hands onto her hips.

"It's a lot more impressive. Maybe I could take you there, too. Make a weekend of it." He lowered his face and kissed her neck, while his hands tried to grab her bottom. His efforts were only thwarted because she was tight against the desk.

Chloe reached back with her left hand, feeling the side of the unit. As his mouth covered hers, deft fingers located a suitable socket and pushed the tiny device into place.

Chloe resisted the initial temptation to knee him in the bollocks as she knew he might still be useful, kissing him back instead while placing her hands on his chest and gracefully guiding him away.

"Easy tiger, I'm not that kind of girl." She reached down, tightly cupping his groin. "But if you play your cards right, we can have that trip to Maine. I like impressive things, so don't disappoint me."

Chloe let go, smiled, and walked past the startled looking Eamon before standing by the door. She looked at him expectantly. "I have to be back by ten, so be a good boy and escort me out of the building."

38

Where are you?

Miley breathed a sigh of relief reading Chloe's message. Not long after Chloe had entered the building, she lost the audio feed, and while she'd suspected it was because of the equipment, it was still good to see her friend leave the building.

Go back to the hotel. I'm going to track your stalker. He waited outside.

Jesus, no. It's too dangerous.

Just go. I know how.

Really?

Well, in theory.

Part of her training with Uncle Jakes's crew had taught her how to spot if she was being tailed and how to shake the tail if she was. In her mind, if she knew how to lose one, then she could use the same theory to follow someone without being spotted.

Uncle Jake and his crew had taken her to Seattle, near the training camp, to allow her to practice in the real world. While she hadn't exactly received top marks, her uncle had considered her good enough for a beginner.

Practice was one thing. Trying to recall what she'd learnt

while tailing someone else was going to be difficult. Miley had slipped into a different coffee house opposite the building Chloe and Eamon had entered. With fewer customers, she'd felt more exposed watching the man outside the building pretending he was on his phone or smoking. After ten minutes, a car pulled up, he jumped in, and another man took his place. The newcomer pressed himself into the shadows, making him difficult to see. A professional move. With a different person following, it was less likely the tail would be spotted.

Miley was already leaving the coffee shop as Chloe and Eamon left the building, glad that her friend didn't look for her, and prepared for the man to follow. She heard Chloe wish Eamon a good night and promise to call him before leaving him standing on the pavement while she hailed a cab.

The man didn't move.

Miley was ready to fall in behind him. She saw Eamon turn towards her, shrug, and mutter to himself before walking passed.

The man followed Eamon.

"Shit." She tried to calm herself, waiting until both men had passed before turning to observe them descending the steps of the nearby subway. Just as the tail vanished, Miley headed after them, hurrying down the stairs and trying to use the thin crowd of people to keep her from view. She soon had the tailing man back in her sights. He was so intent on his prey that he wasn't taking any precautions, filling Miley with confidence she wouldn't be spotted.

But, she wasn't going to be so careless.

As the men passed through the barriers, she positioned herself to see if anybody was watching her before realising she needed to get a ticket. Glancing at the boards, Miley tried to figure out if there was a city-wide ticket like in London. Fishing in her pocket for her small purse, she purchased a Metro card before hurrying after the men who were almost out of sight.

Reaching the top of the escalators, Miley saw the tail pretending to look at his phone, while Eamon was a few metres ahead almost at the platforms. Miley whipped out a portable makeup mirror, angling it so she could see the people on the escalator as she brushed the strands of hair behind her ear.

Stepping off the escalator, Miley walked onto the left-hand platform where both men jumped onto the waiting train. With few people on board, she did the same and took a seat in a carriage further down, making sure she could still see them.

The doors hissed shut before the regular rumble of the train ensued as it entered the tunnel. Miley checked her phone, but as there was no signal, she used the opportunity to examine the tail. Angling the phone discreetly, Miley took two pictures.

He looked as if he was in his mid-forties with close-cropped brown hair and a few days of stubble. Dressed in dark trousers and a brown jacket with a high collar, he was slumped back on the blue seat as if he was trying to look casual as he read one of the abandoned newspapers.

As the train slowed at another stop, the phone signal returned. Miley quickly typed out a message.

On the subway, he followed Eamon, not you.

She then emailed one of the photographs to Adam, asking him to check the guy out if he could. She didn't tell Adam where she was as didn't fancy having to explain to her dad why she was alone on a subway following bad guys. She already thought it wasn't a smart move herself.

Before there was any chance to reply, the train moved off, and the signal again vanished. Chloe's response was received at the next stop. It told her to get the hell off the train.

Miley ignored it.

Three stops later, Eamon rose and moved towards the train doors. She smiled remembering being told it made life so much easier when the mark revealed their intentions early. Miley observed the man with the close-cropped hair fold his newspaper, while she continued to appear concentrated on her phone. The train stopped, and after watching both men depart, she slipped between the doors just as they were closing. After plugging in her earphones, she shoved her hands in her jacket pockets before following them up the stairs.

The men departed the station, and Miley hung back trying to appear disinterested in the world around her like any typical teenager. She knew her age and gender were an advantage when trying to blend in. Who would be expecting a cute teen to be pulling such a stunt?

Miley stepped into a doorway for a few seconds to confirm no one else was following out of the subway station. All three of them carried on for another couple blocks, moving deeper into the city where the lights were not as bright and welcoming. Miley felt her heart pounding as the surroundings changed from the opulence she'd seen in Manhattan to those where she didn't think a teenager should be on her own at night. They were the kind of dark streets her age and gender might not be an advantage after all.

Then the tail stopped.

Raising his phone to his ear, he stepped to the edge of the sidewalk. Caught by surprise, Miley made a split-second decision to carry on walking. With her head down; she passed the man as he barked into his phone in a foreign language. A few yards further, she brought her own phone to hand and, reversing the camera, she filmed a car rolling to a halt and the tail climbing in.

Slipping the phone up her sleeve as the dark saloon screeched down the street, she continued walking. Eamon had vanished, and Miley had no idea where she was.

39

"There, at the bar," Terry indicated to Zack, "with another guy and two women."

"Looks like they're moving in." Zack looked at the photo on his phone. It was the man they were after. A trader named Harvey Gibbons. "Tricky if he's a little busy."

"Yea, might not be so friendly if we bust his moves." It sounded awkward coming from Terry, he was not used to talking in any sort of cool manner. They'd missed their target at the Callooh Callay bar, but one of the staff had informed them the Hoxton Pony was where most people were headed, and after forking out for the entrance fee, they'd gone inside. With the thumping music and club-like atmosphere, Zack was surprised at the age range. Forty somethings were acting like teenagers. Being single, wealthy, and high probably had that effect.

After collecting a couple of cold lagers from the bar, they circulated, looking for Harvey. It only took a few minutes to find the arrogant-looking city trader leaning against the rear bar chatting to a couple of bombshells. Probably trying to dazzle them with stories of his financial prowess. Harvey was more than likely going to be pissed if they broke up a sure thing. But, Zack didn't have time for finesse.

"Should we wait?" Terry asked. "See how it unfolds?"

"Be tactful, you mean?"

Terry nodded taking a swig of his lager.

"Not really my thing." Zack made a beeline for the group leaving Terry to hurry after him. As he approached, Zack thrust out his hand.

"Hi, Zack Carter, pleased to meet you." The two men gave him a disgusted look. "Oh, and this is my friend Terry," Zack continued as Terry stepped up beside him.

"No offence, pal." Harvey's companion brought himself upright and broadened his shoulders as if it made him look like a hard case. "But fuck off. We're a little busy here." He indicated to the two ladies who both smiled at Zack.

"I hear you're going to be the trader of the month." Zack pointedly looked at Harvey. "Well done, mate; it's always nice when you hit a lucky streak."

"Listen, whoever the fuck you are." The companion widened his aggressive stance. "This is a private conversation."

"Hey, okay." Zack raised his hands in a submissive manner. "I just wanted to congratulate your friend Harvey here on his epic work, but it's cool. We'll fuck off. I had a warning for him too, but if he doesn't want to hear it, that's fine. Who cares what the FCA thinks on a night like this?"

Zack stepped away, and Terry followed as they grabbed a free table over at the other side of the bar.

"You think he'll bite?" Terry said.

"Right now, I'm gambling that he's going to want to take a leak." Zack indicated the toilets close by; it was why he'd chosen the table they were sitting at.

Sure enough, a few minutes later, Harvey worked his way through the crowd, at first towards the toilets before he stepped over to their table.

"Who are you?" he demanded.

"I'm Zack Carter from the Angel Detective Agency. My colleague here works for people who've discovered some interesting trading figures."

Harvey swallowed and start edging back. "The FCA? Look, I've got nothing to say, guys."

"We're not here to bust you, Harvey." Zack remained casual and sipped his lager. "We want to warn you to get the fuck out of the city, but we need to know where you got the info."

Harvey glanced around and slid into one of the free chairs. "Shut the fuck up, man; people overhear things in a place like this."

"Really?" Zack laughed. They had to shout just to be heard a few feet away. "Then tell us what you know, and we'll leave you alone."

Harvey looked as though he was deciding whether to leave or not. "How do you know?"

"You got greedy today, Harvey, and people noticed. Only we're the right people for you to speak to. We want to help you out of a tight spot. The sort of people you're involved with could seriously fuck up your health if you know what I mean."

Harvey wiped his brow. "Double vodka," he called to a passing waitress. "Fuck man, I just wanted to get out early. I know they'll catch us, and I don't want to be the first."

"Us?" Though Zack suspected he already knew the answer.

"I checked some other trades, and people are doing the same as me. I guess I wasn't so special after all." His drink came, and he swallowed it down in two gulps.

"Do you know who sent the information?"

Harvey considered them both carefully. "I think I should wait until I have a lawyer." He started to rise.

"Listen, Harvey," Zack said. "We don't give a fuck about what you've been doing. What we care about is who's been sending you the info because we believe they're behind some nasty shit that's gone down in the city."

"What do you mean?"

"Like the bombing."

"Shit. You don't mean it's them." Harvey sat back down. "Fuck me, I heard that was fucking ISIS."

Zack nodded.

"Fuck, no way. They don't mess with the markets." Harvey was shaking, and there was confusion written all over his face.

"How do you know?" Zack tilted his head.

"I need another drink."

"No, Harvey; what you need to do is give us everything you have, even your laptop and phone. Then, you should go away for a long holiday and forget about working in the city ever again. Do you understand me? We can book you a ticket right now, then we can all go to your house and get your stuff. It's either them or us, Harvey, and you've probably seen the YouTube videos of what they do to people who fuck up their plans." Zack ran his finger across his throat.

Harvey took a deep breath and looked as though he was about to vomit. "Come with me."

40

"What the hell were you thinking?"

As soon as the hotel door opened, Miley was confronted by a furious Chloe. She felt the tears well up. Once the dark sedan had gone, and she was on her own, Miley had been terrified. The bravado she'd felt tailing the two men had vanished.

As she'd turned to try to find her way back to the subway, a group of young men had appeared on her street from a side alley. Although they seemed to be on a night out, she'd been frightened when they called out to her, inviting her to join their party.

It had taken a call from Chloe to calm her down. After that, Miley hurried to the nearest busy street, hailed a cab, and jumped into it with her heart racing. All the while describing to Chloe where she was as her friend reassured her it was going to be okay. Only when she was in the back of the cab and on her way to the Regis had Miley begun to feel silly for panicking so easily. Here, Dad was right about her lack of experience.

And she already knew Chloe wasn't happy.

In the hotel room, Chloe's verbal onslaught was quickly followed up by a massive hug.

"I was so worried about you."

"It was mostly okay." Miley returned the hug. The warmth of her friend's love was more than welcome. "I just freaked when I found myself in the middle of nowhere."

"Your dad is going to be so mad." Chloe released the embrace and shook her head.

"Not if he doesn't know." Miley stepped over to the bed and dropped her bag. She realised that probably wasn't going to happen.

"He's a private investigator, an ex-detective, an ex-military intelligence analyst, and your dad," Chloe said. "You really think you're going to keep this from him?"

"I suppose not." Miley pulled her laptop from her bag and kicked off her shoes. "I better think of a clever way to spin it. I got the plates of the car that picked up the tail."

"Then let's get Adam onto it." Chloe pulled one of the chairs across to the large desk as Miley set up her computer. "He's been working on the data we've extracted from the servers."

"You managed to get the drive in there with your dignity intact. I couldn't hear a thing once you got into the lift. They had some serious shielding."

"It was a close-run thing. I get the feeling Eamon likes to take his conquests there and screw them in the server room surrounded by virtual money. I saw the cameras were still switched on. So, it wouldn't surprise me if those videos appeared on the net."

"Ew." Miley brought everything up on the large screen. "Has Adam found anything?"

"Adam says there's some dormant malware, but he hasn't worked out what it is yet, and I don't really know what he's talking about."

"Their systems didn't detect it?" Miley knew it was a type

of computer virus, no doubt waiting for something to trigger it into life.

Chloe shrugged. "Adam says something added from inside the system with full privileges can easily be hidden."

Miley brought up the images she'd collected. With a little bit of zooming, they could pick up the license plate of the sedan.

"Bingo," she said. "Do you think Adam can trace this?"

"Not sure we have that sort of access, but we could try," Chloe said. "I think we should send this to Special Agent Bennett. They'd be able to trace it even if they don't tell us anything. I'll send him the picture of the man, too. On the phone, you said they were speaking another language."

"Sounded Eastern European," Miley said. "But I'm only going off films I've seen."

"Same as I did with bastards who attacked the limo."

"Linked to Alex?"

Chloe brushed her hair back and sighed. "I've no idea."

Miley's phone rang.

"Oh shit."

"Who is it?"

"My dad."

Chloe smiled, rose from her chair, and gave Miley a peck on the top of the head. "Well, I'm off back to my cheap hotel. Good luck with your dad."

Miley noticed Chloe ignored her pleading looks as she left the room.

Taking a deep breath, the teenager answered the phone.

41

The Russians were undoubtedly trying to intimidate him. Alex wanted to laugh at how inept their efforts were. He wasn't to be threatened by a group who were no better than street thugs who considered bulging jackets and thick necks was a sufficient demonstration of strength to command respect. The Russian man sitting between his two brutes was a lot smaller, almost wiry, and with a weaselly face and pointed nose, his glasses precariously balanced on. Alex knew it was an amusing attempt at intimidation by contrast. Pathetic, but amusing.

Alex's response was to relax and smile as he sat opposite in a comfortable, brown-leather chair.

"Why should we listen to you, Mr Anderson?" the thin man asked.

"Our agreement is based on a mutual need. So, out of respect for each other, we both need to listen."

"You Americans."

Alex held up his hand to cut the man off. "I am not American Anton; I am not of any country anymore."

"You're in no position to dictate to us."

"Who said anything about dictating?" Alex smoothed down his trousers. "You're getting everything that you want. The fact is, you'll be getting far more than our agreement, but when I say the English woman is off limits, then she's off limits. Your botched attack could have ruined everything."

"Are you trying to threaten us?"

"Threatening you with what, Anton?"

The man pushed his glasses higher up his nose. "To withhold your information."

"Did I say that, Anton? Did I even imply that?" Alex raised his eyebrows and glanced at the men standing on either side of their boss. "We have an agreement, and I'll honour that agreement, despite the incompetence your team has demonstrated so far."

Anton laughed and looked at his two colleagues, who smiled even though Alex thought they probably had no idea what the joke was supposed to be.

"Our friend is amusing. You expect us to listen to you out of the goodness of our heart?"

"I expect you to listen because I am delivering everything I've promised." Alex was growing tired of dealing with this arrogant little prick. He thought too much of himself, having inherited a small-time operation after the previous owner had met an unfortunate end. An end Alex had engineered.

Anton had KGB pedigree. He was one of many cuts from the old Soviet security services when things had gone south in the nineties. Since then, they'd rebuilt in America and became particularly successful when there was a clamour for Russian software developers after the finance houses turned digital. The influx of technical resource was bolstered by ex-security services down on their luck and seeking easy money. Anton had been using a legitimate software company as a front for his illicit activities. While he'd proved adept at financial fraud, he also wanted to be respected like a mafia boss.

"I've always delivered. Lilly will be yours as promised. The information will be released, and the software attack will go ahead as planned. But the English girl remains off limits."

"We have provided you with manpower. We have provided the skills to build your software. Do not talk to me about delivery. Do not tell us what to do. Why should we, from the great mother Russia, respect someone with no loyalties?"

Alex laughed out loud. Russia had rejected him years ago. Anton still hankered after his homeland, but Alex knew he'd never give up the money and power America provided. Anton claimed he hated everything about America and its people while happily living a life of privilege.

"Out of respect for your well-being." Alex concentrated his stare on the thin man.

"You are threatening us, Mr Anderson. You have many balls. My friends, Mr Anderson says we should be in fear of our lives." The two men chuckled again. This time, they probably understood the joke. Alex guessed they saw him as easy prey. He adjusted his position in the chair slightly. He knew his life wasn't in danger; they needed him too much, but it wasn't beyond them to administer some sort of lesson if Anton saw fit. If they moved against him, Alex would be ready.

"You know why I'm helping you; you know the tools I bring. Even your beloved mother Russia can't accomplish what I have. And, you know what I am capable of. Any notions you have about trying to dispose of me when this is over, forget about them now." Alex saw the reaction on the Russian's face before Anton regained his composure. "You don't think I haven't detected your crude attempts at infiltrating me? But what has it brought you, Anton? How far have you got? You don't think I know how many other goons you have scattered around this place other than these two meatheads? You think you have the power, Anton? You think I'm just one man?"

"It is not wise to use that tone." Anton kept his voice quiet and measured.

"I'm sitting here talking. You're the ones plotting my demise when this is over. I'm a man of respect, and I'm a man of my word." Alex rose quickly and gracefully from the chair with a speed that saw the two thugs reach for the guns. He ignored their moves, keeping his gaze fixed on the thin Russian.

"The girl is off limits. If any harm comes to her, I will end your organisation. And don't look for me afterwards because you'll never find me. There will only be whispers. And if you seek me, the last thing you might hear is my whisper in your ears as I cut your fucking throat." He stepped away from the scene, pausing when he reached the door. "We'll make history, Anton; savour that moment. But remember, you are just a fucking pawn in a game that is far greater than you could possibly imagine."

Alex was ready for anything as he walked through the main bar, feeling the eyes on him, knowing the owners carried guns. But no one stopped him leaving. The cab still waited outside. He stepped to the window, paid the driver, and told him to go without him. A few minutes later, an Uber arrived; Alex climbed in with a curt nod to the driver before the car smoothly accelerated away.

He would change his transport again and take a trip on the subway before the day was over. Meeting the Russians in person was always a risk, but he was sure the message had gotten through.

Alex wondered if he would have to deal with them when

this was over.

42

"They've declared a Jihad on London," Mike said.

Zack was sitting with Terry and Adam in a briefing room at the detective's station viewing messages posted from the so-called ISIS splinter group. "We're pretty convinced there's going to a major terrorist attack in London, so expect the alert state to go to critical today. There are some big events this weekend; we think it's going to be one of them."

"Hyde Park concert on Sunday and the American football game at Wembley, some juicy targets there," Adam concurred. "Any intel on which?"

"Nothing yet, but we're preparing for the worst. All leave cancelled. Guys, I thought I'd let you know as everything is geared towards this now. We think the financial fraud was to bankroll these plans. The brass is convinced the attack on the pub was to stop the information leaking out. As was the murder of Mr Walsh. My boss is looking to shut down our co-operation with your agency because they can't see any further benefit. There's no more fraud occurring at Global Money, and the company that wrote the program is tearing it apart to find the source of the software exploit that was used. They won't be able to do it properly until the weekend, but by Monday, we think it will be confirmed that elements of ISIS have stepped up their cyber game."

"It's a misdirection," Zack said quietly. He was picturing the board in their office.

"Are you trying to say there's not going to be an attack?" Mike looked at him as though he'd gone out of his mind.

"There'll be an attack. But that's not the greater purpose."

"That's a pretty fucking good purpose." Mike's feathers had been ruffled.

"Look, Mike, I'm not belittling the attack, or the work counter-terrorism are doing. The threat is real, but we think it's to conceal something bigger. To hide an attack on the markets. Does any of the intel point towards a threat to the city, the financial district?"

"I've not seen everything," Mike admitted. "But what I'm aware of is an attack on a public event this weekend. With probably more than one person."

Zack spent a few more minutes turning over the information in his mind. He pointed to one of the sheets of paper they'd brought for Mike. It was a list of names.

"These are people we believe have recently traded on insider information. It's profit declaration week for some companies. An appropriate time to make money if you have the right info."

"All insider trading?" Mike stood and went over to the list. "Shit, I haven't heard about this."

"Because all of them but one sailed close to the wind but weren't doing enough to trigger an investigation. They don't even know we are on to them. The trader we spoke to was contacted anonymously, and all the information handed to him was encrypted."

"Where were the tips coming from?" Mike sat back down and looked at the laptop they had open.

"We can't trace it. One-time Dropbox or WhatsApp accounts, you know the drill."

"Too easy for them to do," Mike said.

"Exactly, and I don't believe that it's a coincidence."

"Anything to link it with terrorists?"

"We're ripping apart the lives of those on the list as much as we can, but so far haven't found a link. If you could run it through your channels, you might find something we can't. But this isn't just happening on this side of the pond, Mike. This is not just about the UK."

"What do you mean?"

"Adam." Zack nodded to the younger man.

"We've got software inside one of the exchanges in the US we suspected might have been tampered with, and we were right. Some of the most sophisticated trades being done in the dark pools over there are being influenced by this software. It's subtle, very fucking subtle, but it's there."

"Chloe went to see the CEO of Global Money," Mike said. "Was this why?"

"No, it's not even their dark pool," Zack answered. "She's there because the CEO has been getting threats which are untraceable, threats to bring the company down and destroy his family."

"And you think it's all linked?"

"After going to see the CEO, Chloe's car was smashed into and shot at by Russians in New York. Yes, so I think it's all linked, and I think there is someone known to us behind this."

"Who?"

"Alex Ryan. Bring up his picture Adam."

Adam flipped his laptop around and produced the picture they had of Alex that was put together from Chloe and Miley's descriptions after Oakwell.

"The guy from the by-election," Mike said. "You've spoken about him before, but that was just speculation."

"We're almost certain now." Zack watched the shock spread across DI Knight's face. "This is the way he works, and we know his desire to avenge Angel is incredibly strong."

"It makes him sound like a criminal mastermind. I know he's evaded us for years, but is he really that good?"

"He is a master at manipulating people, at getting things done. For example, he had incendiary devices made by an ex-bomb maker who had been a mercenary after leaving the British Army. It looked as though this guy had turned over a new leaf, but instead, he was laundering money through the various charities he was involved with. Alex discovered his secret and forced the man to build the devices that were used in the attacks."

"The pub bombing." Mike was nodding his head.

"Exactly. From everything you have found, this was no suicide bomber, but Alex could've manipulated someone into a position he couldn't get himself out of to make or carry the bomb. We know he has the kind of contacts that can get hold of serious hardware."

"And his motive is to avenge what happened to Angel's family through the money markets?" Mike started pulling at this lip. Zack hoped they could keep him on-board despite what his boss ordered.

"That's our theory. He's already be targeting the CEO, threatening him. We know Alex likes to taunt his victims. We saw that in Oakwell."

"I'll need to take this to major crimes," Mike said. "But as I've said, everyone is focused on the terror attacks. It's going to be difficult to get resources on this."

"I know." Zack nodded to Adam. "We've prepared a file." Adam reached into his shirt pocket and handed over a small flash drive.

"Everything we've got," Adam assured him.

"We agree the terror threat is real, so at least keep working with us. What we don't yet know," Zack said, "is how he's going to execute his end game."

Mike looked at the file and nodded. "I'll see what I can do."

43

"Why me? What have I done?" Lilly's contorted face looked up at Alex as she yanked on the restraints.

Alex had expected someone with her privileged upbringing to have already descended into a blubbering wreck. He could see Lilly still didn't quite believe what was happening to her. The surprise on her face as he'd turned from loving boyfriend to captor as they'd walked around the abandoned ranch was precious.

They'd driven along the I95 to the old farmhouse that had been left for ruin after the financial crash years ago. Lilly had talked about how she'd first learned to ride a horse among the rolling grassland, and Alex had like the idea of the irony it would add to his plans. After his enquiries had found the place on the market for a reasonable price, he'd bought it.

"You were born into an evil family, Lilly. A family more concerned about money than people. A bank isn't just a business; it's the lifeblood of the economy, and all your father does is grind every penny out of its customers and every ounce of blood out of its employees. So long as profit margins are maintained, your father and the shareholders don't give a fuck."

Her arms were chained to an iron pipe running through

the ample basement. It wasn't soundproof, but the house was three kilometres from its nearest neighbour, and no one was likely to come by, not in the brief time that mattered.

"It's not true. That's not what my father is about. Why are you doing this? What about the people we help with the charity? The lives we save. My father funds it all." Lilly hauled at her chains again, the veins throbbing in her neck as she focused her anger into giving her arms more strength.

After a few attempts, she collapsed onto her knees exhausted. "I loved you, Darren. I thought you loved me."

"Oh, Lilly, you're so naive. Your father supports your pet projects, so you look the other way. How many people have suffered while the greed of Global Money sucks up wealth around the world, regardless of the poverty it leaves behind? Irrespective of the shattered lives. I never loved you, Lilly. You were there to be used just as your father uses other people. As your father used the software I wrote to make the company billions."

"Is this what this is about? You want money?" she screamed throwing herself towards him with a fresh bout of anger. "Well, you can have more fucking money. You can have all mine. You could have had it all anyway."

Alex smiled and squatted down on his haunches to her eye level. The perfect makeup had been smeared by the sweat from her exertions. Lilly hadn't struggled at first. Thinking it was some sort of kinky game. But when she'd realised she was being chained up for real, she'd fought like a hellcat. The side of her face was swelling where Alex had back handed her.

"Money made from the misery of others."

"People benefit from what we do."

"That's what you have been brainwashed to believe. But

tell that to the little girl who walked into her home to see her father hanging in the garage. A father who'd worked hard for ten years. A father who'd scrimped and saved for his family only to have it ripped away from him."

"I don't understand." Lilly was back on her knees panting heavily. It looked as if the fight was finally draining from her.

"His six-year-old daughter found him swinging. Angel's life was ruined because all her family's shares were worthless after your father sacked him and left them with nothing. Her daddy couldn't take the shame.

"Do you know how shit her life was after that, Lilly?" Alex clenched his fists wishing it was James Goldstein shackled in front of him and not his daughter. "Seven years after living a life of abuse and neglect in a shitty neighbourhood, she was slaughtered by monsters desperate to make a few bucks from drugs. She was trying to stop them selling that shit in her neighbourhood, and she died for it. Angel was a good person, and she fucking died because of your father."

"That's terrible." Lilly shrank back until she was sitting against the exposed brickwork behind the piped she was chained to.

"This is the price of what your father does while you walk down the streets in your designer clothes and your thousand-dollar perfume," Alex spat. "Families on the streets. Children with nothing."

"If my father had known, he would have helped." Lilly's tone was weak and unconvincing. There were tears now.

"He did fucking know. He didn't give a fuck, you dumb bitch. He still doesn't. No profit in it. Every time the banks take someone's house away, it destroys lives. Every time they call in the overdraft on a business, it destroys lives."

Alex remembered seeing Angel walking towards her uncle's car. She was clutching her mum's hand while looking 'round to where Alex had stood on their drive, pleading with his mum to let her stay with them. Desperate his best friend didn't have to go away. At the same time, some bastard was erecting a for sale sign in the house Angel had grown up in. If he could have saved her then, she would still have been alive now. His Angel wouldn't have had to suffer.

"People win and lose in business; the fact that things like this happen is horrible. You know I run a charity that tries to help people in trouble, people in need." Lilly sobbed. "Father gives me money for it."

Tears poured down her face. Alex knew Lilly wasn't a bad person, but she was blind to the real harm her lifestyle caused. She had no idea what it was like to struggle in life, not to know where the next meal was coming from. He took a deep breath trying to gain control.

"Very commendable, Lilly, but why don't you stop the greed in the first place? Why do you still work for a system that sucks the life out of people, so the bottom line can be maintained? Why don't you see the shattered families, the drugs they end up taking just to cope, and the death it leads to?"

"I'll try harder," Lilly wept. "I'll change."

"You think your father will change?"

"I'll talk to him; he's a good man. He donates money now. Can't you see that?"

"He's not a good man, Lilly. He never will be. He only gives to charity because it's tax deductible and makes for good PR. Only when you take away what is most precious to men like him can you force them to change."

"But what about you?" She pointed an accusing finger at

43

Alex, a face contorted again, eyes narrowing as she looked at him. "You run a business. You've made millions off the money markets. What makes you so different?"

"My money, my business, is dedicated to destroying your father and people like him. Global Money and the whole fucking corrupt financial system will be brought to its knees. My business was to be inside the system."

"How many people will that hurt?" Lilly wiped away her tears. "How many will suffer? It will be the poorest; you know that, don't you? Those who've invested their hard-earned money that will be left with nothing. Like your friend's father all over again."

Alex smiled. Lilly was far stronger than he'd expected. "The system will be reset for good. There'll be no going back. No bailouts keeping the same corrupt leaders in power. They didn't learn the lessons last time. They'll be sure to learn them now."

"Who are you to judge us, to judge people like my father? Who are you to decide where the money should go? Does this make you any better?"

"I am but a humble servant of the people." Alex rose from his haunches and bowed theatrically in front of Lilly. The beautiful face that once looked upon him with adoration was filled with horror and rage. "I will expose the system to the people, and they can do with it what they will. But there'll be no more Global Money, no more banks that are too big to fail. There will be a chance for people to start again."

"My father won't negotiate with the likes of you." She spat towards him.

"Is the flow of money among the wealthiest of the world more important than his own daughter?"

"No, because to deal with scum like you legitimises all you stand for."

"That may be true, my lovely. But there's one thing you should know. Whether you live or die is of no consequence to what I'm doing. I told your father not to contact the police, but I know he's talking to the FBI right now. Already putting your life in danger."

"What do you mean?"

"People are so predictable. Only now is he showing his daughter any real attention."

"He's a good father." But Lilly didn't sound so sure.

"Really?" Alex laughed. Her gaze fell downwards. "Haven't I heard you drone on about the way he has treated you? Didn't you tell me you think he would have preferred a boy? Or was it just pillow-talk to make you a more interesting person?"

"He will know it was you," Lilly said. "They'll hunt you down."

"They'll know it was me, Lilly. But not who I am." Alex switched to his British accent. "Am I the American business-man you've always known?" He smiled at the shock registered on her face. "Have I spent all my life in the States? Is Darren my real name?" Alex laughed at her confusion.

"What are you? You sick fuck," Lilly screamed and yanked at the chains again until they strained against the metal pipe.

"I'm an avenging angel, my love." Alex turned and walked out of the door. Closing it behind him, he drew the freshly oiled bolts across as Lilly screamed incomprehensible utterances from her prison. Climbing up the stairs of the basement, he nodded to the two Russians sprawled on the mouldy sofas in the lounge before leaving. He didn't need to speak to the two men as instructions had already been issued. It was a shame to think they probably wouldn't be able to contain themselves with such a lovely woman under their control.

But she was no longer Alex's concern. Her only use was to be a distraction, to have everybody looking in the wrong direction.

Alex had become fascinated with magic over the last few years. Especially illusionists who could seemingly pull off visual feats that defied reality. Yet, most of their skill was in making people look in one direction while the real trick was being performed elsewhere. Kidnapping Lilly was the ultimate distraction for the American side of his operation.

44

"They told me not to involve the FBI." James clutched a printout of the original Russian version of the email. Since getting it translated, he could recall every word. On the screen, there was a picture of his daughter shackled to rusty pipes. The image turned his stomach. For the first time in his life, he felt out of control.

"You've done the right thing." Special Agent Bennett stood next to his partner in James's opulent front room. They'd gathered as much information as they could about possible Russian activity in New York. But it hadn't revealed enough to help James make sense of what was happening. He'd had no contact with any Russian agencies, never mind done something to piss them off. "Better in our hands than that of private investigators."

"Do you really think it's the Russians?" Chloe was sitting on one of the white leather sofas next to Rose Goldstein holding a translated copy of the letter.

"It seems the obvious connection." Special Agent Mandy Smith was wearing a beige pantsuit. "Mr Goldstein, may I suggest we have this conversation alone?" She pointedly glanced at Chloe, who smiled back.

"We can help, you know." Chloe pointedly looked at James.

"Alex Ryan is behind this."

"It's something we will take into consideration, Miss Evans," Leon said.

"But not seriously." Chloe shook her head.

"I still want her here." James moved to sit on the large chair opposite Chloe and his wife. He knew Rose wanted the investigators involved. Chloe not only offered his wife comfort but was convinced about the involvement of the man who'd kidnapped her.

Chloe had told James about the surveillance, which had unearthed more possible tampering of financial software on the exchanges, and that insider trading had been uncovered in London. While the FBI seemed slow to react, James was becoming increasingly convinced that Chloe's agency was getting to the truth of matters.

"Your call, Mr Goldstein." Special Agent Bennet shrugged. "We need copies of all the previous letters and any messages you think might be related." The FBI agent paused as though considering his next words carefully. "Of course, it would be better if we had unrestricted access to what we need."

James's first thought was telling them they were out of their minds before he fell back into the chair with a resigned air. Typically, they wouldn't let any government officials near their records without a handful of warrants that had been scrutinised and challenged by the company's army of lawyers. But while the company board might demand his head for so easily allowing the FBI unfettered access, James didn't give a damn if it was going to help get back his daughter.

"Yes, of course. My assistant can furnish you with whatever you need at the office. She's there now."

"Thank you, Sir," Special Agent Smith said. "That will be of immense help."

"Should we get the money ready?" James's wife asked.

"It never does any harm to make the arrangements," Leon said softly. "In the end, it's your call if you pay or not. While we never advocate the paying of criminals, the handover of ransom money is sometimes our best chance of getting the people behind a kidnap."

"There was no ransom in your case, was there, Miss Evans?" Mandy said, obviously making a point of the differences between the kidnap cases.

"No, but he likes to mess with people, and he's certainly been doing that." Chloe didn't rise to the bait despite the fact the female agent really pissed her off.

"The messages and the kidnap may well not be related," Leon said. "They don't appear to be the same MO."

"I wouldn't bet on it," Chloe muttered. James could see the FBI agents weren't taking her seriously. "Why was the message in Russian? Wasn't that a bit obvious?"

Both Agents stared at her. While Special Agent Smith looked dismissive, James could see Leon was considering her question.

"How many kidnap and ransoms have the FBI dealt with where the demand was in another language?" Chloe continued, and the other two shrugged. "Alex Ryan wants you to think she's been kidnapped by the Russians. He wants you looking the wrong way. It's what he does."

"To do what exactly?" Agent Smith asked.

"To bring down Global Money. And the financial system with it."

"Not a lot then, really." Special Agent Smith didn't hide the sarcasm from her voice.

"We're not ignoring what you say, Miss Evans," Leon used a more diplomatic tone, and James saw him glance at his partner. "But the credible threat is to Lilly Goldstein, and we have to work with what we know."

"I can't get hold of Darren either," Lilly's mother said. She was clasping her hands tightly on her lap, her whole body rigid with tension.

Leon looked at his notes. "Who's Darren?"

"Darren Anderson," James said. "Lilly's current boyfriend." James tried to keep the disapproval out of his voice. He quite liked Darren and couldn't deny the genius of the software upon which the recent fortune of Global Money had been based. But, he wasn't the right sort of society gentlemen James had envisioned for Lilly. "He owns the company that built a lot of our software, Austin Trading Solutions."

"His phone keeps going to voicemail," Rose said. "Maybe he's been taken, too?"

"He'd mentioned going back to London," James said. "He often commutes between New York and London as he's setting up a European office."

"What does he look like?" Chloe asked.

"Average height and build." James looked at his wife for confirmation, knowing she was better at remembering faces.

Rose nodded. "Grey eyes and slicked back black hair. He's Texas born and bred. Austin, I think."

"Loves himself a bit too much, as well."

"James, don't be like that," his wife said. "We'll have to let him know; he'll be worried sick."

"Unless he's taken her," Chloe said.

"No, that wouldn't be possible." Lilly's mother looked surprised at the suggestion.

"Until he's eliminated from the investigation, then it's always possible," Special Agent Bennett said. "Do you know if his company is in any financial trouble at all?"

"Making money hand over fist, as far as I'm aware," James said. "They should be with the amount we pay them."

"We need all his contact numbers and details," Leon said. "It may be he was the last person to see her, so it's important we speak to him."

"I'll get them for you now." James retrieved his tablet from a sideboard and started flicking through his contact list.

"Please get our daughter back," Rose pleaded, and James felt his rip in two.

45

Alex passed smoothly through the Gatwick security checks using the false identity of Darren Anderson for the last time. He expected even the sluggish authorities to start hunting for Darren soon as the primary suspect in Lilly Goldstein's kidnapping. He wasn't afraid of them knowing he'd flown into London. It would cause further confusion as to his involvement since the trip had been planned.

Of course, when they checked to see if he was at the London office like he was supposed to be, they would discover Mr Anderson had vanished. They'd try to trace him through his credit cards. Darren had been booked into a suite at the Rosewood Hotel near the Holborn tube station. The police would visit only to find the room occupied by a man contacted on Craigslist who'd been paid to use the room for a few days, giving him a free trip to London. The place Alex was staying for the night had been paid for in person in cash a few weeks ago. A place where building contractors usually hung out, not high-class businessmen.

There was the issue of the CCTV cameras that pervaded the streets of London. Once his picture was shared across agencies, they would be trawling the CCTV network to find him. They would attempt to locate him using the airport surveillance cameras to see where he went after passing through security.

While Alex left the terminal doing his best to avoid being filmed, he had to base his plans on being identified. He joined the taxi rank, pulling out his phone to aimlessly check random sites as were the other bored passengers. When a taxi drew up, he jumped in, giving the driver an address and postcode that the burly Asian man punched into his navigation system.

The driver wanted to make small talk, and Alex obliged, keeping with the American business persona and accent. He didn't want to come over sullen and broody or act in any manner that might have the driver scouring the news for any sign of who his passenger might have been.

They followed the M23 north before joining the slow traffic on the M25 ring road. The driver talked about American football; he was going to watch a match at Wembley over the weekend. Big Giants fan. Alex knew enough about the game to seem credible. He had no interest in sports of that nature, but it was wise to have knowledge of the latest happenings of the sports world. If you wanted to make small talk with guys, then sports were a good subject.

It worked with some ladies too, but often knowing what the latest celebrities or pop stars were up to was enough. And Alex Ryan knew a hell of a lot about the decadent behaviour of the powerful celebrity elite.

Their time would come soon enough. Alex would make sure of that.

Swinging off the M25, he watched the dark grey clouds roll across the outer suburbs of London. He hated the city and all it stood for. Not just the financial sector, that was only one form of cancer which needed to be eradicated, but also the anonymity of the residents who didn't give a shit about who their neighbours were and probably didn't even speak to them. An old woman could freeze to death in the flat above them, and they wouldn't know because Londoners only gave a damn about themselves.

The taxi pulled up outside the Travel Lodge in Hounslow. Alex handed over the fare and gave him an American style tip rather than a meagre English one. Despite his bulk, the driver hauled himself out of his cab and opened the boot to retrieve Alex's case before offering him a smile and a nice day.

Alex headed to the lobby, using the self-check-in and booking under the name of a UK businessman who probably didn't even know his card had been stolen. The machine spat out the plastic key, and Alex found the room.

He showered before changing into a set of clothes he'd brought across from the States, black boots and jeans with a dark blue plain T-shirt under a thick Logan Paul hoody. There were a few unique additions. He donned a body suit, which added thirty pounds to his look. His grey-coloured contacts were changed out for brown ones. His hair was trimmed back. The black dye washed out. The beard was also shaved off before he set to work with the prosthetics and makeup to make sure his face matched his new heavy-set look. It wasn't so over the top it looked false, but it altered his shape enough that people wouldn't place him, even if his photo was shown on media outlets.

Happy with his look, Alex made sure the hotel room was clean, wiping away as much trace of himself as he could. He put on the TV, setting the timer to switch off at eleven. Then turned the lights on over the bed. Leaving the key card, he left the hotel via a fire escape and plunged into the darkness of the car park.

There was a large bin outside and, ensuring no one was around, he hurled his case inside before covering it with some of the rubbish. There was a risk they might find the case before the trash was taken, but it only contained his old clothes. On entering the street, Alex took care only to use back roads with no CCTV coverage. It was quite a distance to the tube stop he wanted to use, but he used the time to get used to walking naturally in his new shape. Alex added a little slump of the shoulders to signify a beaten man of no consequence.

Darren Anderson had vanished forever.

46

"It's got to be Alex." Chloe threw herself on the chair in Miley's suite. "Did you come clean with your dad? I take it he's still talking to you. How long was the lecture?"

"About fifteen minutes," Miley answered ruefully. "He insisted I either go back or I'm not to leave the hotel."

"I take it you didn't promise anything?"

"He gave up in the end." Miley smiled. "Ran out of steam and just wanted me to stay safe. I've started to pull together everything I can find about Austin Trading Solutions and its founder. For somebody born and bred in Austin, Texas there is scant information online."

"Facebook, LinkedIn, Twitter?" Chloe suggested.

"Nothing," Miley said. "This is a tech CEO who keeps himself to himself despite the company being valued at well over a hundred million dollars."

"James said his contract with them was worth twenty-five million dollars a year, and he knew of three other organisations who'd already bought the software. So, no magazine articles, online blogs, interviews?"

"Well, there are some for the company." Miley brought a few interviews up on the main screen. "But these have been done by the Tech Director and even by some of the researchers.

Darren, or Alex, has remained behind the scenes as the brains, hence recruiting other people to front the company. I'm already trying to check some of the data on his background we're supposed to have. But, I might need to wait until Adam is around to help with that."

Chloe was holding the printout of a picture they'd found of Darren from a company blog post after a Christmas party a few years back. She wondered if the image still being accessible to the public was a mistake. Even Lilly's social media feeds didn't have any pictures of her with her boyfriend. He was an expert at keeping himself off the internet even when in disguise.

The description the Goldstein's had given hadn't flagged Alex at the time to Chloe. But then, that was the advantage Alex had with his standard build and height. It meant he didn't stand out and changing hair and eye colour was simple.

But the image was him. Take away the glasses, facial hair, and changes to his nose, and it was the Alex Ryan they'd both been imprisoned by in Oakwell. Chloe had to admit if they'd passed him in the street, she probably wouldn't have recognised him.

"I've sent the stuff we have to Special Agent Bennett," Chloe said. "Even he's admitted the similarity in the photos, but they can run far more sophisticated analysis to make the match. Though, I doubt they'll tell us anything."

"Ongoing investigation," Miley agreed. "We're just civilians that get in the way. Do you think he's going to kill her?"

"If he wants to, he will. We know that." Chloe felt a shiver go down her spine. The memories of being trapped in a house three years ago were still vivid. She moved closer to Miley, not just to be of more support to the teenager but for her own comfort. Those hours had been a shared experience neither wanted anybody else to suffer.

"We've got to get her back," Miley said quietly.

Chloe squeezed her arm. "There's a bigger picture. He wants us distracted. Alex wants the FBI to be focused on the kidnapping. Your dad is convinced he's going after the entire system. Adam and Terry are working out how he's going to do it."

"We have to find out where she is." Miley looked at Chloe. "I know what he's doing. I know your right. But we don't know anything about the financial markets. What we do know is what it's like being held by this bastard."

Chloe nodded and looked again at the picture of Alex Ryan. "We'll find her, Miley. We'll keep her safe."

47

The Zack walked into the makeshift office with DI knight Adam gave him a disgusted look. Fortunately, there was no one else from the complex in their small workplace, and Zack had also taken the precaution of instructing Mike to dress down before he arrived. Even in plain clothes, most coppers were easy to spot. Zack knew he'd get a lecture from Adam later about the sanctity of the place and how bringing the law could get them kicked out. Or the whole complex shut down.

"Jesus, guys. What is this place?" DI Knight looked as though he'd just walked into a drug den and didn't know who to bust first.

"A technology incubator for startups with no cash," Zack said.

"Or hygiene." Mike stepped up to shake Adam and Terry's hands.

"And it's worth forgetting you know about this place," Zack reiterated what he'd said on the phone when Mike had asked to meet. Adam threw him another disgusted glare, but with the clock ticking, Zack wasn't about to let anything get in the way of stopping Alex Ryan.

"Hey, I understand." Mike raised his hands in supplication. "You know the score, Zack. The number of times we look the other way would surprise most of the public."

"Well, let's keep the police talk to the minimum." Adam appeared somewhat placated. "Coffee? We've got some quality stuff."

"Anything as long as it smells good." Mike pulled up one of the cheap plastic chairs and sat against the back wall, so he was facing the incident board. "So, if your Alex Ryan theory is true, how is he going to do it?"

DI Knight had asked the million-dollar question that Zack knew they were still working on. Asking anybody in the banking sector if one man could cause financial Armageddon resulted in being laughed out of the room. Of course, they were the same individuals who called those predicting a housing crash Chicken Little.

"We're still working out the details," Terry answered. "The market's run on confidence. If he shatters that confidence, investors will run for the hills and panic sell. He could flood the markets with mis-information to shake that confidence. Alex might have control of trillions of dollars' worth of stock he could offload. There are hundreds of possible scenarios, but they're all almost impossible to implement. We do have a few ideas."

"You need to come up with a plausible scenario if you want more attention from the police." Mike took a mug of coffee from Adam. "We've got tabs on all those identified as possible insider traders," Terry said. "Harvey gave us the passwords to the accounts he was using to get the information, and we're controlling them now. If they go for something big, we'll know."

"Well I have to say Financial Crimes, and the FCA are getting excited about those traders." Mike took a sip of coffee. "We're getting warrants to raid their houses as soon as we can. The FCA want us to go now, but if you really think we might catch the person feeding them data, I can hold off the raids."

"I can't prove it," Zack said. "But it's what I believe."

Mike nodded. "We haven't been able to trace the origin of the messages or files either. As you predicted."

"What about the software at Global Money?" Zack asked. "Have the engineers arrived from Austin?"

"Yes, but the company is stalling until trading ends on Friday. We've tried to follow the money from the transactions Terry identified. But most of it vanishes into thin air. The only money we can identify has been donated to children charities around the world. Our teams are getting tied in knots trying to work out if they are legit organisation. We've never seen anything like it before. If this is one guy, he's fucking brilliant. That's why it's almost impossible to believe."

Zack understood. Adam and Terry had used all the resources at their disposal, including some of the other companies in the complex that Adam had charmed into helping them. But even they hadn't managed to find more than the police. "You can't link it to ISIS?"

Mike shook his head. Zack thought he looked tired and probably pulled more than one all-nighter that week. "Nothing. So even that's just supposition on our part."

"He's in London," Zack said. "Alex Ryan is in London."

The DI drained the rest of his mug and pushed it onto the table. "Really?"

"He was the founder of Austin Trading Solutions, the company who put the software in Global Money they run their trading models on." Zack nodded to Adam, who brought up an image of Alex from Oakwell, as well as Darren Anderson.

"He's altered his appearance, but even the FBI's computers have matched with eighty-five percent confidence."

Mike whistled. "Where is he now?"

"Off the grid," Zack answered. "He'd emailed his London office to tell them he had another appointment and wouldn't be in for a couple of days, but his phone is off."

"Could be a legit excuse."

"He's a man who seems to be acting very casually considering his current girlfriend, the daughter of James Goldstein, has been kidnapped." A still image of Lilly Goldstein chained to the pipes was brought onto the screen.

Mike sat upright in his chair. "How do you know this?"

"We were helping James Goldstein."

"So, this shit is real." Mike's brow furrowed as he studied the images of Alex Ryan. "Is he that good? It's still impossible, right?"

"Everything about Alex Ryan is impossible." Adam handed Mike a printout of all they had gathered regarding Darren Anderson. "He stayed anonymous while living in plain sight. The company was started three years before Oakwell, which means he's been playing a hell of a long game and got himself positioned inside the system years ago."

"Jesus." Mike took the information and read through it. "No one could believe how he vanished so easily after Oakwell. Or that they couldn't find evidence of his existence before the incident."

"There were some breadcrumbs," Zack said. "If you followed the trail of the people who'd been affected by Alex. Old school companions for example. We investigated their lives and found some mysterious figures or contacts in each of the cases. It's there; we saw his first crude efforts as he learned his craft, and we traced a house he'd rented years ago. Had we been on it at the time, we would've found him. But years after, the trail was cold. He doesn't seem to be making mistakes anymore.

"Alex Ryan is a master manipulator who's upped his game to the highest level. He's been planning this for at least six years. He's moved all his pieces into position, just as he did at Oakwell, and is about to launch his end game. Everything else is a distraction."

"I'm convinced," Mike said, and Zack could see it in his eyes. "But it still doesn't tell us how he's going to do it."

Zack nodded to Adam, who pushed another sheaf of paper across the table. He saw enough in Mike's reaction that gave him confidence the DI would be amenable to the next revelation. Up until this point, Zack hadn't wanted to show their full hand.

Adam cleared his throat. "We might have figured it out."

48

James looked at the two young women sitting in his office. Head in hands, he'd spent the last hours wrestling with the decision to pay the ransom. The FBI didn't want him to. The FBI didn't want any outside agencies involved. But, his wife had begged him to pay, and Rose firmly believed the agency could help them. Even his security chief, Brad, admitted Chloe and her London colleagues had discovered vital information others had missed.

But when Chloe arrived with a teenager in tow, it made it hard to take them seriously with his daughter's life at stake. Yet, James had been taken aback by the fierce determination of the girl who had also been an abductee of Alex Ryan. Her confidence belied her stature and age. When Miley had told him and his wife that she was going to get their daughter back, James believed her.

Neither could he ignore the data on Darren they'd unearthed. The FBI concurred it was most likely the Alex Ryan the detective agency had talked about, which meant they'd been on the money with everything so far.

"So, have the FBI found anything?" It was the second time Miley had asked the question, while James had been lost in thought.

He shook his head. "They know he's flown to London, but he'd informed the office he would be away a few days. Look, he was never my favourite guy, and I know everything you say seems to be becoming a reality. But, he had to be working for the Russian mob. He can't be doing it on his own."

"Is that what the FBI is saying?" Chloe asked.

"They think his company must be in some serious financial trouble they're hiding. Probably took mob money to get started, and now, they are looking for a payback he can't handle." James was smart enough to know the FBI's theory was all supposition. But, it did seem plausible.

"Are they telling you to pay?" Chloe cocked her head as she spoke.

"No, but I want to. Rose wants me to."

"Then let us do the drop," Miley said.

"They asked for your wife," Chloe pointed out. "I can pose as her."

"What do you think?" James looked at Brad.

"I think you should listen to the FBI, Sir." The tall man shuffled from foot to foot while continually adjusting the blue tie of his equally dark blue suit. He looked very much out of his depth.

James sighed. Five hundred grand wasn't easy to get hold of, but James had the connections. His wife had already said she wanted to do the drop and was getting the money together. James didn't want to put his wife in harm's way or do anything stupid that might get Lilly hurt.

"At least if you're going to do the drop, you should let the FBI handle it," Brad added.

"That would be the right thing to do," James muttered. Yet the Feds hadn't got a damn thing right so far, and putting his faith in them alone was not something he was prepared to do.

"They'll be expecting the FBI," Miley said as though she could read his thoughts. "They won't be expecting an eighteen-year-old girl to be doing any sort of surveillance, and once the drop has been made, we'll find out where Lilly is."

"You still think this is a distraction?" James climbed from his chair and turned to look out of the office window. Was his daughter in the city? Was she close? Was she scared? He wanted her back so badly that for the first time in his life, he didn't give a shit about Global Money. Maybe that was the trouble all along.

"Definitely," Chloe said. "But it's a distraction we have to negotiate. We've other people dealing with Alex's plans. We need to concentrate on Lilly."

"He really wants to shut us down." James was speaking as much to himself as the others in the room. Had he brought this on his family in his quest to be the best? Having spent all night awake reviewing his life, James was regretting a lot of his decisions. He hoped it wasn't too late to put certain things right.

"And the whole of the finance sector," Miley added.

James turned and faced the two women again. "Our best techs are ripping through the software as quickly as they can. We've got engineers from ATS on their way to look at the code, but so far, they've found nothing, so the board won't even consider closing trading until we can offer good evidence. It means we can't examine our servers until Friday night."

"What about the anomalies in London?" Chloe questioned. "Isn't that enough?"

James shook his head and leaned against his desk. "It's still just a numbers problem we can't trace to the software, so it could still have a human element. It's still possible someone has been manipulating the trades in a way we've never seen before, making it an inside job. We suspect Brandon's boss might be involved as he's been off sick since your partner was arrested."

"We're checking into his affairs," Brad said. "And there's the other insider traders you told us about. None of them has connections to Global Money."

"Exactly," James nodded.

"But if you find something in the software," Miley said, "then you'll shut it down?"

"We've got one day until the weekend," Brad said with a defensive air. "We've already called it scheduled maintenance. They won't have time to scour every line of code, but they may be able to see some differences if they are to be found."

The techs had described what they thought they might find to James, but it had been over his head. He trusted if they discovered anything, he'd be the first to know.

"Zack thinks it will be before the weekend," Chloe said quietly. There was a snort from Brad.

"On what basis?"

"The threat to London from the terror group is for the weekend." Miley gave the security chief a cold stare. "And we know Alex has gone dark in London. With the police looking for anything that will threaten the high-profile events taking place in the next few days, he can make his moves right under their noses. Dad says if it's going to happen, it's going to be Friday."

"Has the extra security been put in place around everything we have?" James quizzed his security chief.

"Yes, Sir. Here and in London. If anybody attempts to get

near our offices, we'll be ready for them."

"Is the finance analyst's plan, what's his name, Adam," James said, "really possible?"

Brad shook his head at first. Then, he looked at the two women and took a deep breath. "Our data chief says highly improbable but not impossible. He would've had to comprise the code at the exchanges in a big way. But, it could be done."

"We know he has software on at least one New York exchange," Chloe pointed out.

The security chief gave a grim nod. "We've alerted the exchanges to the possibility. They're investigating."

"It would be nice if they'd listen to us instead of threatening us with legal action for compromising their servers," Chloe said.

"You think they could be right don't you Brad?" James nodded to the two women.

Brad glanced at them before replying. "Yes." The security chief swallowed. "Too many things all happening at once to be pure coincidence. But, I still think you should leave it to the FBI."

James paced the room again. He knew how hard it had been for Brad Reynolds to admit the outside agency might be right. It meant his own people had failed. But it was an admission that tipped James's decision.

There was a missed call on his phone from Special Agent Bennett. No doubt he wanted to check what was happening about the money drop. James looked at Chloe. "You know this Alex, so if he is behind it, I want you involved. But I want the FBI in the loop because I can't take chances with amateurs running the whole show."

49

MOHAMMAD: Is everything ready for the great day?

AHMED: Allah has provided. We are ready.

MOHAMMAD: Have you spoken the rituals?

AHMED: We will do so tonight.

MOHAMMAD: Allah will shine down upon you all and welcome you into his dominion. The Caliph is rising.

AHMED: We will do you proud.

MOHAMMAD: You do yourselves proud, brothers.

AHMED: Allah Akbar.

MOHAMMAD: Allah Akbar.

Alex didn't give a damn if they succeeded. But they had turned out more competent than expected. Alex had altered his plans to use the group to create a much bigger distraction. It had meant having to source weapons and equipment at short notice, and while he'd cultivated the contacts to do so, it had come at a high price and more questions than Alex would have liked.

He was beginning to have confidence the shambolic group might actually pull it off. Even if they were caught as they approached the area, it would provide enough disruption for Alex to deliver the final payload. Just when everyone would think the worst was over, financial Armageddon would begin.

While his next actions would place him in the direct line of fire, it was a part of the plan he couldn't risk leaving to anyone else. It could be the difference between success and failure.

The coffee shop he was working in was closing for the night. Alex cursed himself for staying too long. He could see the looks of the staff wanting him to leave. He closed his laptop, and as he passed the counter, added a generous tip to the jar. That brought more appreciative glances from the final two staff members, and maybe they wouldn't remember him.

Into the night, Alex raised his hood against the cold and continued his practised walk through the streets of London to his hotel. He wondered how Lilly was doing and whether the ransom would be paid. Someone would be there to pick it up, and Alex had contemplated hacking the New York CCTV network to see what happened. Would the FBI spend all night running around the city trying to figure out where the man was going?

If the individual he'd chosen was smart and followed his instructions, he might be able to keep hold of the money.

There were a few hardy souls on the streets despite the cold. A stiff breeze meant coats were tightly fastened, scarfs and hats covering bare flesh. There was talk of snow by the weekend. It amused Alex to walk among folk with no idea what was about to happen. People who filled their lives with small talk and worries about how respectable their lives looked to others. Soon, they wouldn't give a damn about how good their holiday photos would look to the so-called friends next door. They would be ripping the neighbours apart fighting for food.

He swung into Charring Cross tube station using the all-day pass he'd purchased earlier. Pulling a book out of his backpack for the journey, Alex clambered onto the train, becoming just another punter trying to ignore the world around him. He'd chosen the latest Jack Reacher paperback. It was a pretty good read.

Exiting the tube station, Alex strode to his latest accommodation, a nondescript guest house more commonly frequented by building contractors. The type of establishment where cash payments and false names were readily accepted. He was sure most of the guests were illegal immigrants from Eastern Europe hired as cheap labour on local building sites. Alex didn't bother with breakfast as it was more of a canteen with long tables where the guests all sat together. That might mean questions, and he didn't like questions. All Alex wanted them to see was an overweight, thirty-something that kept to himself.

In his room, Alex showered and lay on the bed going through the plans for the following day.

It was going to be a glorious moment in history.

50

"I can hear you," Chloe whispered even though there was no need as she hadn't yet left the confines of the SUV the FBI was using as their command post for the money drop.

"Okay, comms all good." Leon adjusted the wiring around Chloe's jacket making sure nothing was visible. She was grateful it was cold enough so wearing warm clothes to conceal the devices didn't cause a problem.

Leon had admitted the FBI was surprised this kind of old-fashioned drop was being used for a kidnap and with cash that could be traced by their serial numbers. He was beginning to doubt there was some sort of sophisticated Russian connection, having confided in Chloe that it all seemed far too amateurish. She hoped the FBI were coming around to their way of thinking. Though the disdain Special Agent Smith still seemed to regard her demonstrated not everyone agreed with Leon.

"Remember your instructions, and follow them to the letter." Special Agent Bennett took her by the shoulder and looked into her eyes. "We don't approve of this, but it's what Mr Goldstein wants. Don't take any chances."

Leon and his partner had argued against two civilians taking part in the money drop with the same vehemence as they'd argued against paying. James had insisted because the two women were the only ones who could identify Alex Ryan, and the FBI had to admit that Alex could have re-entered the country with a different passport as there was no trace of Darren in London.

"I gotcha." Chloe gave Leon a thumbs up.

"You okay?" Leon looked concerned.

"Nervous as hell," she said. "It's good to know America's finest are there as back up."

Miley had been trying to get hold of her Uncle Jake. He was someone Chloe wanted to be covering her back from the legendary tales Miley had told her. A sniper on overwatch sounded just the ticket even if she wasn't quite sure what it meant.

"Okay, its game time," Leon said. "We're good to go."

Chloe heard other voices checking in on her earpiece as she was bundled from the van outside a branch of the Chase Bank. Her instructions were to walk up Broadway towards Union Square before sitting on a bench in the centre of the park area.

Despite the late hour, the streets were crowded, and Chloe found it easy to feel lost among the bodies, so she didn't stand out. The money was in a blue and green rucksack slung over her shoulder over a heavy winter jacket they'd bought that afternoon. With her jeans and Ugg boots, Miley had told Chloe she fit right in with the New York scene. Chloe didn't believe her; the money felt like a great weight, and she had to strain to walk normally.

Chloe resisted the temptation to glance around to see if she could spot Miley. Of course, the FBI would've been against a teenager being involved if they'd been made aware. Zack had been on the phone to forbid her. Even James had said it wouldn't be a good idea and Miley had stomped off to her hotel with language that had turned the air blue.

So, where was she?

Miley knew the location of the drop and was probably already in the area. Despite not wanting Zack's daughter in danger, Chloe hoped she was out there watching her back.

She continued down Broadway. There was a cinema on her right showing the latest John Milton movie, and Chloe thought how useful it would be to have someone like him on her side.

It wasn't long before she reached a mobile vendor where she waited a moment or two, buying a pack of mints, before using the crosswalk until she was in Union Square itself. The FBI had told her to pause and buy something. They'd told her to walk casually so as not to draw attention to herself, just another woman about town.

Taking the first few stone steps, Chloe kept to the left side of the square, passing the dog run. The people inside the compound were desperately trying to tire their dogs at the end of the day. She liked dogs but didn't understand why people would keep them when they lived in a big city like New York. There was barking, shouting, growling, and the sound of laughter from the fenced off area. Chloe pulled her coat a little tighter as the breeze picked up. But, she wasn't sure that was the sole cause of the shiver going down her spine.

Then Chloe saw her. She looked like any other New York teenager with ripped blue jeans and a casual olive-coloured jacket with a high collar. Her hood was up too, but Chloe could make out the sizable headphones she wore similar to others who walked the streets solo. Miley was once again doing her own thing.

Chloe avoided looking at her friend and hurried along the path before cutting across a grassed area until she found a free bench in the centre of the trees. As instructed, Chloe sat on a bench facing the central monument. She unslung the rucksack and placed it on the wooden slats beside her. Chloe glanced at her watch. It was ten minutes before the contact was due.

"See anything?" It was Leon in her ear. Chloe pulled out her phone and stabbed the screen to life, so if people saw her mumbling to herself, she wouldn't be considered some kind of nut.

"Nothing."

"Okay." She wanted to look around to see if she could make out any of the people as agents, or even to see where Miley had disappeared to, but she'd been told to look as inconspicuous as possible. Chloe didn't want to attract the attention of anyone who might want to see what she was carrying.

As her phone ticked over to twenty-two hundred, there was a shuffle of feet a lot closer than any others had been. Chloe looked up as a large man with an impressive beard sat beside her, on the other side of the rucksack.

"You have something for me?" The man didn't look at her. She noted his hands were buried deep in his pockets. Did he have a gun?

"In the bag." She nodded down to the rucksack trying to sound as if she did this kind of thing every day.

"It's all there?"

"Yes." Chloe assumed so, but did he expect her to have counted it herself?

Picking up the rucksack, the man walked off.

She tensed and held her breath, expecting a dozen agents to pounce on him as he walked away. She looked for somewhere to take cover in case a gunfight broke out.

"Okay, we are on him," Leon said in her ear. "Give it five minutes and get back to us."

Instead of some movie-style action, the man vanished, and life in the square carried on as usual.

51

"So how did it feel to be carrying around half a million dollars in cash?" Miley slid onto the seat next to Chloe.

"It was heavy but kind of awesome." Chloe nodded. "I thought you'd be out there doing your cool spy stuff. You not following him?"

"Nah," Miley shuffled closer to Chloe and watched what looked like a group of evening dog walkers pass having finally given up trying to tire out their pets. "Dad said I wasn't allowed." Miley smiled to herself. Her dad had told her she wasn't allowed anywhere near the operation. Of course, she'd ignored him and made her way to the square.

"Now wait a minute." Chloe turned to face the younger woman. "Since when do you do what your dad says? If I remember rightly he wants you back on your island guarded by Hades."

"Well, even dads are right sometimes, and the FBI is following."

"So, what do you know that they don't?"

"Dad reckons the guy's a bust." While Miley had once more defied her father to be out during the operation, she'd kept in touch. She could rely on her dad not to cut her loose, even when she went against his wishes. "Did he speak to you?"

"Yes," Chloe nodded.

"An American accent?"

"How do you know?"

"I didn't, but Dad reckons it would be some deadbeat Alex had roped into picking up the bag. Probably doesn't even know what's in there. Right now, he's likely doing a load of cab hops or train changes to confuse the hell out of anyone following."

"Misdirection," Chloe said.

It was Miley's turn to nod. "Dad doesn't doubt Alex wants James to suffer, and that Lilly is in danger. But the ransom was another way of pulling everyone from the real moves in his game."

"But that means we're no nearer to finding her," Chloe said. "She could be anywhere in the city."

"New York is a big place," Miley agreed. When her dad had first said this would be a bust, Miley was despondent. "Dad says the FBI is ripping Alex's alter ego's life apart to find something. They'll be looking for places he might have owned or rented, etc. Something that would give him a place to hold Lilly hostage. But we don't think that will go anywhere either."

"Why?"

"Not Alex's style, and if he has bought anything, there will be nothing to trace it back to Darren. We know he's that good. Remember the house we were held in?"

"Hard to forget."

"I know, but who owned it?"

"My old head teacher and his wife," Chloe said. "They were supposed to be on a cruise. Or that's what the neighbours thought. But they were dead in the basement."

"Nothing was tying Alex to the house. No reason for anyone

to look there for me."

"No. I only went there with Liam because he already knew about it. Alex wanted me there."

"If we think about the same thing here, what do we get?"

"Lilly won't be any place we can associate with Darren or Alex," Chloe said.

"Not quite." Miley had been startled at the level of her dad's thinking as they'd talked it through. While she obviously knew about his work in military intelligence during his time in the Army, she hadn't understood much about it until she'd been talking with Uncle Jake. It was then that Miley found out how good her dad had been. There was more than one story of how his insights had saved both military and civilian lives. Apparently, Jake had wanted his brother to join him when they'd left the army. By then, Zack had been madly in love with Miley's mother and was determined to try to live a normal life.

"Alex would want it to be a place that connects to James. It would be part of the punishment. What better way of finding his daughter dead in a place dear to him."

"Of course." Chloe nodded emphatically. "It might be in the basement of one of the businesses."

"Exactly. Not one of the businesses though."

"Too difficult." Chloe was following the chain of thought. "It has to be personal. I bet James has a lot of property. Have the FBI searched them?"

Miley shook her head. "Don't know what he owns yet, and Adam reckons there could be a lot off the books for tax reasons. Might even be something he used to own that Alex has taken over."

"Then we talk to James." Chloe jumped off the bench and

pulled out her phone. "We'll get everything we can off him."

"And when they FBI realise they are following a nobody, they might help us." Miley stood to join her friend and for the first time felt confident they were going to get Lilly safely back.

52

Zack walked down the street to a coffee shop he knew would be open before the sun had even thought about making its daily appearance. It was a place for workers who'd just rolled out from under warm duvets not entirely sure they really wanted to face another frigid day. A few people were already inside nursing huge mugs of tea or coffee. Giant breakfast drinks and sandwiches were a speciality of the establishment.

After ordering a more modest black coffee, Zack took a seat in one of the orange plastic chairs next to the window, so he could watch the world go by. It wasn't unusual for him to be in so early. No one knew how much he struggled to sleep most nights. If they did, they'd probably pack him off to a therapist. He knew Chloe suspected. Even though she had seen his stash of pills one night when she'd been 'round his flat.

The truly insane thing was how he felt sitting nursing his caffeine injection. While most times he stared out into the dark streets with confused, upsetting thoughts about the state of his life, they'd been replaced by excitement and anticipation.

It was no boring divorce case he was handling today. There wasn't an uber-rich client who wants him to trace stolen items because the police were, in their opinion, too incompetent.

Instead, he was once again on the trail of one of the most dangerous men in the world. And that made him feel more alive than ever. It also meant he hadn't reached for those pills when he awoke.

It didn't fill the hole left by the loss of his beloved wife or not having a daughter that needed him anymore. But, it was something he could focus his mind on. Because it was something he was good at. He'd loved his time in military intelligence, piecing together the clues that saved the lives of soldiers and civilians alike. It was those moments when it went wrong he'd struggled to cope with. When the intelligence hadn't been accurate in the first place. When the recommendations he gave only made things worse. When innocent lives were lost.

There were times where the good couldn't outweigh the bad any more.

Despite wanting a regular life with a family after leaving, Zack had found it hard to adapt to civilian life. Mary tried to keep him straight by providing a loving base anchoring him in reality. Then there was Miley, and he'd thrown his energy into the small family to make it work. But, as a stray bullet can end the life of a soldier who was about to head home after an active tour, then malignant cancer cells can strike the ordinary civilian at any moment. Happy family dreams shattered in a moment.

Then Mary was gone.

But now, there was another mission, another chance to catch the person who'd eluded him since Oakwell. When Zack had set his mind on an objective in the army, he invariably achieved his goal. A dogged determination that had traced one of the most feared insurgent leaders in Iraq while even his superiors were telling him it was impossible.

Only Jake had listened to him. He'd detoured from his mission to scope out the objective, and the insurgent leader was where Zack had predicted he would be. There was a shitstorm after Jake's team had taken him out. If Zack's boss had wanted him court-martialled. But the top brass had recognised the insurgent was a highly prized scalp they'd found before the Yanks. He sometimes thought that some of his superiors were more concerned with looking good in front of the Americans than getting the job done.

It was almost the same with Alex. No one wanted to hear he was back; no one believed he was going to cause a financial meltdown because the prospect of a terrorist cell attacking at the weekend was on everybody's minds. Zack had already seen on the news the police raids across London trying to collect any information they could. It was possible they'd already found the people Alex had been working with, and that would be a good thing.

But everything was a misdirection, an illusion.

He sighed and drained his cup. After talking with Miley, Zack hadn't been able to sleep. She wouldn't listen to him when he told her to stay out of danger. There seemed almost a reckless abandon about her actions. As though she was putting herself in harm's way on purpose. Was that the price Miley was paying for what she'd been through with Alex? He wanted to blame his brother for putting these thoughts into her head, but Zack knew it was more than that. They should have gotten her proper counselling after Oakwell. How was a fifteen-year-old supposed to cope with seeing a man's brains spattered over a breakfast table?

But who was he to talk? Had had he ever listened when he

was told to see a therapist? So, why should his daughter be any different?

Behind the counter, the early morning cafe staff turned up the television as the news came on, and what was once background noise became the centre of attention. He withdrew from his thoughts to listen to a breaking story lighting up America.

Zack fished out his phone and navigated to the BBC news site where the released papers about the financial affairs of the President of the United States were the glaring headline. The media had long speculated he'd been using Russian money, but the level of debt he owed to one of America's oldest enemies was staggering. It appeared most of the President's business interests were in some way reliant on this money making him hugely obligated to those that were already accused of trying to affect the election.

There was already talk of possible collusion. The clamour for him to step down would be deafening. Zack smiled and looked out of the window. He hadn't seen this one coming, but what a move. America was now focused on their beleaguered President, and if the people took to the streets, then all the better for Alex.

Zack knew they wouldn't be able to stop everything Alex had planned. They probably only knew a fraction of his intentions. But if they could prevent him from collapsing the whole system and bring him to justice, it would be enough. Zack only wished he had more help.

His phone vibrated and lit up.

He looked at the number flashing and smiled for a second time that morning before answering the phone.

"You've got a lot to answer for brother. But right now, I

need your help."

53

Sandra was excited. She'd been lurking in the forums for a while trying to get accepted. Two attempts with a female name resulted in getting inundated with unsavoury offers or lewd comments. It had nearly made her leave and not want to go back, but her curiosity had been piqued, and eventually, she was accepted as one of them.

It was one of the boys in computer club who'd told her about the forum where if you were approved, you could get access to some pretty cool code. It had taken three months with her male username to gain that acceptance, and it had meant a lot of late nights posting and helping people on the forum with their coding problems.

And last night, it paid off.

Sandra re-read the instructions in the notepad file downloaded with the software she'd been given access to. It was easy to use, but there were some security precautions she needed to take. Flicking open a browser, she brought up a suggested website that hid her identity and fixed some of the settings on her computer.

Hands trembling with excitement, she started the software and inputted the required parameters before opening a new tab in her browser and logging into the forum. Her username allowed access to an area previously hidden. Finding the right thread, she created a post indicating she was ready.

Another thirty users had already checked in with more arriving as Sandra glanced at her computer clock and saw there were only a few minutes to go. She knew they were just one of the forums involved in the attack. Someone had posted that up to a thousand people might be doing the same. It seemed unlikely to Sandra. Wouldn't that many people attract attention?

There were sounds outside her bedroom. Footsteps on the landing. Sandra heard the bathroom light switched on and her older brother clearing his nose before spitting.

"Gross," she said quietly before checking her screen was turned away from the door so the light wouldn't seep out and attract his attention. Her folks knew Sandra was a night owl and certainly would show an interest in her being up so early.

But she wasn't going to miss this for the world. Little old Sandra Deacon from Atlanta, Georgia being part of the anonymous movement to strike a blow against globalisation. She wasn't supposed to say anything at school, but she'd already let slip to her friend Graham that she was doing something big this morning. He'd been trying to get out of her what it was about, and she'd loved the attention. Graham was the best-looking boy in the computer club.

The moderator posted in the forum. He wanted to know if everyone was ready. Sandra knew he was building up his part, but why not? This was history in the making. A flurry of people posted revolutionary comments. Sandra tried to come up with a snazzy one of her own but just ended up typing yes.

It would have to do. She was too nervous.

There was a brief pause as the moderator asked them to

wait. Her mouth was dry. She knew she should have gotten a drink before she started. Her brother flushed the toilet and padded passed her door again. Sandra held her breath. Was he listening outside or had flushing masked him entering his own room?

She almost missed the go post. Scrabbling for the mouse, Sandra brought up the software and hit the button aptly named "Novice attack." Immediately, the graphs exploded into life, telling how many data packets were being fired out from her software.

Sandra called up the CNN website and saw there was a big fuss going on about the president and his money. It was something to do with the Russians, and she hoped it wasn't important enough to keep what she was doing from being a big story.

54

Chloe had taken a while to realise something was happening in the news. They'd grabbed a few hours' sleep before going to meet with James at his apartment. She'd already phoned him about getting the property information they needed while he was desperately waiting for news from the FBI. They would've gone over straight away, but the FBI had convinced James they'd find his daughter. And the girls had needed the rest.

They were supposed to have been taking a cab to James's home but found themselves climbing into the back of a Grey Ford Taurus provided by Global Money. Brad had collected them from their early breakfast.

"What's going on?" Chloe asked as they pulled out into traffic that seemed more substantial than it should have been for the time of day. She moved towards the blast of the heater to get warm. The temperature had dropped sharply overnight.

"Massive revelations about President Doyle's finances and business dealings." Brad turned so he could see them. "Some are saying it could destroy his presidency."

"What've they got on him?"

"Huge debts to the Russians across almost all of his business."

"Is it true?" Chloe asked. "We've heard it talked about for

ages."

Brad shrugged. "He's already tweeted denials. The usual fake news claim. But the clamour for him to release his own finances to prove otherwise is huge. Could bring him down this time."

"I take it the free taxi service is because you haven't found Lilly?" Miley asked. She was rubbing her bare hands together to get some warmth into them.

"No sign." Brad turned to face the front again as the driver expertly navigated the cold dark streets towards James's apartment. "The boss is frantic and wants all the help he can get."

"What happened last night?" Chloe asked.

"The pickup guy led the FBI a merry dance around the subway until they got pissed off and pulled him in. Turns out, he'd been paid to get the rucksack and keep on the move in New York until the morning. Then, if he hadn't been pulled over, he was going to be allowed to keep the contents of the bag. They're still questioning him, but Special Agent Bennett believes his story. The guy is just a small-time perp hired to waste time and divert the FBI."

Chloe glanced 'round to Miley. "Score one for your dad."

"And today, we got to score two." The younger woman nodded. "Lilly needs us more than ever."

"That's not all," Brad said. "James got another message this morning on his personal cell. If he doesn't shut down Global Money and send all their profits to a series of children's charities by the time the markets open this morning, then Lilly will die."

"Was it in Russian?" Chloe asked.

"No." Brad shook his head, concentrating on the traffic. "It was the same as the previous messages. Signed off the same way."

"The Angel of Money," Chloe said.

"Exactly. The Feds are in a real spin. You seem to be the only ones with a handle on what's going on."

"When do the markets open?" Miley asked.

"Nine thirty," Brad said. "So that gives us three hours."

A few minutes later, the car pulled up outside the impressive building on Central Park West that served as James's home. Two serious looking doormen waved an electronic surveillance wand over Chloe and Miley before allowing them upstairs.

As they entered the main reception room, where James was pacing, and Rose was crying, Miley moved straight over and sat beside her on the white leather sofa, taking her hand.

"We'll find her Mrs Goldstein. With your help, we'll get Lilly back."

"Is this him?" James pointed at the early edition of the New York Times on the broad, mahogany coffee table.

"Without a doubt," Chloe said.

"Should've listened to you all along," he muttered before taking a drink from his glass, which Chloe suspected to be whiskey from its strong smell. It didn't look like he'd had any sleep, which was hardly surprising under the circumstances. There was two days of growth on his usually immaculately shaved face and dark patches under his eyes.

"You need to take it easy, James," his wife said with tenderness in her voice.

James waved her off with his hand but not unkindly. "Can you still find her?"

"We think she'll be somewhere associated with you personally. Which is why we want to know about any property you have, either of you," Chloe said.

"It might also have been special to Lilly," Miley added.

"We've got everything ready." Brad produced a sheaf of papers and photographs from a briefcase and laid them out on the table. Chloe shuffled forward in her seat to start the examination. It appeared the Goldstein's owned a lot of property.

"Will the FBI still help?" Chloe looked up at James. "Can you get them looking at some of these?"

"I'll call Special Agent Bennett." James put down his glass and took his phone from his jacket pocket. "They've already been searching the business properties."

"Let's hit the New York ones first." Chloe was rifling through what looked like an impressive portfolio. "If you have tenants, find out if they're in and go for the those that are empty. If there is no answer, don't just assume they're away."

"How do you mean?" Rose asked.

"We were held in a house where people thought the owners were on a cruise," Miley said. "But they'd been killed, and Alex was using the house as a base."

"Oh, my." Rose covered her face.

As James contacted the FBI, Chloe went through the reams of papers and photos that had been provided, becoming despondent at the sheer number they'd have to search. There just wasn't the time.

"We need to narrow it down." Chloe retied her hair in a loose ponytail feeling frustrated.

"Holiday getaways," Miley said holding a photo in her hand depicting a large residence that looked to be in a secluded area. "Especially ones that Lilly loved."

"She loved that place." Lilly's mother took the photo, and Chloe could her see her reminiscing about days gone by. "Isn't that where she first learned to ride, James?" Rose handed the photo over to her husband. "Do we still own this?"

James shook his head sitting next to his wife. "No, we let that go a long time back now for quite a profit. I think I could find who owned it. I remember Lilly being mad when we sold it, but we needed the money to buy the place in London."

"Some of our best memories of Lilly when she was younger were made there," Rose said.

"How far is it?" Chloe asked.

"It's a way, out up the I95," James said.

"Find out about the owners and contact them," Chloe said. She looked at Miley who was nodding.

"It could be," she said.

The teenager's phone started to ring.

Miley looked at the screen, smiled, and then glanced back at Chloe.

"We've got help."

55

"There's more action." Adam's voice came through on Zack's headphones. He didn't generally like wearing the fiddly things, but he needed to stay in constant communication. The younger man was in their makeshift office monitoring everything he could while Zack sat with Terry in yet another coffee shop. This time, he was outside St Paul's tube station in the heart of London's financial sector.

News of the revelations in the US had swept around the patrons of the shop that morning before the suited financial gurus had hurried off to begin the day's work. Zack had waited in anticipation, but the morning passed without incident. Terry joined him in case he could spot something amiss Zack might overlook. He was sitting opposite, eyes glued to his tablet while nursing a second large Americano.

Terry had been in touch with former colleagues from Global Money, which wasn't many since most of his floor had been killed in the explosion. But Zack wanted to get a handle on what was going on. The stocks had been spooked by the news of the president, and there were fluctuations, but everyone was waiting for the US markets to open to see how they would react. Most saw the possible ousting of the president as a good and bad thing at the same time.

"A DDOS attack is taking out a lot of sites," Adam said. "I can hear shouting in the corridors. It's a big one; we're trying to trace the source."

"DDOS?" Zack asked.

"Distributed Denial of Service attack," Adam explained. "Basically, it's a coordinated attempt to access particular sites at the same time by thousands of people. Do it well, and you can crash a server. Even a low-level attack can stop people accessing a website. A lot of sites use services to defend against it, but it's still hard to entirely stop."

"How do people do it?"

"Co-ordinate enough users to run specialist written software at the same time and on the same net addresses. They get newbies in the world of cybercrime to download software as it only takes a few clicks to get going. Each person can simulate thousands of accesses to a site, swamping the servers. The difficulty is coordinating it. That can take some doing. I'm on 4chan now, which is where the media say most of these people hang out. They don't really; it's a myth allowing the media to think they can go and look, but folks are posting about the attack on there, and I might get a lucky hit that sends me to where the real action is. There are a few other forums I know that might have info."

Zack still didn't quite get it, but he'd gleaned enough to know it was bad. "Which sites are being attacked?"

"The big banks," Terry cut in staring intently at his tablet. "The consumer side, so people can't do their internet banking."

"These attacks are often used to hide something else, such as a hack after passwords," Adam said. "Yes, the forums are going crazy with excitement over this."

The news was obviously spreading as the businessmen and

women around them started barking into their phones. It was lunchtime, and the place was crowded.

"What good will this do Alex?" Zack said as much to himself as the others.

"More misdirection," Terry said. "It's attracting everyone's attention right now."

"He needs those protocols down," Adam said. "That's how he can crash the system. If he gets into the Stock Exchange, there'll be computers connecting to the main software running on cloud-based servers. With the right permissions, it would be wide open to someone with his skills."

"Should I do another walk by?" Terry asked.

Periodically, one of them had gone out and walked passed the London Stock Exchange. They'd printed a photo of Alex as he'd been as Darren Anderson, but they didn't have much hope of spotting him. Zack doubted he looked the same.

"No, there's going to be something more," Zack replied.

"The terror cell?"

"Got to be. Ultimate distraction. Bigger than this." A message appeared on Zack's phone. It was from DI Knight.

The attack on the banks?

It's him. It's got to be.

"Zack, something is happening." Looking up from his phone, Zack could see people racing passed the shop. They were coming from Paternoster Square, right outside the entrance to the Stock Exchange.

"This is it. Adam, we've got something going down here. Check the news and keep us updated."

"Where are you going?" Terry asked as Zack jumped to his feet.

"This is the distraction he needs. He's going for the exchange."

"So, you're going there, too?"

"I've got to stop him. You'd best make your way back to the office."

"No, I'm coming with you." Terry packed away his tablet as he rose to join Zack.

"This could be dangerous, Terry, very dangerous. I don't know what the terror cell or Alex will be armed with."

"I'll still feel safer with you."

"Your call." Zack wasn't going to waste any time arguing. With luck, if things got too heated, Terry would see sense and bug out. As it was, Zack wished he was armed. But the chances of getting hold of another gun after Oakwell were non-existent.

"Reports of a van smashing into bollards off Oxford Road and taking out some pedestrians," Adam said in his ear as Zack ran into the street and started to push against the flow. "News of shooting, too. Zack, I think you should just get out of there."

"Just keep me updated, Adam."

"Okay."

"You heard that, get out of here." Zack turned to Terry as the popping sound of gunshots sounded ahead of them.

"I want to help," Terry shouted. It was getting difficult to navigate their way through the crowd. "He killed my friends."

Zack didn't reply as he pushed across the road and raced through another passageway leading to the square outside the exchange.

"Get down."

He shoved Terry into a doorway just as bullets smashed into

the wall where, a moment before, they'd been standing.

56

Despite the prayers and readings, Ahmed knew the others were as scared as he was. Though, no one would admit as much as they drove the van through the busy streets to their destination. No one dared say they didn't want to go through with it. But Ahmed was having those thoughts, and he considered himself the strongest of the group.

He knew when the doubts were consuming his brothers as, one by one, they would mumble words from the scriptures. Ahmed did the same as he navigated the streets of London in the white van. It was the same vehicle they'd used to collect the items for the attack, just with different number plates.

Apart from the quiet prayers, no one was talking. Ahmed had Emir beside him in the passenger seat. It was a plain white van a few years old, and it was a typical enough sight driving through the streets of London with an Asian driver. They'd filled it with boxes of fruit and veg, so if they were stopped, they could tell the police they were making deliveries. The weapons hidden among the fresh goods would hopefully go unnoticed.

The other two members of their crew sat on the crates holding onto the sides of the van to stop themselves falling. Syed was spending most of his time reciting the religious passages, his eyes fixed firmly on a space between his feet.

Despite their fears, glory awaited. For Ahmed, this would be the ultimate redemption. His family, so disappointed in his life so far, would see how great and glorious he was. He might never bring them the sons and grandsons they so desperately wanted, but he would bring magnificence to the family name as he struck a blow against the tyranny that killed so many brothers from their homeland.

They drove down Oxford-Street, following the A40, which would take them to their attack point. Hordes of workers spilt out of offices, descending on the street for their lunches or to head off to the more decadent shops nearby. More money wasted on frivolities while people in Ahmed's motherland died for want of food.

Ahmed had been brought up to live frugally by a family who had emigrated from Iraq to London twenty-five years ago, after the first Gulf War. His parents had hoarded every penny to build a future for Ahmed and his two sisters. Their father had continuously talked about the decadence around him. His mother aghast at the show of female flesh which surely offended Allah. They believed in the scriptures and believed the world would soon see that Islam was the only way.

The traffic eased a little as they passed further along Oxford Street. He questioned the wisdom of an attack this time of day. While there would be plenty of people, it would be hard to get the van up to any sort of speed to force their way to their destination. But Mohammad had insisted, hinting this would not be the only glorious mission today.

"Get ready my brothers," Ahmed shouted as they passed a Starbucks on their right. The starting point of the next phase.

255

The two brothers in the back rooted through the boxes pulling out the Russian-made AK47s. There had been no time to train with the weapons other than watch YouTube videos and take instruction from Emir on the loading and reloading. But this would not be a pitched battle where with precision shooting. All they had to do was kill as many of the infidels as possible.

The prayers grew louder as the men ensured the weapons were loaded, and two were passed to Emir. Ahmed felt the sweat on his palms inside his gloves as he gripped the steering wheel tighter and looked for the next point.

"Stay steady, brothers," he said out loud as much to calm his own nerves.

The next point came. The Merrill Lynch building on his left. An apt sign of a decadent society. Ahmed steeled himself and looked for a suitable moment to cross the opposing traffic and floored the accelerator.

He chose a small Ford Ka to cut in front of. Clipping the side of the blue car and sending it spinning, their van mounted the pavement. Ahmed felt the thuds of bodies against the front of their vehicle as he wrestled with the steering wheel to keep the van from veering into the nearest building. The panicked crowds tried to scatter ahead of him. Some threw themselves into the road to avoid the van hurtling along the pavement. Even inside the cab, he could hear their screams. His brothers shouted in triumphant joy.

"Hold on," Ahmed commanded.

The van rammed into a solid metal post.

The posts were to stop attacks from getting any further into pedestrian areas, designed to prevent the very thing Ahmed and his brothers were attempting. Fruit from an unsecured box smashed against the front windscreen and Ahmed couldn't help wondering if it looked like an exploded head from outside the van.

The pedestrian walkway to Paternoster Square was in front of them. The heart of the infidel's power. The centre of their greed and tyranny.

"For Allah."

The rear doors burst open, releasing Bhavik and Syed into the streets. Even before their feet hit the pavement, the two men were firing into the crowd with short bursts.

Emir handed Ahmed a rifle, and they both jumped from the van. Ahmed flicked off the safety and fired his own burst. A group of three women had been trying to flee down the walkway. Two fell as bullets thudded into their backs. The third carried on running, her terrified screams drowning out the cries of her injured companions.

Ahmed felt a surge of adrenalin as he cut down two more women wearing short skirts. Their bare thighs exploded into a pulp of blood and flesh.

"For Allah," he raged, but it was surprising how quickly people had scattered leaving few targets. He could understand why other brothers had chosen packed areas with few places for the infidels to flee. Those they did see were raked with bursts of gunfire. He heard the other two reload. Emir had been screaming as he emptied his magazine into a wine bar. There were hideous cries of people caught in the hail of bullets. Emir roared with laughter.

"Keep moving," Ahmed shouted. They were making their way down the passage.

Above all other sounds, he heard sirens as the authorities responded. They'd predicted armed units would be with them in a matter of minutes. Minutes they had to make count. Ahmed urged them along the passage, Emir keeping pace beside him. Moments later, they emerged into the large, open square in front of the London Stock Exchange. Panicked civilians, rushing across each other as they tried to find a safe exit, became their targets.

Ahmed thought it was a pity they hadn't decided to attack from all three entranceways, driving the infidels into the square. That would have been a truly wonderous slaughter.

Changing his magazine, he fired into any small group of people to achieve the maximum casualties. He heard Syed curse as his weapon jammed. His younger brother fought to pull the magazine clear.

"Remember the videos," is all Ahmed could say, but at least Emir was beside them adding his own firepower.

Syed called out. Ahmed turned and saw him fold to the floor clutching his stomach.

57

"Adam, is my dad okay?" Miley shouted into the phone. They were back in the Taurus heading north on the I95 for New Haven. After making frantic phone calls, James had discovered the old farmhouse had been abandoned a few years ago after the owner had died. The place had been left to one of the children who hadn't been in the country for years. Though recently, it had been purchased by a shell company they couldn't trace, and Miley knew what that meant. After viewing it on Google maps, she realised it was the perfect place for Alex to have taken Lilly.

Across the car radio, word came through of the attack in London.

"I don't know, Miles," Adam said. "I'm sorry. He asked me to get hold of Mike before he hung up."

"Where was he?"

"At the exchange. Right where the attack was. He was spot on."

"Have you got hold of Mike?" Chloe shouted above the engine noise into the speakerphone.

"Not yet, I'm still trying. I think the network is struggling to cope. The guys here are saying the DDOS attack has spread to the American banks as they were opening."

"That's right," James said. He was sitting in the front and hadn't been off the phone since they'd started driving. He was trying to deal with the fallout of the attacks at the same time as talking to the FBI about where they were going. Special Agent Bennett had been trying to persuade them to hang back and give more time for the FBI to gather intel and assemble a squad.

None of them wanted to wait.

"Hang on, Mike's on the line; I gotta go," Adam said.

"Let me know as soon as you hear from Dad," Miley insisted.

"I will. Don't worry; he'll be alright." He tried to reassure her.

Miley wasn't convinced. She tried her dad's phone again, but the network was still busy. Had they cut the cell towers to prevent the terrorists from communicating? She was frightened he was hurt and terrified he was going to be going up against not only the terrorists but also Alex. He wouldn't even have a gun this time. She hoped Alex would be at the farmhouse as at least they were going to have armed assistance.

"Can you get the news on?" Miley said. "Can we see what's happening?"

There was a TV in the car that Brad, who was sitting in the back with the two women, switched on. CNN was broadcasting the images from London. At the same time, red flashes crossed the bottom of the screen regarding the allegations about the president and the attacks crashing the major banking websites. People were already talking about how the US markets would react when they opened.

The reports from London spoke of multiple casualties and an ongoing situation. Eyewitnesses claimed to have seen at least two of the gunmen shot. The press reported the gunshots had ceased and were speculating as to whether the incident was over.

Most of the coverage showed ambulances and police racing to and from the scene trying to piece together what had happened with the scant information they had. Another flash across the bottom of the screen spoke of ISIS already claiming responsibility.

Miley tried to call again but still couldn't through.

"He's resilient, Miles." Chloe gripped her free hand. "He'll be okay."

"He's bloody stupid." Miley shook her head and looked out of the window as the countryside of North America flashed passed the window. It seemed hard to believe the milkshake drinking man who'd held her in the house three years ago was back. Miley remembered the screens in the dining rooms rotating through the various financial markets. Even then, Alex had been planning all this.

Looking at her phone, she offered a silent prayer to any deity that might listen and keep her dad safe. Was Alex there? Or would they find him in the house with Lilly, using it as his lair? It gave Miley an appreciation of how her father felt when she put herself in harm's way, and she vowed to be more thoughtful when this was over.

"Okay, that was Special Agent Bennett," James said coming off the phone. "He's sending a team to meet us at the house. When we arrive, they want us to sit tight and not do anything."

"Will they make the deadline?" Chloe asked.

"They're working on it."

"If they're not there, we have to act," Miley said.

"We don't know who we're up against Miles," Chloe said.

"We could just as easily get her killed than save her if he's left her with other people."

Miley shook her head. "Can we get the FBI to send the information on the known people of interest?" she said to James. "Tell them we may have seen them. Or at least Chloe has."

"Okay, but can I ask why?" James said.

"So I can send them to my uncle."

"Then we'll know what we're up against." Chloe rested her head against the back of the seat.

Miley looked at her and offered a small smile. "And they won't have a clue what's about to hit them."

58

"Terry get down, get down."

The younger man was too slow. Zack tried desperately to pull him behind the thick wall as bullets peppered the other side; ricochets bounced off the brick columns they were next to. He saw a woman collapse beside him, blood spurting from a severed artery on her leg.

For a moment, the hail of bullets stopped. Zack let go of Terry and dragged the woman by her coat until she too was behind the wall. Throwing off his own jacket, Zack wrapped it around her leg. The woman stared at both him and her leg in shock. She wasn't screaming, but Zack could see her face was a deathly shade of white.

"Terry, are you okay?"

"I don't know," the man whimpered, pushing himself to his knees. "I don't know."

"Come here and hold this tight on her leg." As Terry followed Zack's instructions, he took a quick moment to scan him for injuries. Some of the chips from the bricks had cut into Terry's face, but they were only superficial marks. "Stay with her, and keep the pressure on until the paramedics get here."

"Okay." Terry nodded mechanically, not taking his eyes off the leg he was pressing down on. "Where are you going?"

"Alex will be here. This is his diversion."

Terry nodded again without looking up. Zack was glad he'd lost his appetite to accompany him.

There were more rattles of gunfire but nothing near them. Zack could tell they weren't professional gunmen. The bursts were random, erratic, wasteful. A brief look and Zack had seen two of the terrorists firing from the hip.

"Everybody stay on the ground." The commands came from two armed police in full tactical armour hurrying down the passageway. The few people still between the buildings pushed themselves into the walls or flopped to the pavement.

Zack stayed in a crouch. He turned to the two men as they came alongside him. "At least two shooters. Three round bursts. Firing from the hip. Opposite side of the square one minute ago."

The nearest of the armed responders paused to look at Zack as if assessing him and the quality of his information. The man then nodded before he and his partner took up firing positions either side of the passageway.

The sound of their shots echoed painfully around the enclosed area. They fired simultaneously, double taps, and Zack had a strong feeling two of the terrorists were down. The men shouted again before going around the wall.

There was the rattle of a gun on automatic.

The terrorists.

Two more sets of controlled double taps, which Zack knew were the police.

Glancing back, Terry was staying low and still with the woman. More armed police swarmed up the passageway. This time, they helped the few remaining civilians away from the scene. Paramedics and fire crews arrived wasting no time in tending to the wounded. The sound of the gunfire had stopped. Were all the terrorists down?

Zack knew he had to act. Stealing between the brick pillars, he stayed behind one offering enough cover but still allowing him to see the front of the exchange building. The armed response units were in the square. Several bodies were on the ground, and the fact the response officers seemed particularly interested in certain ones led Zack to believe they were the downed gunmen. None of the bodies were moving.

They never would.

He was in an awkward position. This was now a crime scene, and while the initial focus would be to preserve life, they would also be protecting the evidence. Not only would they not want a civilian in the way but might treat him as a potential hostile.

He fished out his phone and saw there was a weak signal but trying to ring only brought a busy network signal. He messaged DI Knight. There were messages from Miley, desperate for news; Zack responded, telling her he was fine without elaborating on where he was or what he was about to do.

Where are you? Mike messaged him back.

I'm outside the Exchange. That's where he's going to be. I need help to keep the police off my back. Can you come?

Already close by. Hang tight. Stay out of trouble.

Be quick.

More emergency services filled the square, which assured Zack that the shooters had been neutralised. He knew it had created the perfect cover for Alex. Probably his plan all along. People from the buildings were streaming into the square and being directed by the police to safety. They were coming from the front of the Stock Exchange building too, though Zack knew most would be led out through other exits, not just to keep them safe but to keep them from seeing the bodies.

His phone went. It was Adam. The call connected.

"You're alive."

"I'm good. Terry has taken a hit, but I think he'll be okay."

"Jesus, it looks fucking bad man. Four terrorists smashed a van across down the pavement before they jumped out and started shooting. Where are you?"

"Paternoster Square looking at the LSE building. I've got to get in there. Mike's on his way."

"I've got the floor plans here," Adam said. "I can see the rooms he's likely to need for access to the network. James was sent a deadline to stop Lilly being killed. It's two thirty, UK time."

"Shit that's thirty minutes away." Zack let it sink in. It meant thirty minutes before Alex planned to unleash hell on the financial system if he wasn't stopped. "Won't the system be locked down in this sort of emergency? Trading stopped?"

"Probably, until he kickstarts it again. They would tell you it can't be done, but if anyone can find a way, then Alex can."

"Fuck me," Zack said. "How can I get in?"

"Right now, through the front door."

"Okay, got to go; Mike is on the other line."

Zack flipped off the call with Adam, so he could speak with Mike.

"I've made some calls, and I can get us in. Meet me outside the front in five."

59

Chaos was Alex's friend, and the confusion caused by the attack had been perfect. The doubts about Ahmed's men following through had evaporated when he heard the first gunshots, and Alex knew the ensuing confusion would be the ideal cover for his plans.

While terrified Londoners fled the shooting, Alex had slipped into the toilets of the London Stock Exchange. Before then, he'd been sitting on the steps outside the building enjoying a milkshake he'd bought from one of the small street stores. The locals had looked at him oddly as, although the sun was out, it was still a cold November day. But he'd smiled as people dashed by him on their way to or from lunch.

He hadn't been concerned about standing out anymore. Perhaps when everyone was interviewed, the barista would mention him. Or anybody who'd seen him on the steps in an overlarge jacket sucking down the delicious strawberry shake. It wouldn't matter because he'd be long gone. There was another persona, years in the making, he had to become for his next task.

When he heard the rattle of gunfire, Alex had tossed what was left of his shake aside and walked up to the wide, main double doors of the Stock Exchange. He entered the reception area, but no one was interested in who he was. The sound of gunshots and screaming saw people rushing towards the large windows to see what was going on.

Nobody paid attention to the man who strode passed the reception desk towards the toilets. Once inside the cubicle, Alex shed the weight suit and prosthetics, stuffing them into the holdall. His coat was changed for a lightweight yellow jacket, which went over black trousers and a white shirt. With the correct flashes on the shoulder, it gave him an official look. Certainly enough to convince panicked civilians who just wanted to escape the carnage.

From the holdall, Alex retrieved his gun before tucking it into the waistband under the fluorescent jacket. There were two devices carefully wrapped in thin hotel towels he brought to the top of the holdall. The contact who'd supplied the bomb vest had provided him with two smaller phone-triggered devices. Each contained enough Semtex to cause enough of a distraction to cover his escape.

Checking his watch, Alex departed the toilets and saw more staff spilling down the stairs. He shouted with authority for them to evacuate. Not that they had any intention of staying, but it gave him a good reason to be rushing up the stairs as though he was clearing the building. Workers merely glanced at him, assumed his importance, and obeyed instructions. Alex didn't care so long as they were out of his way.

Having memorised every detail from the plans and photographs he'd acquired, Alex moved swiftly up the levels to the relevant floor. A few well-worded emails to their IT department had also revealed what he needed to know about the server room he was heading for. It was always astonishing how much information people would give up over email after being duped into believing they were talking to a someone who had the right to know the information they were asking for.

After a few minutes, Alex was outside the IT rooms. The doors opened, and a white-shirted, middle-aged man emerged seemingly oblivious to the attack. He looked around in confusion. Probably wondering where everyone had gone.

"You need to get out of here," Alex shouted. He then realised the man was wearing a lanyard key card around his neck that might be useful.

Pulling the gun from his waistband, he shot the man twice in the chest. As the body crumpled to the ground, Alex ripped the key card from around his neck.

Moments later, he was inside the server room with complete access to everything he needed to complete his end game.

60

Lilly had been through every possible emotion since Darren had left. She realised she didn't know the man she'd fallen in love with. At first, she'd convinced herself it was a practical joke, that Darren would appear at the door smiling and let her go. None of it made any sense.

When the first Russian stomped into the basement, she knew how dangerous her situation was. The men looking after her were sadistic bastards who leered and pawed at her body, boasting about what they would do if her precious daddy didn't comply with their demands.

Knowing there was a ransom allowed Lilly hope her father would pay whatever it took to get her back. There was something of a sour taste at the thought of what he'd been doing if Darren was to be believed, especially if it had put her in danger. Deep down, Lilly knew the truth of Darren's words.

Her father had always been ruthless when it came to money. She'd been at dinner parties where he'd boasted about another company takeover, which had seen a loss turned to profit because they'd got rid of thousands of workers. She'd often thought about the workers and their families. Only, her negativity was dismissed because her father spoke about how they wouldn't have had a job anyway if the bank hadn't intervened. She'd set up a charity to help the homeless, having seen so many of them on the streets of New York. But had she done it just to make herself feel better when she was on yet another shopping trip? Had her father donated money because it was tax deductible and made him look good?

Global Money generated so much wealth that rarely went to those needing it the most. She didn't know the true extent of what her father had done to attain the position of CEO in such a massive corporation, and it didn't justify her imprisonment. But it served to make her mad at her father for acting in a way that made people want to do this to her.

Lilly vowed if she were freed, then at least she would change. Perhaps she could persuade her father to give up being a CEO, give back to some of the people they'd made their wealth from. But her captors would be made to pay, cowardly bastards who also preyed on the weak themselves to get what they wanted.

She'd pleaded with one of them as he'd sat on a wooden box facing her during the night, an ugly man with a thick neck and muscled shoulders giving him an ape-like stance. He and his companion spoke with a strong accent she assumed was Russian. They would use their language if they spoke together. She knew they were talking about her by the way they leered and laughed.

The one with the thick neck was seated, playing with a long knife, the blade of which he rolled up and down his trousers as he told her how he hoped her father would refuse their demands. When that happened, he was going to take her to one of the rooms upstairs and have a whole lot of fun before sending a few pieces to her father to persuade him to be compliant. She wouldn't be killed if she behaved; she just might be missing a few pieces.

"You won't let me go," Lilly shouted pulling at the chains even though she knew it was futile. "I've seen your faces. You can't let me go."

The ugly man had laughed. "We'll be going back to our motherland. Our debt will be paid. We will be free."

"So, kidnapping and torturing a woman will make you free?"

"Stopping the American dogs makes us free." The brute spat on the floor near her. Lilly moved her legs out of the way.

"We could pay you a lot more," she said. "You could stay in America or go to another country and live like kings."

The man rose from his box and stepped over her. Lilly shuffled as far back to the wall as she could. He squatted down, the knife held out before him. His head pressed forwards until Lilly felt hot, stinking breath on her face. He sniffed at her cheeks.

"The very smell of you rich Americans disgusts me." The brute held the knife to her neck. "You think you're better than us. You think you rule the world." The knife blade slid down her chest between her blouse, passing the already torn buttons where his friend had decided he needed a better look. "You wear your fancy. You wear fancy perfumes while your planes smash hospitals and schools for your freedom."

"I don't do that." Lilly felt tears tumble down her face despite her best efforts to be brave.

"No, like all Americans, you want good life. You don't give a fuck about anyone else." The spittle from his angry tirade landed on her face as he pressed the knife against her breastbone so hard she knew he'd drawn blood.

"Please don't."

His eyes seemed to glaze over for a moment as though

recalling a vivid memory that was causing such pain. Then, looking down, he backed off and left the room.

There was enough play with her chain allowing Lilly to rub the spit off her face with a shaking hand before checking to see the damage he'd done. It was only a small nick between her breasts, but a faint trickle of blood fell beneath the white of her blouse.

Resting her head back against the rough stones, Lilly let the sobs come unhindered as she contemplated the worst.

61

DI Knight's badge might not have had the authority to let him go anywhere within a terrorist crime scene, but his force of personality, reasoning, and a judicious phone call to his superiors seemed to make a difference. No one believed there was still anyone to pose any danger, but neither did they want to stand in his way. Zack assumed the building would be cordoned off soon enough, but for now, they had access.

"I've got the floor plans up," Adam said in his ear as Zack and Mike entered the reception. "You need to get to level three. The server farm is there."

"Okay." Zack looked around seeing lifts and the stairs. He indicated to Mike they were going to use the stairs. The Detective nodded and hurried alongside. "Could there be anywhere else he might use?"

"Probably any of the terminals on the upper floors," Adam admitted. "It's possible some of them could've been left logged on in the evacuation and give him the access he needs."

"Then why the server farm?"

"He's a tech head, and if there is access there, it will give full admin rights, making his life easier."

"I get your logic." Zack looked up. "There are camera's here. Any chance of getting feeds?"

"Not without the world's best hackers or some permission. It's a good point, though. If he's inside the system, then he could be watching you."

"Copy that." Zack slowed his pace as they hit level one.

"Oh, and Zack, there is something else you might want to know."

"Go ahead, any information is valuable."

"It's Chloe and Miley." Zack had a sinking feeling. "They think they've found Lilly."

"That's good. Are the FBI going in?"

"Well, sort of."

"Adam, what's going on?"

"Miley insisted they go. She says they've got help."

"For Christ's sakes. Hang on."

Zack rang off and dialled his daughter's number. It was a couple of rings before she answered as Zack and Mike reached the third floor.

"Not a great time now, dad," Miley answered the phone in a whisper.

"What are you doing Miley? Leave it to the FBI."

"They won't get here in time, and the deadline is nearly up. In ten minutes, she's supposed to be killed if Global Money doesn't dump their stocks."

"Jesus, what do you think you can do?" Zack's heart was racing.

"Uncle Jake is here."

While Zack was panicking, he couldn't help but note Miley's calm demeanour.

"Jake?" Zack's thoughts whirled in confusion. After he'd spoken to his brother on the phone, Zack had expected him to help but not directly. And especially not get Miley involved.

"Put him on."

"Can't right now, but he's brought some goodies. We're watching the farmhouse now, and we think there's only two of them. Not very professional either, and they don't know we're here. They keep showing themselves at the window. Real amateurs."

If Zack hadn't been so worried, he could have laughed at her cockiness. "Miley, stay out of it. Let Jake take care of things. Is his crew there?"

"He couldn't get them at short notice, Dad. He needs my help. I'm on overwatch. Like a proper sniper."

A term Zack had never thought to hear from his daughter. Or any other eighteen-year-old for that matter.

"Zack, which way?" Mike said, and Zack realised he'd just stopped at the top of the stairs. "Miley, the FBI, it's their job."

"Did you wait when it was me?"

"That's different. Jake can take care of it."

"I'll be okay, dad. Gotta go. Game time. Love you." With that, she hung up, and Zack found himself leaning against the wall breathing heavily against the rising panic in his chest.

"What's wrong?" Mike said. He was agitated, looking back and forth down the corridors.

"My daughter in the States." Zack shook his head before reaching back to his phone to reconnect with Adam. "There's nothing I can do about it now. Come on." Taking a deep breath, he had to control his fear and set his mind to the task at hand. Zack could feel the sweat pop out on his brow as he fought the urge to get the hell out of there.

As Adam came back on the line, Zack led Mike down a long corridor until they came to a set of metal doors with tinted glass.

"Get low," he indicated to the detective, and they both crouched behind a set of metal panels that still allowed them to see into the room.

"See anyone?" Mike said.

"Nothing." Zack tried to keep this breathing steady. "Wait. Movement."

"And something else." Mike pointed towards another door at the end of the corridor. Zack looked and saw a body crumpled on the floor, blood spread across the smooth white tiles.

"We need back up," Mike said.

Zack nodded. "Go back down the corridor and call it in. I'll keep an eye on things here."

Mike stayed low as he scampered back to the top of the stairs, and Zack could hear the faint whispering as he spoke on the radio. Checking his watch, he saw there were only five minutes to the deadline. Which meant there were five minutes until Alex Ryan was going to carry out the central part of his plan.

Not enough time for help to reach. Despite what Zack had said to his daughter, he knew he too needed to act on his own.

Ignoring the fierce whispers of Mike demanding what the hell he was doing as the armed response was on their way, Zack pushed open the nearest door. He created a gap only wide enough to slip into the cold room. The noise of the air conditioning drowned any other sound, meaning staying quiet wasn't an issue. Tall metal racks stretching from floor to ceiling were filled with small rectangular boxes. Lights danced up and down the black and grey devices in a manner that Zack knew must mean something to somebody.

It wasn't a large room, and with machines stacked around the edges and in front of him, there was only space to walk around the perimeter. It was the same distance whichever way he went. About four metres. It had two choices, left or right.

He chose right.

62

"Remember what we taught you. Nice and steady."

Miley took a deep, calming breath as she concentrated on looking down the powerful scope. Her weapon was a lightweight Dragunov sniper rifle with a slightly shortened stock to accommodate her stature.

The joy at seeing Uncle Jake had been short lived as he'd quickly disengaged from her hug and become serious. This was no social visit. They had to focus on the job at hand, or someone could get hurt. Miley had nodded trying to suppress her excitement, especially when Jake revealed the rifle he'd brought her even though he knew it might mean his brother never spoke to him again.

The rifle was made for another woman who'd not collected it and was about Miley's height and arm reach. One of his crew, Mitch, had a legitimate day job when he wasn't working with Uncle Jake, making custom weapons in Washington State. For gun nuts mainly, hunters and target shooters who'd watched *American Sniper* and thought it was the coolest thing in the world.

She knew Mitch made weapons for other mercenary crews around the world. Only so many though because his guns were some of the finest and most accurate money could buy.

They'd stayed at Mitch's ranch for a few weeks before she'd gone back to school. It was where she'd learnt to shoot several types of guns. The sniper rifle had been her favourite, and it hadn't taken Miley long to show she had some aptitude.

Through the scope, she could clearly see the house, and more than once, a figure was visible in the window. She'd watched one of the abductors go outside for a smoke. He'd wandered away from the building without even bothering to check his surroundings. Jake had shaken his head and told Miley how inept the kidnappers were.

Miley realised they didn't think anyone would find out where Lilly was held. Or they didn't care. Even so, Jake said they acted like common thugs rather than professionals. It was good news; their amateurish behaviour made them easy targets. The bad news was that it made them unpredictable. Jake told her stupid people did stupid things, which tended to cost lives.

Miley was in the prone position on a slightly elevated piece of grassland to the west of the farmhouse with a clear view of the front door. Jake had crawled further north to cover the rear, and having followed his movements to see where he went, Miley couldn't now make him out. Using the tall, wiry grass as best she could, Miley hoped she was as well hidden.

"We're in position," she spoke into her mike. As with the conversation with her dad, Miley tried to sound a lot calmer than she really was. Despite the instructions and breathing exercises, her heart was hammering; Miley was sure if she loosened her grip on the rifle, her hands would be shaking. How the hell was she going to make a good shot? The idea of getting involved had seemed a lot more appealing before they'd crawled their way through the fields to get into position.

Now, it was all too real.

"Okay, we're starting to walk up the drive," Chloe said. They couldn't be sure Lilly was in the house, and the thermal scanner Jake had brought only showed two bodies. From the plans and James's recollection, they knew there was a large basement. If she was in the house, Lilly would be there.

Jake and Brad, pooling both their security expertise, had conferred and were confident this was the place, not only because of Miley and Chloe's research but the presence of the two men. Why else would such rough looking individuals be holed up in an abandoned farmhouse?

"You have got us covered?"

"We've got you, Chloe," Jake answered. "If they so much as twitch, we'll take them down."

"Good to know."

Miley raised her head from the scope and saw Chloe strolling down the long drive wearing wellington boots and a large coat they'd bought in a stop off just shy of the farmhouse. She was holding James's hand as part of the plan, and they would pass themselves off as a couple out on a country walk. Brad had wanted to be the one walking with Chloe because he said it was his job. But James was the boss, and it was his daughter in the house. He wasn't going to leave this to someone else.

"Leon says they are twenty minutes out." Brad came over the airways. He was with the Taurus out of sight of the farmhouse and ready to come charging down the road with the vehicle if he was needed. "They're telling us not to do anything stupid as they have an ATF team on its way."

"They won't be here in time." James sounded desperate.

"Just passing on the message."

"Received and understood," James said.

"Any movement in the house?" Chloe asked. "Have they seen us?"

"That's a negative," Jake said. "Looks like both tangos are in the front room. Wish I could've got some sound in there."

"I've got eyes on one tango." Miley wondered if that was the right jargon. It sounded cool, though she couldn't help imagining a huge, fat orange man was in her sights.

"Hold fire until we know the threat is real."

"Okay." She couldn't think of anything more military sounding.

"Twenty yards from the door." The tension was apparent in Chloe's voice. They were both wearing bulletproof vests under their large jackets, but with no idea what the two in the house were armed with, it might not be enough.

"No movement yet," Miley said. "They haven't seen you."

"Okay," Chloe whispered. "Knocking on the door now."

63

Alex spun around.

Something had attracted his attention.

He looked near the central server rack and saw movement through the gaps in the machines.

There was someone in the room.

Glancing back at the console Alex was using, he could see the penetration software was almost through the security. It would take two minutes to load the next part of the program and another minute or two for the code to take effect.

Alex faced a dilemma. Did he continue and risk getting caught or abandon the mission when he was so close. The police radio in his ear helped make his decision as he heard the call for back up at LSE. They knew he was there, but it meant he still had a little time if he could deal with whoever was in the room. It was probably just some security guard or rogue copper who'd been clearing the building.

He turned back to the console.

Alex put his gun by the side of the keyboard.

He might just be able to get the job done.

Seconds later, Alex turned and fired. A figure emerging from behind the server stack dived out of the way. Alex wasn't sure if he'd scored a hit.

Looking at the console in frustration, Alex knew he had to be bold and trust the program would run its course. There wasn't time to deal with the intruder and get the payload in play. It sounded like the man was scrambling to his feet where he'd dived behind the central racks. Abandoning the console, Alex backed away in the opposite direction while keeping his gun trained towards the sounds.

The man in front leapt from behind the shelves before hurling a server at Alex. Ducking low, Alex fired and then felt somebody grab him from behind.

He immediately thrust his elbow back and felt it connect with something soft. There was a groan from his assailant, the grip loosening. Glancing down, Alex smashed his right foot into the instep of the large man who'd grabbed him before throwing his head back at whatever he could hit.

The head butt struck home, and Alex heard the crunch of what he hoped was the man's nose. Released from the hold, Alex saw the other man in front of him.

He recognised Zack.

Smiling, Alex just managed to bring up his gun and let off a shot before Zack jumped him. Alex knew he'd scored a hit.

Zack fell forward as the bullet penetrated his shoulder and spun him around.

Before the second assailant could recover, Alex dodged aside from the falling Zack, went into a crouch, and rolled himself along the ground, clearing both men. Then he was up, circling the outside of the room towards the main door.

For a moment, Alex considered waiting to make sure they weren't following. It was tempting to go back and finish Zack. But the armed response teams would be entering the building. Perhaps the wound would be enough to ensure that Zack wouldn't be able to thwart his plans again. He was astonished at the appearance of Miley's father. How had he known Alex would be there?

Alex hauled open the door to make his escape. The other assailant appeared but ducked away once he saw the gun pointed towards him. Alex let off two shots for good measure. His Berrata's magazine held ten 9mm rounds, but he wasn't concerned about conserving them. This wasn't a situation he was going to shoot his way out of.

Once through the door, he sprinted along the corridor. Alex slipped the Beretta under his jacket before retrieving a phone. It was connected to the two devices he'd strategically positioned earlier. Powering up the phone, Alex held it ready as he reached the stairs. He had only to go down one level to reach the fire escape and just made it before the police started swarming up the stairs. If they'd heard the gunshots, it would be adding to their urgency.

Slipping through a set of doors, Alex put as much distance between him and the response unit as he could. Turning right, the fire escape was at the end of the corridor, and he burst through into the daylight before sliding down the metal stairs to the ground. Faces turned towards him but most looked away at the sight of his fluorescent jacket and air of authority.

"This is supposed to be a secured area." As Alex approached the barrier, an officer approached him.

"What are you doing here?"

"They're in the building," Alex said. "Response team told me to get out."

The officer looked at him with suspicion. "Who are you with?"

"I can't hear properly," Alex shouted tapping his ear. "Gunshots have made me deaf." With his other hand, he pressed the pre-dialled number on the phone.

"Can I see some ID, Sir?"

Alex fumbled about his hi-vis jacket as if complying with the officer's instructions.

Seconds later, the historic London Stock Exchange was rocked by two massive explosions. The officer turned. The crowd started to scream and began fleeing from yet more drama. Alex slipped under the cordon and disappeared into the panicking mass of people.

64

Chloe took a deep breath as she knocked on the door.

For a while, there was silence on the other side, and she could feel James's tension. She couldn't imagine what it was like to know your daughter was likely being held prisoner inside the building. If it was her, she might not have been able to refrain from simply barging through the door in desperation.

Chloe knocked again. They hadn't really planned for a no answer scenario. Did they just walk back down the drive?

"I hear something," James whispered. Chloe felt his hand grip hers a little tighter. It did nothing to calm her own nerves.

"One of them is moving towards the door." It was Miley in her ear. Chloe had her hair down to cover any sign of a wire. James had wanted to be the one in communication, but there'd been no way to affix it to him without it being evident to anyone who came close.

The front door opened.

A tall man with broad shoulders stepped through the gap he'd created and pulled the door closed behind him. He had the type of shifty look that made Chloe think he was up to no good, even if they weren't Lilly's kidnappers. His wide, bearded face and narrow eyes looked out of place compared to the people Chloe had seen on the drive along the I95. An image that wasn't helped by his strong accent when he spoke.

"What do you want?"

"Hi, my boyfriend and I have been walking all day, and I really need to use a toilet." Chloe threw out her best embarrassed smile. "Sorry, but you don't have many neighbours to ask."

The man looked her up and down, barely glanced at James, and then slightly opened the door again. "Go away."

"I promise I won't be a minute." Chloe hopped from foot to foot. "Hey, what's that accent, by the way, it's pretty cool. I'm Chloe." She stuck out her hand. "I'm from England."

"I don't care. Go away." The man started to shuffle through the door.

"The lady asked nicely."

Chloe gasped as she realised James was holding a gun. This hadn't been part of the plan, and he hadn't mentioned anything about carrying.

"What's going on, Chloe?" It was Miley. Only Chloe couldn't answer her.

"Let's just step out onto the porch, mister, and we can sort this out." James gesticulated with the weapon.

"Is this a good idea?" Chloe knew it wasn't because it was obvious James was having difficulty holding the gun steady.

"We just need to check the house for a missing person," James continued. "Then we'll be on our way."

The man stepped out onto the porch leaving the door ajar. Chloe could see he was observing James. Even Chloe could work out he was looking for an opening.

"Put your hands up."

The man complied.

"Jesus, what the fuck are you two doing?" Jake's urgent whisper was in Chloe's ear.

"Chloe, pat him down. Check for a gun."

While she didn't think it was wise, Chloe stepped forward to begin her search. The man moved with such speed that before Chloe could react, she was twisted 'round a massive arm engulfing her neck and a gun pointing at James. Without warning, the Russian fired, and Chloe saw James crumple to the ground.

Terrified, Chloe did the only thing she could think of and bit down hard into the Russian's bare arm. The man grunted with surprise and loosened his grip enough for Chloe to slip his hold and throw herself away from him.

There was another crack of gunfire. This time from a distance and some of the wooden panels exploded near the door.

"Shit, missed," Miley hissed.

Another shot struck the door. Chloe saw the man turn his gun in the direction of the fire and let off two shots before he dived into the doorway.

"Both men inside, Jake," Miley said. "I missed."

"Remember what we taught you, Miley, stay calm. If you get a shot through the window, then take it."

"Okay."

"What's going on?" Brad thundered on the airwaves. She pulled her mike up as she went over to James. For the second time in her life, Chloe saw the damage to someone's face when a bullet tore through it from close range.

"James is dead," she said.

"Jesus," Brad said.

"Quiet," Jake hissed. "Miley, tell me when you have a shot."

It was hard to hear Jake with the shouting going on from inside the farmhouse. One of the windows was smashed, and Chloe dived down by the porch fearing they were going to shoot at her.

"Got a shot." Miley's voice sounded calm and composed.

"Take it, Miles, squeeze the trigger real gentle now."

There were a few more seconds of shouting. One of the men inside fired towards Miley's position, but Chloe knew she was safely out of range. Then, there was the crack of a rifle, and Chloe saw the remaining glass splattered with blood.

"I'm going in." Jake's voice came through her earpiece. "Hold your fire, Miley."

"Yes, Uncle Jake."

A moment later, there was a crash from inside the farmhouse, and Chloe heard three more shots.

"Two men down. Securing the building. Miley, keep it covered. Chloe, stay outside until I say."

Both girls acknowledged, and Chloe could still feel her heart beating so fast in her chest, she struggled to breathe normally. It had all happened so quickly, and three people were dead.

"House secure. There is one white female in the cellar chained to the wall."

"Lilly," Brad said. "I'm coming up. Leon says they are ten minutes out."

"I feel sick," Miley said. "Did I?"

"It was a great shot, Miley," Jake said. "But now, we've got to get out of here. Your teacher said something about an important chemistry test you've got to get back for. Start packing your rifle; I'll make my way to you."

"How you going to get out of here?" Chloe entered the front room of the farmhouse house trying to avoid the two dead bodies sprawled on the mouldy brown carpet.

"Not your problem, Miss Evans." She could hear the smile in Jake's voice.

"Will we see you at your dad's?" Chloe asked.

"I don't think he'll ever let me away from the school again," Miley said. "But we'll meet up soon."

Chloe saw Jake was examining the bodies. Pulling something from one of the corpses, he tossed a set of keys to Chloe. Catching them, she realised what they were for.

"I'm out of here," Jake said. "Take care of Lilly."

Chloe nodded as Jake headed out of the back door. She found the stairs to the cellar and took them three at a time until she came to a large room. Lilly was at the far end chained to a set of rusty pipes.

"Oh, thank god." There was a look of relief on her dirt streaked face. "I heard shooting. Who are you?"

"I'm Chloe. A friend." She was about to say of her father's when Chloe realised this was not going to be a happy ending for the Goldstein family. Chloe found the padlocks linked through the large chain rings, and after a few attempts, located the right key. "Are you hurt? Did they touch you?"

"They said they were going to." Lilly shook her head as she was able to pull her wrists free and flex them. She shuddered. "They said they were going to do all sorts of things. I'm so glad you came for me."

"Then let's get out of here." Chloe helped her to her feet. "The FBI are on their way."

65

"Zack, can you hear me?"

Mike's blurred face came into view. Zack felt the pain in his shoulder and on the side of his head. He remembered rushing Alex, the shot, and him tumbling to the ground before smashing onto the base of one of the cabinets. Zack thought he'd only been out for a few seconds but wasn't sure.

"Where is he?" He climbed to his feet with Mike's assistance. The hurt ripped through his shoulder, and he nearly passed out again.

"He's gone. The response teams are on their way."

Zack looked at the console Alex had been working on. "Pull the stuff out. We don't know what he's been doing." Mike left Zack leaning against the server racks as he went over and ripped out the wires from what looked like a small laptop. To make sure, Mike smashed the laptop into the floor.

"Evidence, Detective Inspector," Zack said.

"Blue tooth or wireless connections." Mike nodded at the laptop which was in pieces. "Can't do any harm now."

"And we need to get out of here." Zack was already considering what backup plans Alex might have in place when he heard and felt an explosion. "Shit, he's covering his way out."

Just as he finished speaking, the second explosion nearly

ripped his eardrums apart as it tore through the server racks in one part of the room. Pieces of hot metal flew towards them, and Zack was only just able to haul Mike to the ground before the force of the blast sent crushed computers crashing into the console Mike had just been standing by.

"Come on," Zack yelled into Mike's ear. "Crawl out." His own ears were filled with a high-pitched squeal. His nose filled with the sharp smell of molten metal and plastic.

Ignoring the agony gripping his body, Zack fell onto his hands and knees before resorting to a commando crawl along the tiled floor. He squeezed under one of the units partially destroyed by the blast. The heat was intensifying. Half of the room was on fire, and Zack wasn't sure if anything in the computers was explosive. Zack just wanted to get out of there as fast as possible.

Glass shards littering the floor dug into his bare arms, but Zack gritted his teeth and crawled on until they reached what was left of the doors. Ears ringing, and nostrils filled with stinging smoke, Zack glanced behind to see Mike's grim face streaked with blood as he tried to keep up. There was another explosion, a smaller one in the room behind them, and flames erupted from one of the sides giving off black smoke. He caught a lungful and nearly choked.

Zack rolled into the corridor before coming up into a crouch allowing him to make faster progress away from the room. As they made their way down the hallway, it didn't take long to see the effect of the first blast. The lift entrance was wide open, and the elevators were ripped apart. A smart move, making sure no one could come up quickly.

Zack looked for Alex. He didn't expect to see him, just hoped he was still around. If the bastard got away, what else did he have planned? Would he disappear again?

They reached the stairs.

"Stop right there, and put your hands in the air."

"Let's see those hands."

Two Heckler & Koch MP5 sub machineguns were trained on Mike and Zack. The armed response officers were in a perfect firing position. Zack could see three more were on the floor not moving. This would make the two covering them scared and nervous. As much as he was glad to see them, Zack knew it was a dangerous situation.

He complied immediately not wishing for any mistakes.

"I've got ID," Mike shouted, but Zack could see he'd also raised his arms and wasn't being so stupid as to try and go for the ID. Instead, he let the team do its job and secure the area. Zack would prefer to be handcuffed in the back of a police van than have a bullet in his head from a jumpy armed officer who might just have seen his first real action.

It only took a few minutes for things to be settled. They both went down on their knees as instructed with hands on heads, while guns were pointed in their faces and efficient men quickly searched them for weapons. More armed officers came up the stairs to help their colleagues while others moved off to clear the building.

Mike's warrant card was retrieved, and radio calls made as they were escorted out of the building. By the time they'd reached the outside, Mike and Zack were on their way for a debrief rather than a custody suite.

"Have they caught him?" Zack was still shouting, not sure if people could hear him as everything sounded muffled. "Have they got Alex?"

Mike shook his head. He'd been briefed by the incident

commander, having given Alex's description. "No one has been arrested. All four gunmen were killed. They're going to search the building and check the CCTV to see if someone came out."

"Too late." Zack shook his head. "He'll be long gone. You need all the cameras in the rest of the city looking for him. You need everybody looking for him, or you'll never find Alex Ryan until next time."

"They're doing all they can," Mike said seeing the stern look on the incident commanders face. "They know what they're doing."

"Not with this guy." Zack slumped into the back of the ambulance feeling woozy. A female paramedic was examining his wounds and talking about the loss of blood. Zack was too weak to resist as he was lifted onto a narrow bed while another paramedic started rigging up an IV and asking him questions.

Zack knew Alex was gone. He knew they would never find him. Trying to reach for his phone, the female medic in a green uniform stopped him. She insisted he answer their questions as he faded in and out of consciousness. He had so many questions of his own. Was Miley okay?

66

"I've lost contact with him," Adam was shouting into his mike out of panic rather than necessity.

"What's happening?" Terry replied. "Have they stopped it?"

"Hang on." Adam scanned the markets having brought them up onto one of the screens as it all kicked off. He wasn't alone in the office. Staff from three other companies in the complex had realised what was going on and come to see if they could help.

Laptops and screens were set up. Coffee and Red Bull flowed by the gallon, and suddenly, Adam found himself at the centre of the excitement with everyone looking to him for an explanation of what was going down.

The DDOS attack had been the biggest they'd ever seen, and some of their services had been affected. They were trying to combat it where they could while attempting to trace the origin. One of the interns had been monitoring the forums to see if they could get a gauge on how and why this was happening. It appeared most of the communities were as perplexed as they were.

Adam knew an attack on this scale would have recruited hundreds of newbies, and they probably would be on the forums boasting about what they'd done. He'd heard about this happening before. Students who thought they were society warriors because they'd run easily downloadable software and followed a few instructions. Only, it would be them who were hauled up in front of the judges, not the real perpetrators.

Terry had called him from behind the police cordon. He'd told Adam he'd stayed with the woman who'd been shot until the paramedics had taken over, and Terry had been shuffled off to safety.

"There are some movements in the markets," Adam said, "but they'd been trying to shut down the London Exchange. It doesn't look too different from normal." He glanced at the clock. It was two minutes past the deadline. He knew Miley and Chloe were safe, and they'd gotten Lilly. Maybe they'd stopped Alex after all.

"The attacks are decreasing." It was Lin, the guy who'd introduced them to the warehouses, who spoke. "It's dying off really quick, too."

"I think we've stopped it." Adam couldn't hide the excitement from his voice as another minute ticked by.

"Jesus, that was an explosion," Terry said.

"Where?"

"Towards the LSE. Shit, I hope Zack is okay. Can you get hold of him?"

"No," Adam replied. "He had a piece of software that was redialling every minute, but it kept going to voicemail."

"I can't get any closer to see anything."

Adam continued to scan the screens trying to figure out if there were any anomalies. On one of the displays, CNN was reporting the events at the farmhouse as they'd had a tip-off that the CEO of Global Money's daughter had been kidnapped. The breaking news was that James Goldstein had been shot during the rescue attempt.

Their news choppers were in the air searching for a snippet of exciting action. Adam watched, hoping to see Chloe or Miley. Though Miley had already messaged that she was getting out of there.

"Something's happening," Lin shouted. "Screens in New York are going red."

"Shit, yes." Adam's eyes were drawn to the swaths of red numbers flashing up across the board on the New York exchange. Then, some of the other boards began to follow suit. "We've not stopped it, Terry. The stocks are going red. A massive sell off."

"We need to see if the safety's cut in," Terry said his voice calm. "That's what he'd have been trying to stop, and if he has, then we are all fucked. If not, then they'll shut down the trading across the board."

"What will that mean?" Adam asked.

"We are not quite as fucked, but it's still going to bad. I'll try to get back to the office. Can you keep trying to get hold of Zack?"

"Am doing all the time. It's red across the board, and the news is flashing about a stock market crash."

"Trading being suspended on the Dow Jones," Lin shouted.

"And on the DAX," one of the girls in the room added. "And it looks like the attack has stopped. Reports are coming in of potential viruses firing at big companies."

"Are the trades stopping, though?" Terry sounded as if he was walking fast and trying to push through the crowds.

"Just wait a few minutes." Adam watched the feeds as though there were a lot of red flashes; the screens were turning black across many of the quarters as trading was stopped. The news was reporting the index had fallen nearly twelve percent in the few minutes it had gone bad. It seemed Global Money was dumping its position on everything. There was already an announcement about Global Money ceasing trading.

"I think we kept all the checks in place," Adam said.

"Thank god for that." He heard the relief in Terry's voice.

"Not everything," Lin said and pointed to one of the central New York exchanges. The figures were still tumbling.

"Shit, it's the one we saw the software on," Adam said slamming the table. "Nobody has done anything about it."

"Guess they had other things on their mind over there."

"How bad is it?" Terry asked.

"They are still dropping like a stone."

"It'll keep going until they can kill everything running it. Are the other exchanges still suspended?"

Adam checked across the screens. "London never got going. The rest of the world is halting everything."

"That's something, at least."

"They're saying this is bad." Adam was looking at the headlines around the screens. "Global Money has plunged to near zero, and people are asking how this could happen."

"It's times like this I'm glad I've got some money in a jar at home," Lin said quietly, and there were nods around the table.

"Or Bitcoin," one of the girls muttered.

67

It wasn't just the police interviews Zack had been forced to endure while trying to recover. The media had wanted to be all over him too, and this time, he couldn't use the police as a front to avoid interviews. He'd been moved to a private hospital after the first intrusion by the press. Paid for by Lilly Goldstein as part of the thanks for what the detective agency had done for her family.

Zack knew it was Lilly's own money. Global Money wouldn't be able to foot the bill with the trouble they were in. It wasn't just the financial losses but the fact they were suspended from any trading on both sides of the Atlantic by the authorities. The software they were using, Alex's software, had managed to offload billions of dollars of stock before trading was brought to a halt.

While Global Money had been worst hit, other companies using the Austin Trading Solutions software had found their portfolios up for grabs at rock bottom prices. All the checks and balances within the organisations that were supposed to stop the software going wrong had failed. While Alex might have been unable to bring down the entire system, the consequences of his actions were still reverberating around the world.

Zack moved his shoulder, tensing at the pain as he tried to do the exercises given to him by the physiotherapist. He'd been in the hospital for five days since the operation. The bullet had done considerable damage to his shoulder blade as it had passed through.

Rested against the pillows, he switched on the news.

It was still dominated by the financial aftershocks. Share prices were down around the world, and trading had been suspended every day. Terry had told him confidence was shattered in the system, and despite the attempted reassurances by the world's governments, people wanted their money out of the markets. Gold and other commodities were seeing their prices skyrocket.

New cryptocurrencies were being announced as the Bitcoin and Ethereum, two of the most popular, prices went through the roof. People were already talking about a financial revolution the world hadn't seen for three hundred years.

There was a message on his phone. Zack looked at it and smiled. He'd asked Miley how her day had been.

MILEY: *Gym, languages, biology and English. In other words, boring!!! When's our next case?*

ZACK: *I've told the Principal not to let you off the island until you're thirty, and I've got you a place in a convent.*

MILEY:

ZACK: *How you doing, really?*

MILEY: *It's hard, Dad. I've seen the pictures on the news, and I think I did that. I killed him.*

ZACK: *I know, baby. You getting the help they promised?*

MILEY: *Twice a week as the doctor ordered. I know it's the right thing.*

ZACK: *But.*

301

MILEY: *Well, it seemed so different on the range. Uncle Jake says that I need to remember they were sick people doing a bad thing, and I helped stop it be even worse.*

ZACK: *He's right.*

Not that it made Zack feel better about his brother and what he'd turned Miley into. When Zack had sent her off to train and learn skills, it was so she'd be able to defend herself. Instead, Miley was now an eighteen-year-old who had to deal with the fact she'd killed a man. Zack shook his head, but he really wanted to shake his brother and ask him what the fuck he'd been doing.

MILEY: *I know. And at least I've got to keep my phone as an edge case for a while. The other girls are jealous.*

ZACK: *You've haven't told them what happened.*

MILEY: *No. They just think I was on holiday in London. No dramas.*

ZACK: *Then keep it that way.*

MILEY: *I will. Love you lots, Dad.*

ZACK: *Love you too, hun.*

Zack switched off his phone before placing it on the small bedside table. Feeling thirsty, he grabbed a drink of water. There was a voice outside the door asking if it was okay to see him. The police had posted officers for security while the investigations were taking place. It was as much to keep the press at bay as for his protection.

Zack smiled as he recognised the voice.

68

Chloe swung open the door to be greeted by Zack's beaming face. It lifted her heart to see he was safe. When she'd first heard that Zack had been shot, Chloe had been desperate to find out if he was okay. It was Mike who'd eventually rang her to say Zack was in the hospital after an operation but was expected to make a full recovery. After having seen James brutally shot, it made Chloe feel so lucky that her friend was alive.

It had broken her heart to see Lilly cradling her father outside the farmhouse. After all the poor woman had been through, it was so terribly tragic. But she's been incredibly stoic and thanked Chloe for everything the agency had done. Both Lilly had her mother insisted all the bills were going to be paid; no blame was going to be levelled at the agency. The Goldsteins seemingly had a lot of their own money in investments not affected by the crash. It was something Rose had always insisted on.

"They let you out of the country." Zack pushed himself upwards. Chloe could see he was still in pain. "You should have called."

"I wanted to surprise you." She rushed over to the bedside and bent over, giving him a big hug while trying to avoid his shoulder. "I seem to remember having to do this last time." She grinned and sat on the edge of the bed holding his hand.

"Yes, but it was you doing the rescuing this time. You took a big chance there, Chloe. It could have been you who got shot."

Chloe shrugged. "Had to get the job done, and Miley insisted instead of waiting for the FBI to show. You've got a hell of a daughter there Zack. She's amazing."

"Not sure I like what she's turning into." Zack's face went serious for a moment.

"What, an independent woman capable of fighting for herself and others? Not to mention super intelligent. All traits I think she must have inherited from her mother."

Chloe felt guilty for not having tried to put her foot down in New York to stop his daughter from being so deeply involved. It was as though it was Miley who was the stronger, more confident one. Chloe was thinking of asking about getting the same sort of training. Alex still being out there, and the fact they'd thwarted him twice, had her worried he would come after them.

"You know what I mean. She's only eighteen."

"She's got you to keep her feet on the ground," Chloe pointed out.

"And you. Thank you for looking after her." Zack placed his other hand on her thigh and squeezed it. Chloe looked at his face and felt a tingle inside her. There was something about Zack that warmed her heart every time she saw him. It had been sad to see how down he'd been when things had been going bad at the agency.

"I tried my best," she said, "but it was Miley who saved me, remember." She closed her eyes for a moment. "It went so wrong so quickly I wasn't able to do anything. If Jake hadn't been there, it would have been a disaster."

"Which is why we leave it to the professionals," Zack said, and the look on her face said everything. "Okay, so I'm a hypocrite."

"No, you are just a man." Chloe laughed.

"The FBI let you go?"

"Lots of fish to fry and I'm just a tiny cog in a big chain wheel at the moment," Chloe joked. "The story is going to be the ATF got there and completed the rescue. There were no news crews around until after the FBI had arrived, and there were no bad guys to talk.

"Lilly and Rose are quite happy to go along with that story if we are. Special Agent Bennett told me before I left Global Money will cease to be and what's left of its assets broken up and sold off."

"So, no one is after Miley or Jake?"

Chloe shook her head. "Weren't even there, as far as the FBI are concerned."

"And James?"

"Died a hero assisting the FBI." Chloe had been shocked at the level of cover-up to keep certain aspects out of the media. It had begun to make her wonder how much she could believe when the government made their announcements.

"Do they accept it was Alex?"

"Some do and some don't. Leon does, but his partner says he must have been working for the Russians; she seems to have them on the brain since the election. The economy is on the brink of collapse, and they've got a lame duck president after the revelations, plus the cyber-attack has the whole country questioning security. Accepting this was the work of one Lex

Luthor style mastermind is hard for most people. And unless you've met him, I can understand."

"It's the same here, from what Mike has been saying." Zack reached over to take a sip of water. "Some in authority acknowledge Alex was probably behind it, while others insist it was ISIS. After all, they are trying to take the credit as they always do. They've found chat logs of a man who was talking to the leader of the terror cell behind the London attack. But funnily enough, they can't trace him."

"And so, Alex is still out there. Planning his next move. If he has one."

"It's just a game to him." Zack shook his head. "A game he's addicted to. I was so close; I was on him. Next time, the son of a bitch won't get away."

"Does this mean the Angel Detective Agency is still a going concern?"

"If we still have some cash in the bank."

"Oh, that reminds me." Chloe tucked her blond hair behind her ear and leaned into Zack. "We've had a call from Hank William's lawyer."

"The American divorce case," Zack groaned. "Have they set a court date?"

"No, he wanted me to know he wouldn't be representing Mr Williams any more. Apparently, our American friend lost everything in the crash. No money to pay a lawyer."

Zack smiled; then his face fell. "Does that mean we're not getting the rest of our money?"

"No much point suing him," Chloe joked. "But, I think we've got enough to stay afloat a while longer."

"I was actually thinking we should be branching out into other countries." Zack was watching her for a reaction.

"United States?"

"I was thinking New York. Of course, it does mean one thing."

"What's that?"

"You are going to have to come and work with me full time."

"I think I can handle that. It would be a pleasure to work with the man who very nearly caught the greatest criminal mastermind the world has ever seen." Chloe leaned forward and kissed Zack on the lips. "But we do need to talk about my salary."

69

Miley pushed the phone back under her pillow after using WhatsApp to message her dad. While she was allowed the app to speak to her father, Miley was wise enough not to flaunt her limited communications with the outside world. It wasn't her own phone. The school wouldn't go that far. It was one they'd provided, which only allowed WhatsApp and only to her dad's account.

"You going to breakfast this morning, panda?" Her roommate Letitia said, slipping on her black shoes.

Miley nodded and moved over to the full-length mirror at the end of the bed. Letitia was one of few people in the school who knew what Miley had been through. Both on her break from the school and before. It was the West Indian pupil who'd helped Miley during her investigation into wrongdoing at the school when she'd first arrived. And while Miley didn't always tell her roommate everything, she tried to keep as few secrets as possible.

Adjusting her black and yellow tie, so it sat correctly against her white blouse, she saw there were still dark marks under her eyes, which was why Letitia had begun to playfully call her panda.

It had taken Miley long enough to get over Oakwell when

she'd seen Alex shoot a man in the head. But knowing she was responsible for another's death, however reprehensible he might have been, was more challenging. While Letitia tried to be understanding, Miley couldn't help thinking her friend found what she'd been up to was cool.

At least there was therapy twice a week where she talked through her emotions, and that helped. All pupils had at least one session a week as it was. They were encouraged to talk about their feelings and work on issues that could impair performance.

How could they be assets to the world if they were still dealing with childhood traumas?

"Stop daydreaming and come on, panda."

Miley tied her hair in a loose pony tail before turning and slipping through the door an impatient Letitia was holding open. They walked down the wooden platform outside their room and joined the mass of pupils from their accommodation heading towards the mess hall.

Even though Miley had only been away for a few days, it seemed like a lifetime. Everything felt different. She was sure the other pupils, and even some of the teachers, saw the change in her.

While she missed her dad and Chloe, and though the adrenaline rush had been awesome, it was good to be back at the school with her friends. These were people tasked with making a positive difference in the world when they graduated. Handpicked, not because their parents were rich and powerful, but because they represented a desire to progress humanity.

The fact Miley could be among them was incredible. And after seeing some of the worst scum humanity had to offer, she wanted to be a part of making the world a better place.

In the mess hall, she stuck with Letitia and a few of the others from her accommodation block. Grabbing a plateful of muesli and fresh fruit, she sat next to her roommate to find the table was already full of gossip from the outside world.

While they weren't allowed unfettered access to the internet or any entertainment channels, neither were they kept in isolation. There was a media centre, where they made their calls, that also served as a cinema and played multiple news channels, so the pupils were kept up to date with world affairs. Often, significant events would be debated in some of the classes as the young people wrestled with their opinions.

The financial chaos engulfing civilisation had dominated these discussions since Miley had returned, but this morning, there was a new story capturing the pupil's imagination.

"Was there anything about this when you were in London, Miley?" Izzy, the daughter of a well-known Hollywood actor, pounced as soon as Miley sat down.

"Wow, what news? Some of us have only just got up."

"The image leaks. All the hotties are there. Didn't you hear anything?" Izzy was looking at her as if Miley had just landed from another planet.

"No," Miley threw up her hands in despair. "And I have no idea what you are talking about."

"Someone has been hacking into the icloud accounts of celebrities. Stolen their photos and published the raunchy ones. I've heard even Jennifer Lawrence has topless pictures out there. I can't wait to speak to my dad and see what's happened. I can't believe you haven't heard anything."

Miley shook her head, looked down at her food, and found she'd lost her appetite. Something in her gut told her there could be only one person behind this.

Alex Ryan was already making his next move.

First to know

Building a relationship with my readers is one of the best things about writing. If you enjoyed this book and would like to find out about further books when they are about to be released, then please sign up below. I'll only ever send you information about my books and never share with third parties. You'll also be the first to know about any new material.

http://www.sjdavison.com/sign-me-up/

I need you

If you enjoyed this book, you could help me.

Reviews are so critical for me to get attention for my books. Not only that it helps the ranking so many more readers can become aware of my books.

So, if you liked Angel of Money I would be grateful if you could spare five minutes to write a review on Amazon. It can be a short as you want.

Thank you very much.

About the author

Having spent ten years in the military, I went on to work in the Cyberworld creating programs and delving deep into the data that drives our lives.

On the side I wrote fiction and explored the mysteries of the human mind.

All of these life threads have come together in my published work as I combine thrillers and technology to weave page-turning stories. Or at least I think so, and I hope you do too.

If you love fast paced thrillers, international action packed adventures or mysterious crime novels then my books are for you.

37326960R00185

Printed in Great Britain
by Amazon